FLIRTATION ACT

THE COMEDY TEAM OF

O'BRIEN
& WILLIAMS

—SHINE—

in their flirtation act

"Will She Love Me!"

For booking information:
Goodman Talent Agency
1270 Sixth Ave., New York City

FLIRTATION ACT

The Story of
a Boy,
a Girl,
and
Vaudeville

A NOVEL

by

Debra L. Davis

BearManor Media

2017

Flirtation Act: The Story of a Boy, a Girl, and Vaudeville. A Novel

For information, address:

BearManor Media
P. O. Box 71426
Albany, GA 31708

bearmanormedia.com

Edited by Lon Davis

Typesetting and layout by John Teehan

Published in the USA by BearManor Media

ISBN—978-1-62933-097-6

[Music cue: "Penthouse Serenade"]

*This book is dedicated, with
profound gratitude, to the man
who graciously contributed his vast
knowledge of vaudeville, served as
a perfect partner for sketch writing,
and respectfully employed his
prodigious editing skills.
My heart.
My soul.
My Lon*

[Fade out music]

TABLE OF CONTENTS

Love Me, and the World Is Mine
by Dave Reed, Jr., and Ernest R. Ball

I wander on as in a dream,
My goal a paradise must be,
For there an angel waits 'twould seem,
Yet lo, dear heart, 'tis only thee.

Suns may shine to light my way, dear,
Wealth be mine for aye, dear,
Queens may pledge their riches too;
Yet the world would still be lonely,
With such virtues only,
Life to me, dear, means just you.

I care not for the stars that shine,
I dare not hope to e'er be thine,
I only know I love you,
Love me, and the world is mine.

Flirtation act: flur•**tey**•sh*uh*•n akt (*n.*)

A vaudeville term for a specific type of routine, one that involves a man and a woman engaging in comical banter, sometimes including a romantic song and dance. Well-known teams who utilized this form of sketch comedy were Burns & Allen, Hyams & McIntyre, and O'Brien & Williams.

CHAPTER ONE

THE BOY

July 1925

The intense light pierced his eyes, getting into his brain and distracting him. He could smell—and taste—the electricity thrown off by the white-hot carbon arc lamp. A small bead of sweat trickled down his temple, finding a pool to jump in just above his collar. The greasepaint baked into his pores and stank. And he was getting one of his headaches.

Damn.

Standing center stage, he heard the opening strains of "Danny Boy" and willed himself to concentrate on the all-too-familiar song. He began singing quietly, forcing the audience to pay greater attention; tricking them into investing more of themselves. Slowly, as the lyrics unfurled, he built to an emotional crescendo, his resonant tenor filling the hall. The older patrons sniffled, the younger girls swooned. He finished big, to an ovation which shook the Palace Theatre walls. Putting his right hand over his heart and bowing into the blinding spotlight, he acknowledged the clapping hands he could only hear; thanked the crowd he would never see. Before the adulation could stop, he sprinted offstage.

He made his way through the wings as hastily as possible, joking with the usual assortment of stagehands, prop men, and performers crowding the already tight passageway. He called people by name, continuing the in-jokes that were the language of vaudeville.

"What are you up to, Danny?"

"Seventeen minutes, Fred."

"Cold house tonight, Danny?"

"Don't worry, Billy, I warmed 'em up for you."

"Hey, Danny, did I hear you hit a bad note out there?"

"Of course not, John. I hit *several* bad ones."

At his replies, however genuinely witty or flat or hackneyed they may have been, these sycophants laughed that insider type of laugh: the kind that was just a little too hard, the kind you earned through experience, the kind that said "I belong here." These everymen, these individuals who had not achieved fame and never would, all wanted to share a single moment of fame with a winner, and everybody wanted to associate with the elusive Danny O'Brien. But he just kept pushing forward.

He saw Thelma from a distance and felt his pasted-on smile slip ever so slightly, then quickly regain its footing. *Not another quarrel,* he thought. Not with this headache threatening to take his body hostage.

"Hi, Danny," she said, clearly a little miffed. She toyed with the feather protruding from her headband, making it bob distractingly. Thelma was the ultimate flapper. She wore excessive make-up, shot craps, treated sex in a casual fashion, smoked, drank bootleg liquor, drove her father's automobile, and did everything she could to shock the status quo. Her bleached platinum hair was bobbed short; her skirts, shorter. She read Dr. Warren Fabian's daring tome *Flaming Youth*, and referred to herself as a "salamander," slang for a flirty girl who liked adventure. In her abnormalities she had become normal, and Danny had grown exceedingly tired of her ilk.

"Hiya, honey," he said offhandedly. "You sure look ritzy." His words were as hollow as a prohibitionist's liquor cabinet.

"Says *you*," she sniffed and walked past him indignantly, hoping the snub would get his attention.

But cursory worked for him tonight, and he continued making his way to his dressing room. He was the headliner—the star of the bill—but he gladly took the smaller of the two rooms located closest to the stage. This would cause most luminaries to angrily call their agents, demanding for the sake of a demand. But not the easygoing Danny: he left such displays to amateurs whose capricious talent needed constant confirmation.

Flicking on the light bulbs which surrounded the mirror above his make-up table, he shut the door and sighed with relief. He couldn't get out of his tuxedo jacket, waist coat, shirt, and tie fast enough. Sitting down at the table he grabbed his ever-present bottle of aspirin, quickly shook out four tablets, and jammed them into his mouth. He chewed the bitter medicine without benefit of water. He liked it that way: it fit his mood. After a few moments he turned his attention to the pile of clutter in front of him, and shoved the green-and-tan tube of Max Factor #5 greasepaint, pot of kohl, liner brush, and tube of lip color out of the way. Opening the jar of Pond's, he dug his hand into the thick cream and smeared the stuff over his face. He closed his eyes, savoring the cool sensation it yielded.

At this point in the evening Danny used to feel like he had an electrical current running through his body. The high he experienced after winning over the audience used to overwhelm him. He used to feel alive. Tonight, and for a long time now, everything seemed meaningless to him. At the age of twenty-eight he was walking through life questioning everything; not having the slightest idea where to find a single answer. He grabbed one of the Pullman towels from a neatly folded stack and began scrubbing off the Pond's.

He paused, staring at the guy in the mirror.

"What the hell do you *want?*" he whispered.

Daniel Timothy O'Brien was born into show business. His grandfather, who was the Timothy of his middle name, was born in Donegal, Ireland, in 1835. He was one of a million Irish who immigrated to America in the 1840s and '50s to escape The Great Hunger—a devastating famine which was responsible for a million deaths. As one immigrant recalled of that time, "I saw the crop. I smelt the fearful stench … the death sign of each field of potatoes … the luxuriant stalks soon withered, the leaves decayed." Once on American soil, Timothy's family migrated to New York, by way of Ellis Island, feeling blessed to be a part of this wonderful new country.

From the time he was a mere boy Timothy believed he belonged in front of people, the center of attention. As a young man, he hopped a train from New York to Chicago to join up with the Hamlin's Wizard Oil Company traveling medicine show. This group journeyed in specially designed wagons which featured pipe organs with just barely enough space for their performers. Their draw was clean, moral, and musical entertainment for the whole family. Timothy would sing songs and do a line of patter that would include pitches for Wizard Oil, guaranteed to "cure rheumatism, neuralgia, sciatica, lame back … lumbago, contracted cords, toothache, sprains, swellings, frost bite, chill blains, bruises, sore throat, bites of animals and insects and reptiles." This miracle medicine, as was true of most of the elixirs sold in this type of exhibition, was actually just a concoction of cocaine, opium, and alcohol. In order to sell this questionable potion, these hucksters were expected to buy a temporary license from the sheriff of a given county. Since that was rarely granted, medicine shows took place clandestinely, only to have the whole operation shut down and fined while the quick-talking salesman was ridden out on a rail—or worse. Fortunately, for Timothy, he always managed to be in a new county when the lawman showed up with the warrant.

Despite (or, perhaps, because of) the risk involved, Timothy took to this shady lifestyle with gusto. He loved life on the road, bringing entertainment into the colorless lives of these tank towns' inhabitants. Prior to giving his pitch (which by all accounts was as stirring as an evangelical tent show sermon) there were acts of varying degrees of quality: acrobats, dancers, magicians, trick shots, storytellers, and even performing dog acts.

One dancer in particular caught his eye: a witty, intelligent, and delicate lass by the name of Bernadette Sweeney. After a quick courtship he married her, and they soon found that she was pregnant. In November of 1872 she gave Timothy a son, Seamus Fergal O'Brien. There were complications, however, and Bernadette was to pass away five days later.

Timothy was a caring, if distracted, father, not knowing quite what to do with the motherless boy. Seamus grew up quickly in the gritty world of traveling show business, and had decided by the age of ten that this would be his life as well. Small for his age, Seamus would get into fistfights with the other boys on the program, as well as those who lived in the towns in which they played. During one such brawl a local broke a whiskey bottle in half, using the weapon to cut a deep gouge in Seamus's cheek. Without pausing, the bleeding Seamus arrested the bottle from the boy and dealt him a worse blow, laughing to the shocked onlookers that it was just a shame to waste the whiskey. Over the years Seamus would develop the reputation as a fearless lad who would take on all who defied him, and soon earned the respect of everyone whose path he crossed. Many took just one look at the Irish boy's wild mop of curly red hair, fierce expression, and angry scar, then quickly conceded the battle. Seamus further disassociated himself from other youths by consciously adopting his father's thick brogue. He grew up with an attentive manner toward those he deemed important, and a hard, cruel streak toward those he considered subordinate.

By the time Timothy passed away in 1890, Seamus was firmly entrenched in the world of performance. A natural dancer, the slight and graceful young man chose this path and honed his skill. He would try on a number of partners until he found his perfect match: Lida Rose McCafferty, a petite, shy Irish girl born in 1874. She was all too willing to join this alluring stranger to escape a bad home life. A devout Catholic, she prayed the rosary daily and attended Mass whenever possible. Lida was a beauty, with thick black hair, light blue eyes, and the fairest porcelain skin Seamus had ever seen. They married in 1891, and soon gave birth—to a sensation of a vaudeville act. They were billed as The Dancing O'Briens and, through hard work and creative choreography, landed a spot on the prestigious Keith-Albee

Circuit. And, more important than gaining a temporary booking, they came to know the man who would control the whole vaudeville industry: Edward Franklin Albee II.

E. F. Albee, as he preferred, had begun his career touring with P. T. Barnum as a roustabout. Albee was a thin man who sported an enormous mustache. He set his sights on being the man in charge and, along with Benjamin Franklin Keith (another Barnum circus employee), would come to form the premier vaudeville dynasty. Despite the fact that the Keith-Albee circuit supplied thousands of acts with steady work, Albee was not liked by those in his employ; some even considered his business tactics questionable. One incontrovertible fact was that he provided performers with unmatched amenities in his two-a-day houses (those theatres which featured only two performances per day, as opposed to the small-time circuits which forced their performers to do three to five shows per day): clean, attractive dressing rooms, private toilets, and bathing facilities.

Albee, a shrewd judge of talent, knew he had an extremely popular act in The Dancing O'Briens, and was, therefore, civil from the start. Seamus tried his old Irish charm on the man in an attempt to forge a friendship, but it fell on deaf ears. Lida's gentle, quiet presence, however, *was* noticed by Albee. Perhaps he knew Seamus's kind and ascertained that hers was not an easy life. Perhaps she reminded him of someone special from his past. At any rate, he showed favoritism toward the team in a way that was most uncharacteristic.

The O'Briens also had another person in their corner: an agent by the name of Patrick Goodman. Born in 1875, he looked like a stock company's version of Ebenezer Scrooge, although he didn't share that character's most notorious trait. Patrick was tall and exceedingly lank. His black hair was parted in the middle, and he wore pince-nez, although his wife and daughters begged him to wear more modern eyeglasses. He was considered to be one of the best talent agents in New York, always unearthing a job—or better yet, a route—for his clients.

The O'Briens played forty-five vaudeville theatres in thirty-six cities throughout the U.S. and Canada, working fifty weeks a year and living in fine hotels and boarding houses. There was no one spot which they called home. Practicing new routines and refining their standard act was an obsession for Seamus who pushed the team to rehearse six hours a day, on top of dancing two performances seven days a week (taking off half of Sunday for Lida to attend Mass). The team specialized in a high-stepping, fast-paced cakewalk to ragtime music, and astounded spectators with their speed and exactitude. They developed original dances: "The O'Brien Novelty Tango," during which, while sublimely in step, they never touched (with Seamus suavely keeping his hands in his pockets); "The O'Brien New Step," a traditional quick step with higher kicks and precision rapid turns; and, always a crowd favorite, "The O'Brien Irish Waltz," set to "Little Nell Waltz." The team was so popular, in fact, that Lida's look (flowing tea-length petal-shaped skirt, tight riding-style jacket, and small veiled riding hat worn at an angle) was copied by fashionable women of the day. Seamus found that, with his hair shaved almost up the sides, clipped on the neck, oiled, and parted in the center, he gained a more elegant appearance, not unlike a matinee idol. With this style his once bright red hair took on a darker hue. Thick grease-paint make-up, he found, could cover the scar he earned as a youth. He usually wore a charcoal cutaway tuxedo and spats, although for daytime performances he was equally elegant in a light taupe ensemble.

Reviewers were filled with praise for their work. One christened them "the most inventive dance team of this century," and called their style "exciting delirious movement. They make the average theatregoer want to rise up from his seat and join in their exuberant gambols."

Seamus was indeed popular—especially inside the pubs of every town they visited. Everyone, it seemed, loved the charming Irishman, and he was quick to buy a drink for a new bar mate. He imbibed to excess, stumbling home late at night to a sleeping Lida. Many were the nights he would just pass out on the floor; still more the times he would awaken his wife with a slap. Once getting her attention, Seamus would take out any and every frustration on her verbally, whispering repugnant phrases while being oh, so very careful that no one in the next room could overhear. She would suffer through these times, relying on her faith to give her strength, and knowing that his stamina would give out soon enough. The next morning, sober and without a tell-tale hangover, he would be full of profuse apologies, making empty promises of empty glasses. Lida's father had been a lot like Seamus, and somehow it seemed strangely normal, unnaturally natural—though she continued, on a daily basis, to pray for a new way of life.

The first glimmer of that life dawned late in 1896 when Lida found that she was pregnant. Not knowing how Seamus would take the news, she put off telling him until she could no longer hide her condition. Remarkably, he was thrilled with this turn of events and treated her with a newfound gentleness. Seamus was excited and hoped for a boy. He got his wish, and was overjoyed as his son came screaming into the world on May 2. He loved Danny dearly, and vowed to be a changed man—for his son.

That promise would only last a few years. While The Dancing O'Briens continued their vaudeville tour barely missing a step (Lida had worn a fuller jacket over her skirt, and was able to dance until almost her seventh month), within two years of Danny's birth Seamus had returned to pubs, drinking, and cruelty. Danny was seven the first time he saw his father strike his mother. He hid; worried that this incident would hurt his mother and disrupt his family, not being able to comprehend that what he had witnessed was a regular occurrence. That night he cried himself to sleep, but these would be the last tears to be shed by the boy for a very long time.

The following day Danny asked his father about the incident, to which Seamus responded, "'Tis marriage, son. T'ain't pretty. But dunna tell your mother ye ken, 'twould break her heart. An' dun't ye be cryin' lad, 'tisn't manly." Danny would never forget this obdurate homily, nor could he blot from his mind the memory of those terrible nights when he could hear his drunken father's angry whispers. He would be especially sweet to his mother the following day, and she took succor in his affection. But fearing her husband's recrimination, Lida never allowed Danny to get too close to her, keeping an emotional distance which only broadened as he grew older.

By 1906, The Dancing O'Briens were known internationally. New dancing teams (called Terp Teams in the business, after Terpsichore, the Greek Muse of dance), however, were gaining ground and becoming more common. In order to add a new dimension to the act and to stay ahead of this ever-increasing competition, Seamus decided that his boy would join them onstage. After all, Danny was already ten years of age: old enough to begin working. Dressed in a miniature tux, a tiny image of his father, he would make his entrance when his parents were halfway through their act, tap his father on the shoulder, and dance away with his mother. The crowd invariably found this charming. The finish included a series of syncopated quick steps performed by all three O'Briens, which always left the audience yelling for more.

The *New York Times* featured this review of their new act:

Dancing into Our Hearts

Wild applause followed The Dancing O'Briens as they debuted their most recent act for those gathered at the Orpheum last Friday night. Along with some updated and thrilling dance steps and a new partner (their adorable son, Daniel), the O'Briens showed us why they are the ultimate vaudeville dance act in the world today. Dazzling, exhilarating, and remarkable, we can only hope that they will be around for a very long time.

Danny, like his father, was a natural dancer. He valued Seamus's praise, and took great satisfaction in the camaraderie the trio shared. But he hated having strangers speak to him about his family. They would tell him what a lucky boy he was to have such a loving father and mother, and that the O'Briens' marriage was an inspiration to them. He thought about the abuse with which his father "gifted" his mother, and vowed that he would never endure that kind of life. Simply put, he would never marry.

As Danny grew up, it was said that he was the spitting image of Lida's father: blond, with sparkling aqua-blue eyes, and a charismatic way about him. Everyone commented on what an exceptional young man he was, and Danny found that it was all too easy to win over just about anyone. His smile was commented on continually: he had white, straight teeth, and two deep dimples which he learned to use to his advantage. He found that the proprietresses of the local sweet shops would gladly sneak him extra chocolates just to see that smile, while the prettiest girls in every town were happy to offer him his "first kiss."

It was when The Dancing O'Briens were in New York playing the Palace that a heavyset gentleman approached Seamus, informing him that the New York Society for the Prevention of Cruelty to Children was checking into the welfare of his son. Seamus, always at his best in a pinch, retained his outwardly calm demeanor, and was quick to assure this fine fellow that his son was indeed keeping the best company; not put into "immoral situations" involving drugs, intoxicants, or prostitution; and was, in fact, being educated by Danny's sainted mother, God bless her. The man asked to meet the boy, which Seamus gladly arranged. Dressed in his finest, Danny charmed the man and passed his inspection with ease. The next day, Seamus told Lida to get some schoolbooks and an atlas, just in case the old buzzard came around again.

Had that representative quizzed Danny on literature, he, in fact, would have been impressed. Danny could read at an early age and had a boundless thirst for knowledge. He would take on Dickens or Shakespeare between rehearsals, and could write exceptionally well— and not just for his age; many of his fellow performers could only read their names on a vaudeville bill. Always willing to share anything he possessed, he offered to teach these uneducated artists reading and writing, and actually did tutor a few. And Danny was just as thirsty for the "immoral situations"—maybe even thirstier. He and a couple of kids would steal cigarettes and a pint of whiskey from their parents and go behind the theatres at night to have a grand old time. Four days after his fourteenth birthday, Seamus took Danny to a house of prostitution. When Seamus tried to settle up with the bleach-blonde twenty-one-year-old girl, she looked at the smiling Danny and told him to consider it a belated birthday present. From that day on, Danny could often be found after the evening performance knocking on the dressing-room doors of the chorines, a couple of bottles of beer by his side. Danny found that these pretty girls were all too willing to let him have their bodies for an evening of his magnetic company.

By the time Danny was fifteen he had accepted the fact that show business was an addiction from which he would never recover. He loved earning the crowd's approval, especially that kind of rare response that felt as though an explosion had gone off, sending wildly applauding people to their feet and programs falling to the floor. That marked a great night. He also loved the dramatic ambience of the theatres on the circuit, appreciating the architecture of the immense vaudeville palaces. Hearing about Danny's interest in this side of the business, E. F. Albee spent several hours with the boy, teaching him about the various components of design which made up the specific look of his theatres. He showed off, with pride, his ventilation system, a more efficient air-cooling system which blew air over large blocks of ice into ducts beneath the seats. Along with the majestic styling of the proscenium arch which framed the stage, Albee utilized paintings, statuary, and grand carpets to give his audiences a taste of extravagance. If such a look was over the top for those with refined palates, the less sophisticated were certainly impressed by the rococo sumptuousness of a big-time Keith-Albee theatre.

Between rehearsals, Danny enjoyed observing the other acts from the wings. His favorite performer by far was W. C. Fields, billed as "The Eccentric Juggler." Fields was a marvel to behold; his skill in manipulating cigar boxes was nothing short of breathtaking. This came from long years of often painful practice, as well as the inspiration of the so-called "Original Tramp Juggler," James Edward Harrigan.

Fields was serious, shy, and spoke with a mild stutter—which he concealed onstage by not speaking during his act, unless it was to mutter an unintelligible aside when he accidentally on purpose dropped one of his boxes. For a number of years Fields traveled the circuit with his wife, Hattie, who served as his onstage assistant. But when Hattie gave birth to their son, Claude, she chose to stay home, away from the road, and, consequently, away from her hard-working husband. Fields became the loneliest, most melancholic of men. It stands to reason, then, that Danny would be a welcome guest in his dressing room—he was even permitted to address the Great Man as Uncle Bill. The two could talk about a shared passion—the writings of Charles Dickens—for hours. And Fields taught the boy the mechanics of juggling, just one more contrivance Danny would learn to use to his advantage. The precocious boy could finesse Indian clubs, beanbags, and other objects with skill and dexterity, while finessing the hearts of the most jaded of girls. Now he would show up at the dressing-room door of the libidinous chorines with three empty bottles of beer to juggle—and a couple stashed away behind the theatre for imbibing.

At one time Danny even thought that he might turn that skill into a solo act, so easy and satisfying was the art to him. At night he would lie in bed and give thought to what shape this could take: a great comedy monologue punctuated by juggling unique articles that he could tie in with his patter. But soon something would happen that changed the course of his life.

On October 8, 1914, the O'Briens were invited to E. F. Albee's home for a dinner party to celebrate Albee's fifty-eighth birthday. They arrived at his ostentatious mansion, located at Seventy-Second Street in Manhattan, and were soon enjoying the impresario's gracious board. At one point during the meal Seamus began sweating profusely, but he somehow managed to hide the embarrassing condition from his fellow diners. By the time the men were smoking cigars in the oak-paneled den, Seamus had severe pain in his chest and down his left arm. He rose to leave the room, but sank to the floor. Albee ran to him, only to find that the thirty-nine-year-old Irishman was dead.

Albee immediately went to Lida and Danny, breaking the news to them as gently as possible. Lida was stunned into silence, and sat with Albee's wife, Lauretta, shedding a few tears. Danny was determined to be strong for his mother, which he found surprisingly easy to do—with Seamus's own words instructing him about being manly running through his head. Albee arranged for the O'Briens to be returned to their hotel immediately, while Seamus's body was taken to Campbell's Funeral Home to be prepared for the viewing. The grand funeral which followed was attended by vaudevillians and fans alike, the large price-tag of which was picked up by Albee himself. By the time Seamus's mahogany coffin was lowered into the cold ground, Lida had come up with a plan for the future. She was going to move upstate to live with her brother Reginald and his family, there to enjoy a peaceful retirement. Now that she was free of her abusive husband, she came to the realization that show business had never been her passion. But Danny was another matter. She arranged a long meeting with Albee and Patrick Goodman behind closed doors, emerging satisfied with their verbal agreement. Danny would stay on the Keith-Albee circuit and be guaranteed work as long as he wished, only in a different capacity—that of a singer. Case closed.

Danny hadn't the heart to argue the merits of a comedy-juggling act with his mother. He never thought he had a particularly good set of pipes, but he did know how to put a song over. Many was the time he performed in the pubs with Seamus, singing "Danny Boy" and getting free beer served by a mustachioed barkeep fighting back a tear. Maybe his mother and Albee were right about this being the best fit for him.

The first order of business was to line up a vocal coach for the young vaudevillian. Danny practiced for several hours a day, learning diaphragmatic breathing and proper methods of projection to avoid vocal strain. He found that, with enough practice, his voice could easily glide to the back row of any theatre. He loved the challenge of this different style of performing.

Danny started in a quartet, singing traditional Americana, usually in the number-two spot. He worked hard and proved to be the

kind of performer vaudeville audiences would happily pay to see—
and the kind of employee highly prized by any house manager. When
the United States joined the Great War in April 1917, Danny was
ineligible for the draft as he was Lida's only son and her sole means of
support. Faithfully, he would tuck a portion of his growing salary into
an envelope and address it to Mrs. Seamus O'Brien, care of Reginald
McCafferty, The Finger Lakes, New York.

After singing hundreds of renditions of "When You Wore a Tu-
lip" with the quartet, he was approached about doing a single and
grabbed the chance. Another closed-door meeting was held in Albee's
office with Patrick Goodman in attendance, this time with Danny on
the inside. Albee decided that the young man would sing traditional
Irish numbers, something he knew would be a draw for all the Irish
immigrants who populated the big cities of America. The young man
would be billed as "Danny O'Brien: Singer of Songs of the Old Sod."

His costume would suit his tall, elegant form: a white tailcoat
with cuffed trousers, white formal shirt, emerald-green waistcoat and
matching bow tie, white gloves, and black leather shoes with spats.
He would give voice to "The Wearing of the Green," "God Save Ireland," "Too-Ra-Loo-Ra-Loo-Ral (That's an Irish Lullaby)," "McCafferty," "The Rising of the Moon," "You Remind Me of My Mother,"
"Nellie Kelly I Love You," "Gee! But I Hate to Go Home Alone,"
"Three O'clock in the Morning," and, of course, "Danny Boy."

He premiered his act on the evening of Friday, August 8, 1917,
at B. F. Keith's New Theatre in Syracuse, and had found himself battling nerves that entire day. Danny arrived at the theatre early feeling
exhausted and nauseated. Wearing his make-up and costume, he sat
in his dressing room staring at a burned-out bulb which created a gap-
tooth in the smile of lights surrounding his make-up table. When the
theatre manager's five-minute knock sounded, a sharp adrenalin spike
kicked in, propelling him downstairs and into the wings. He all but ran
to the center of the stage upon hearing his cue, standing at first awkwardly with his hands in his pockets, then with them hanging limply at
his side. He hadn't thought about what to do with his hands: Just what

does one do? The stage felt huge to him, like an expanse of an unfamiliar and unfriendly wasteland; a sensation he hadn't experienced while dancing with his parents. The nerves that hit him anew constricted his throat to the point of his barely having a voice. When he somehow made it to the finish of the first song, the audience didn't bother being polite. A shout came from the gallery that suggested he get out his old dancing shoes. This jeering remark brought a repellent roar from the horde. Danny labored through his set, ending his debut with a quick and unrewarded bow. Backstage, Albee, who had witnessed the less-than-stellar performance, was kind to the boy. "This is why we start out in Syracuse," he said while lighting up a thin cigar. Danny thought of ending his solo career before it began, but knew better than to suggest reneging on a contract.

The following afternoon he made a second attempt. He had worked out some choreography for his hands, taking some cues from performers with whom he had worked in the past, and concentrated on a solid vocal warm-up routine. This seemed to be paying off as he found that the audience was much more amenable. What he didn't know was that the matinee was full of young girls who didn't care if he could sing or not: they were there to see the handsome Danny O'Brien. No matter the reason, the ovations at the end of each song gave him much-needed confidence to do his best. His prodigious abilities now in place, he began winning over older audiences as well.

His versions of the revered Irish ballads became standards, and sheet music featuring his image sold well in Tin Pan Alley and in music stores across the country. Albee was thrilled he had a new act that was destined to become even more popular than The Dancing O'Briens.

The *New York Times* gifted him with praise:

DANNY O'—My!

Danny O'Brien, no longer the dancing dandy of the famous Terp trio, burst onto the vaudeville stage last year as the ultimate Irish tenor, and the New York Irish rejoiced. Here at last is a worthy purveyor of the ancient melodies of Ireland. His superb presence, magnetic personality, and rare voice are about as potent an influence for the conservation of what is distinctly Irish as any that has appeared in our time. Be prepared to smile in equal measure with shedding tears, for his sincerity of song will affect you thusly. Thank you, our Danny Boy, for reminding us that a song can touch the heart like nothing else.

And so it was that Danny sang and traveled. He met new people, stayed at ever-changing hotels and boarding houses on the road, and played theatres he had seen as a child. He threw himself into the grind, not noticing as the loneliness of his new life slowly corroded his soul. In just a few short years his star in the vaudeville firmament rose, taking him to the coveted headliner spot—next-to-closing on the bill. He became more popular than he had ever thought possible, but emptier than he ever feared imaginable.

⇥⇤

Danny inserted the key into the battered doorknob and turned it. Renting this apartment in the Osborne, built in 1885 and located right next to Carnegie Hall, was one of the best decisions he had ever made. Unlike his father, who was nomadic by nature and liked living boarding house to boarding house and hotel room to hotel room, Danny relished having the security of a home base for those times not on the road or when playing local theatres. He also liked the fact that the building was said to be haunted by a notable ghost—an architect by the name of Alfredo Taylor, the designer who created an addition to the apartment building in 1906. The architect's ghost was believed to roam the building's halls as well as ride the elevator, and those who saw him said he liked to hang a watch fob from his hand. Danny had not seen Alfredo, but was not opposed to making his acquaintance.

Danny switched on the electric lights and walked into the kitchen. He set his dinner—a sandwich he picked up from his favorite deli, Katz's—his copy of *Variety*, and the day's mail on the tile counter next to the sink. This surface overflowed with life's accumulations: most unnecessary, some imperative. He shuffled through the mail, finding only bills and a small, flat package from his mother. Opening the latter, he found a pair of socks she made for him, along with a note of gratitude for his thoughtfulness. He shook his head and felt a surge of guilt: he could do more. Setting the package down, he almost knocked over the ubiquitous bottle of aspirin. *His headache was almost entirely gone,* he thought with relief. Best news of the day.

From behind him, two green eyes glowed ominously in the semi-gloom of the living-room couch. They blinked twice, then emerged as part of a large gray, brown, and tan tabby. He stretched luxuriantly and yawned, splaying his toes.

"There you are, old man," Danny said, greeting his cat. "I was wondering if you had lost your sense of smell. I have not-so-hot pastrami."

The tabby, named Murray, had roomed with Danny since the cat was a kitten, eight years before. Walking out of the backstage door one afternoon, Danny had overheard some dimwit laughing about seeing a cat hit by a car. Said the cat flew through the air like a football. While the guy was still laughing, Danny punched him in the nose and set out to find the cat—which he did, several blocks over, cowering behind a trash bin. After coaxing the limping and bleeding kitten out, Danny gingerly picked him up and took him to a veterinarian. The doctor administered sodium phenobarbital, then cleaned and stitched up the cat, doing his best to set a broken rear leg and bind it between a couple of tongue depressors and cotton padding. Over the padding he formed a cast using cornstarch paste and muslin strips. Danny was so grateful for the expert treatment that he sent the kind vet tickets to the vaudeville show for his whole family. He even invited the family to meet him backstage, much to the veterinarian's squealing daughters' delight.

After a lengthy and difficult recovery, during which time Danny fussed over the skinny stray, Murray slowly came around and was soon getting into as much mischief as any kitten and then some: the halting limp in his back leg being the only lingering reminder of the accident. The cat mellowed with age and became affectionate and interactive. Danny even played catch with him, throwing small wadded pieces of paper which Murray would retrieve and place at Danny's feet. This was the kind of connection which proved a tonic for the stress often plaguing Danny's life, and he couldn't imagine living without this perfect roommate.

Murray wound himself around Danny's legs and meowed loudly.

"I will make you, monsieur, the house specialty," Danny intoned in a bloated French accent. He bent down and scooped Murray into his arms, scratching behind his ears and kissing the tabby "M" on his forehead. While Murray enjoyed the affection, his eyes never left the wrapped pastrami sandwich. After listening for the low, rumbling purr, Danny put Murray down and grabbed a can of Spratt's Cat Food from the white cupboard.

"Tonight monsieur shall have the tuna *foie gras* with a *remoulade* of pastrami." Danny looked at Murray, who granted his approval with a silent meow from a serious expression. Danny chuckled—first time all day he had smiled with veracity.

He opened the can, keeping it at a safe distance from his nose, and plopped its pungent contents into a bowl. Danny then unwrapped his sandwich, removed a center piece of pastrami (center, to avoid the offending mustard), shredded it with his fingers, and placed it atop the brown pile of cat food.

"Here you go, old man." Danny set the bowl down and watched as Murray first sniffed the offering, took a tentative taste, then settled in to dine. Danny walked over to his latest mechanical pride and joy: a small, white Frigidaire, and removed a bottle of Dr. Pepper for himself and a cold bottle of milk for Murray. After pouring some milk for the feline, he sat down at the counter to eat.

Danny consumed the sandwich quickly and read the paper slowly. He looked for the latest shows that were opening, who was in town, and what was going on in the news. This was his security; these familiar names and places, keeping alive the world in which he thrived. The profession was good to Danny, in no small part because of his relationship with Albee, paying him three thousand dollars per week. After rent and other miscellaneous expenses (five hundred of which he sent to Lida), Danny was left with a hefty monthly savings. And because he didn't gamble (either on horses or Wall Street), drink, or travel beyond his vaudeville routes, he had quite a nest egg. A small amount rested in a bank, but the majority slept in a safe he had in his bedroom closet. His father always wanted to have a safe at his disposal, often describing it as "a cozy fat and wealthy man, al'ays there to lend ye a hand." This may have been Seamus's desire, but he drank up any extra money the family had at the end of the month, so there was nothing to save. Danny wanted something to fall back upon in case—well, just in case. And by this point Danny's safe was as full as a campus quad watching a flag-pole sitter.

He grabbed the pack of Camels and silver lighter that resided on the counter, pulled out a cigarette, lit it, and took a long first draw. He closed his eyes and contemplated his nascent desire to change his act. Getting out of the role of singer and taking on something new might be professional suicide, but it might also be just the matchstick he needed to reignite the fire that had long since burned out. He was determined to take on something challenging, perhaps as a monologist. But no, he reasoned, not another act where he would be onstage alone. He reflected on the days when he worked with his parents, thinking of the good times they experienced while honing the act. He realized that he wanted that sense of intimacy, of having a partner who shares every success—and failure—in equal measure. Someone you rehearse with, perform with, travel with, eat with—someone who could be counted on for encouragement, having been with you every step of the way. Someone who, just perhaps, could offer that sense of belonging. Someone on whom he could depend. Maybe, just maybe, this was the basis of his emptiness.

He thought and thought: What kind of two-act could he come up with that would show off his comic chops and his Irish charm? He could play a doctor … no, that's Smith & Dale's department, and, besides, it's been done to death. He was good with accents, and could do an Irish or Dutch dialect act … but that's where Weber & Fields shine.

He got up and started pacing the length of the kitchen. Murray, still working on his meal, didn't bother to look up, so used was he to this habitual schlep. Danny knocked the burnt end off of his cigarette into the ashtray on the counter. He looked at the pile of mail—and the package.

A delivery boy.

A delivery boy—someone who just shows up in an office, package in hand, and maybe drops it off at the desk of a pretty receptionist. The guy could be brash, and the sketch could revolve around how he gets knocked down by the girl, but wins her in the end. A flirtation act. Could work; could work. He would file this away, knowing that he was too tired this evening to get anywhere with the idea. And, most importantly, he didn't want that headache back. But this concept was definitely worth revisiting. He cleared away the remnants of dinner and proceeded to the living room, Murray following him, having licked his bowl clean.

"Okay, old man, and now it's—'The Culture Hour,'" Danny informed him, utilizing a thick British accent, "brought to you by Spratt's Cat Food. Always Spratt's, always the best." Murray rewarded Danny's pitch with a loud purr. Danny walked to the bookcase which held his 78s, and pulled out several possibilities before settling on what he wanted to hear. "So, friends, tonight we will hear from Enrico himself—from 1911." Danny carefully slipped the record from its thick, tan sleeve, glancing at the familiar burgundy label with its gold lettering and image of the dog staring with piqued interest into the Victrola's bell-shaped horn. "Herein we have an Italian who is singing in French and recording in New Jersey," he stated, the irony completely lost on Murray who was taking the moment to groom. Danny opened the top of his Victrola XII (he was wont to say that this was the best $150 he ever spent), placed the thick shellac record on the turntable, rotated the crank several times, and moved the arm onto the spinning disc. He opened the small doors at the bottom of the player for optimum sound, and out from the machine emanated a prelude of crackle and hiss. Shortly, the strains of the Victor Orchestra could he heard, followed by Caruso's controlled beginning to Massenet's haunting aria "Ah! fuyez, douce image" from *Manon*. Danny knew every note, every syllable, every pop and scratch. He sat down on his favorite deep-green horsehair chair located right next to the Victrola table to listen. Murray immediately leapt onto Danny's lap, stretching up and softly rubbing his muzzle against Danny's cheek. After a while he settled down, closing his eyes and dozing off.

Danny marveled as Caruso's remarkable voice built with the lyrical drama. He had never felt envious of the opera singers he so admired; his lack of jealousy was something for which he was grateful, having seen what that useless emotion could do to people and careers. And, to him, he was just singing Irish schmaltz in a popular-style voice, whereas Caruso was a *real* singer. Listening to this powerful aria of frustration and pain, Danny once again got caught up in Caruso's passion; his overwhelming love expressed so perfectly in this unearthly music. Would Danny ever have a Manon of his own? Would he ever feel that kind of yearning? Sure, he'd had his share of women—plenty of them—but no lasting relationships. He let go too easily. Whenever a girl would say, "You change your ways or else," Danny would always choose "or else." Like Thelma. They had a few dates, shared some laughs. But he certainly didn't want to spend more time with this girl who attempted to fight her way into a relationship. No, he had never felt an all-consuming drive and fervidness for someone. Some*thing*, yes: vaudeville, at least at one time, long ago. But romantic ardor is for the French and Italian tenors. And, after all, it didn't end so well for them, he reasoned as he contemplated the ending of *Manon*. Danny was a seasoned pro in the entertainment business. That is what he knew; what he trusted. The Massenets, the Puccinis, the Verdis—they had to make love seem do or die. That was *their* business.

In the real world it simply didn't exist.

He was much more level headed. In his life he was seeking—what *was* he looking for? Succinctly: a reason. A reason to keep working on the stage. A reason to get up in the morning. A reason to even have a heart, let alone use it. Just … a reason.

The song ended with the repeated hiss of the needle in the lead-out groove. He took a final drag from his cigarette, rubbed it out in the ashtray, then slowly rewound the crank and moved the arm back to the beginning.

CHAPTER TWO

THE GIRL

July 1925

The music which flowed from the small Victrola's horn matched her lugubrious mood. Bessie Smith's earthy rendition of "Baby Won't You Please Come Home" was sheer perfection; a song performed honestly, but with a voice so sweet and well-modulated that one could get lost in its beauty.

Violet walked from the phonograph stand in her bedroom to the embrasure of the window overlooking her parents' backyard, and traced the fat raindrop making its way down the pane. She was bored and had that unmistakable sense of restlessness; a feeling she experienced far too often these days. And this wasn't in the least like her. But since leaving business school she had felt at sixes and sevens, not really being able to figure out—well, *anything* about her life: what she wanted, who she wanted to be, who she wanted to be with. She surmised that this was because her life was full of "endless possibilities," and that she could do anything she put her mind to, as her father liked to say. He was very free with his pep talks, which only succeeded in making her feel all wound up—with no place to spring.

As the music continued, with Bessie singing to her lost love to please come back, Violet stared out her window, her forehead pressed against the cool glass; her world condensed to that porthole's view. The July rain pooled in her mother's rose bed and turned the velvet grass into a sopping-wet sponge. But then, precipitation is as common in Portland, Oregon, as crooked politicos in Washington, D. C. Old-timers always annoyed their listeners by calling it "liquid sunshine," and most Oregonians obliviously went about their business as usual even in a downpour. Violet loved the rainfall, and the promise of verdant landscapes it brought.

Her attention was arrested by a commotion from the steps of the back porch. Two scrub-jays were hopping and dancing around a stick, showing off their deep azure-blue backs and wings. Soon another joined in the gathering, adding his harsh, scratchy squawk to the mounting chorus. She loved these assertive, vocal birds with the dusty gray-brown breasts as they could be most entertaining. As one of the birds advanced toward the stick and gave it a swift peck, Violet noted that the stick moved ever so slightly and revealed itself to be a small garden snake. She quickly threw open the window, yelling, "Get out of here, you bullies! Leave that poor little snake alone!" Up flew the tormenting trio, leaving the snake to swiftly slither under the porch step to safety. Violet smiled as she shut the window with a loud thud.

"Not on my watch."

Violet's father, Charles Willoughby Williams, was born in November of 1880, in Portland, Oregon, of French and Scots lineage. Portland was known in the 1840s as "The Clearing," as it was just a small stopping place along the west bank of the Willamette River, used by travelers en route from Oregon City to Fort Vancouver. At the time, the deed to this land was held by Asa Lovejoy, of Boston, and Francis W. Pettygrove, of Portland, Maine. When the time came to christen this new town, both men wanted to name it after their home towns. A flip of a coin decided the moniker.

Portland developed a reputation early on as a hard-edged and gritty port town. Some historians have described the city's early establishment as being a "scion of New England; an ends-of-the-earth home for the exiled spawn of the eastern established elite." In 1889, the *Oregonian* called Portland "the most filthy city in the Northern States," due to its unsanitary sewers and gutters, and, at the turn of the twentieth century, was considered one of the most dangerous port cities in the world. The city housed a large number of saloons, bordellos, gambling dens, and boarding houses which were populated with miners after the California Gold Rush, as well as a horde of sailors passing through the port.

It was, in fact, the notorious gold rush that brought Charles's parents, John and Suzanne (Susan) Williams, to Oregon in the first place. Although they found this city challenging, and sometimes longed for the comfort of the East, they established a solid home among those who possessed what would be known as the "Oregon Spirit."

But unlike those who came to the West and found financial success, John and Susan's wealth would not be achieved in worldly goods, but rather in a tight family bond. They had five children, Charles being the youngest, and instilled in them at an early age the importance of treating one's fellow human beings with dignity and kindness. They stressed the importance of helping those to whom the government would not listen: the unfortunates who got lost in the "progression" of the new century dawning in 1900. Throughout their lives, this loving family would take in urchins, boys and girls who found themselves destitute and working in brothels in order to feed themselves and their family members. Many young souls were healed, and many lives were turned around because of John and Susan's kind and healing spirits.

Charles was a handsome boy, with warm brown eyes and dark, wavy hair. He had a great sense of humor and, although shy, was easily caught up in the excitement of those around him. Privately, he found some of the dangerous aspects of the city to be thrilling, although just a little of this kind of stimulation to a boy as perceptive as Charles went a long way. He had a good mind, and his parents were determined that he have a solid education to ensure his ease—and, therefore, success— in business. After his schooling was completed, his parents suggested a career in banking, and Charles began an apprenticeship at Ladd & Tilton Bank. Ladd operated their business in a building at First and Stark, and was the first bank to be established north of Sacramento and west of Salt Lake City. The bank had received its first deposit of $50 in June of 1859. Charles would enjoy his employment at the bank, rising from bank teller (wearing armbands to blouse his sleeves, and thereby avoid soiling them with ink), to loan assistant, to loan manager.

During his off hours, Charles, taking to heart his parents' message of community involvement, determined a way to distinguish himself. He joined with other men in becoming a women's suffragette advocate, and proudly wore a pin sporting the colors of the movement: violet, for dignity; white, for purity; and green, for hope. He befriended Senator Aaron A. Sargent of California who had met, and was inspired by, Susan B. Anthony. Failing to achieve a federal amendment allowing women the same right to vote as men, the suffragists pressed for the right to vote in the laws of individual states and territories while retaining the goal of federal recognition.

It was during one such Oregon rally in 1902 that he met the woman who would become his wife: Beryl Shureen Goodman. Beryl was born in May of 1878 into a good English family with a large estate. She was tall, curvaceous, and carried herself with pride; her bright blue eyes shining out from an intelligent face. Beryl possessed high cheekbones and a full mouth, both qualities of which were overshadowed by her lustrous, thick mane of auburn hair, piled high upon her head in the contemporary bouffant "waterfall of curls" Gibson Girl fashion. She possessed a quick wit, and was known for being able to debate anyone on any topic, knowing how to utilize tact and common sense when the situation necessitated. She had one older brother, Patrick, with whom she was very close. Patrick journeyed to New York to find success as a talent agent, but Beryl stayed in Oregon and, after getting a good education, was on track for becoming a business woman. But an additional pursuit became appealing to her when she met Charles: that of being a wife and mother.

Beryl and Charles had chemistry right from the start. Charles discovered a wealth of newfound romanticism which beat within his heart, and he spent hours upon end writing sonnets to Beryl of a florid, passionate style; something that he would continue to do throughout their enduring relationship. She called him "my Poet," and thoroughly enjoyed the outpouring of this young man's heart. He also read poetry to her, from the great romantic writers of the early nineteenth century: John Keats, Percy Bysshe Shelley, William Wordsworth, Emily Dickinson, and Ralph Waldo Emerson. Holding hands and indulging in an occasional kiss, they would sit on a whitewashed bench in her parents' garden, sheltered by a large arborvitae hedge, viewed only by flitting butterflies and an occasional errant hummingbird.

They were married almost exactly a year after meeting and lived in a large house located in the Irvington community of Portland. The house, a wedding present from her parents, was to become a treasured family home. With its unique mix of Queen Anne and Colonial styles, it stood three stories tall, with majestic gables and a large turret over the front porch. From the street, with the tall oak and willow trees surrounding it, the aqua-and-white house took on the appearance of a country inn. Charles personally hired a housemaid and gardening personnel to help with the chores of such a large property. Beryl decided that she indeed liked being free of the domestic responsibilities and took on other pursuits. Possessing a good head for mathematics, she became the resident bookkeeper for a neighboring milliner's shop.

One afternoon Charles was having lunch at a local restaurant which specialized in German cuisine. The proprietor, an immigrant by the name of Fritz Glück, was a large man with an ingratiating manner. He knew Charles by sight, always greeting him with a warm "*Willkommen!*" More than once Charles invited Fritz to join him in a stein of beer, and they would converse for an hour or more, with Fritz lapsing into German and Charles piecing together his meaning by studying his friend's expressive face. One day Fritz asked Charles if he would be interested in hiring a girl to cook and run errands for the household. Thinking of Beryl's growing duties outside the home, he answered in the affirmative, and asked Fritz if he knew anyone.

"You are in luck, *mein guter Freund* Charles," Fritz said, wiping the beer foam from his thick mustache. "My daughter, Mary, is as good a *Koch* as you will find anywhere. Her *Schmorbraten*, you would say German pot roast, will make you sing, *es ist* so *gut*. She is looking for work, and I know you and *deine Familie* would provide a good *Haus* for her." That evening, Charles excitedly told Beryl about the chance conversation, and both agreed that the help would be most welcome.

The next morning the doorbell rang. Beryl opened it to find the back of a short girl, suitcase in hand. She slowly turned around, revealing herself as the new family chef, Mary Glück. Although her German surname translated to *joy*, that was hardly the emotion she exuded. She had the countenance of one perpetually surprised and slightly afraid, as if everything in life took her off guard. Her large green eyes were always open wide, and her mouth, even in repose, formed a perfect "O." She wore her thin, brown hair plaited and wrapped about her head; her clothes were baggy, and her stockings sagged.

"May I help you?" Beryl questioned.

The girl looked at Beryl, then at a paper in her hand. She began a sentence twice, and then looked around at the other houses.

"Are you the cook?" Beryl asked, trying to help the young girl.

After a good stretch of indecision, Mary finally spoke. "Yes."

Beryl felt sorry for the girl, and softened her voice to a whisper. "Come along then, and we shall get you settled. What is your name?"

A pause of an undue length commenced, during which Beryl couldn't help but huff. After the girl recovered from the huff, she said so quietly that she could scarcely be heard: "Mary."

Mary was shown the room toward the back of the house which would be hers, and Beryl took her on a tour of the kitchen, mentioning the family's dietary habits and preferences. Throughout this orientation Mary's hands were constantly in motion, looking like small, nervous birds attempting to take flight. But the girl seemed to understand the lay of the land, and, much to Beryl's surprise and relief, would settle in and prove herself to be an excellent cook indeed.

The first time Beryl went to Mary to compliment her on the evening's pot roast, Mary acted as though she would be getting the boot any minute. When it slowly dawned on her that this was an accolade, she was silenced by the praise. Beryl, unfortunately, soon found her halting and nervous manner irritating, and quickly learned that the less said to her the better. She gave Mary full reign to plan and execute meals, which was an arrangement equitable to both parties. The only time the Williamses ever saw the girl was upon the rare occasion when she would take an evening walk around the property; stepping in a halting fashion, hands fluttering, Mary looked around the grounds as if at any moment she expected to come face to face with a vampire.

Not a month after Mary had started work at the Williams' home, Charles paid a visit to his favorite German restaurant. Fritz came over to his table and clapped him on the back.

"My Mary, *sie erzählt mir, wie wunderbar du bist!*"

"Please, in English, Fritz!" Charles requested.

"She tells me how *wunderbar* you are, you and your family. She is so happy, und *das tut meiner Seele gut*, uh, my soul is good."

When Charles got home that evening he told Beryl about the conversation regarding their cook. They had a chuckle thinking of how the girl no doubt communicated this message to her father, and how he then relayed the message in his own fashion to Charles.

Beryl was justifiably proud of her home, feeling that the sprawling backyard was what made it truly special. Under her loving care a garden was created that was the envy of all who called themselves horticultural enthusiasts. It seemed as if there wasn't a variety of flower that wouldn't grow in this sanctuary. Along with the usual assortment of blossoms could be found hydrangeas, which were especially plentiful and of the most vivid blues and pinks, and rhododendrons of all colors, from snow white to crimson red, which thrived in several sunny spots. One purple rhododendron was so huge, in fact, that it took on the shape of a tree, easily reaching over a man's head. Teas were held outside on the sprawling lawn, and guests often said that the air was perfumed like heaven itself.

Beryl had to admit that these lavish teas were a definite pleasure for her to host. She approached them with businesslike professionalism: ordering the food from one local merchant (much to the relief of Mary), arranging a serving staff from a local employment agency, writing invitations in her own beautiful hand, and ordering her landscaping staff to make sure the gardens were in perfect shape come that day. Women attired in long, flowing day dresses and large-brimmed hats graced the Williams' property on the arms of gentlemen wearing formal morning attire. God in His infinite wisdom dared not allow a drop of rain to fall during one of these gatherings. Everyone who attended felt as if they had been to the social event of the year, and truly admired the abundant violets, roses, and daisies, causing Beryl to blush under their prodigious praise.

But it would be another grouping of violets, roses, and daisies which would be Charles and Beryl's most successful endeavor: their children. Violet Charline Williams was born on November 4, 1905, and immediately became the apple of her father's eye. Along with being named after the graceful flower, *violet* served also as a nod to one of the colors of the women's suffragette organization that brought the couple together. The brunette-haired, brown-eyed beauty followed Charles around everywhere, and would often stand at the door and cry for some time after he left for work. Beryl would scoop her into her arms and explain to her that Father had to go to work, and that he would be home later in the afternoon. But wooden puzzles assembled in her room and books read in the library didn't fully distract her from his absence. A few minutes before five she would camp out at the front door, rewarding her weary father with a hug and many kisses. For both, this was the highlight of their day.

Violet would get two sisters with whom to play: Rose Bernice came along in 1907, followed by Daisy LeAnn in 1910. She mothered these new, very lifelike dolls, helping Beryl whenever she could. But it was to her father's side that the five-year-old naturally migrated, begging him to take her with him to his bank. Charles always replied that little girls simply did not accompany their fathers to their places of business; that she would be quite bored sitting still all day in the office. But, after multiple requests and rejections, she finally wore him down. A date was set for the following day.

Dressed in her best pink cotton frock reaching just to her knees, white sash, white stockings, and white patent-leather shoes, Violet was the very picture of a Daddy's Girl. Her mother took extra care to curl her eager daughter's hair in ringlets and tied a large bow atop her head. She then put a pack of colored pencils and a few sheets of drawing paper in a small white purse and placed it over the girl's arm as she was walking out the door. Her mother, the strict disciplinarian of the family, warned her to be on her best behavior, to which Violet nodded agreement enthusiastically.

Violet loved every minute of this exciting journey, from the carriage ride downtown to the trip up the marble staircase in the huge bank building. Charles's office was just off that of the manager's, the rather severe-looking Mr. Daniels. When Charles and Violet were in front of his office, he stepped out, looked down at her and grimaced. Violet hid behind her father.

"She's with me. You won't hear a peep, sir," Charles assured his boss.

Once in Father's office, however, Violet felt safe and secure. This large room featured dark wood paneling and huge windows overlooking the city. Center stage was his massive, imposing desk covered with documents of all kinds, dark brown leather-covered books, fountain pens, and a large green lamp. Violet was given a small desk in the corner and told to stay there while Father worked. She smiled, retrieving the colored pencils and paper from her purse. She soon was drawing contentedly, glancing up now and then to see him attending to what must be important business. How she loved the air of excitement as employees would come into the room one by one, arms burdened with stacks of paper, serious expressions darkening their faces. But they would all smile at her and tell Charles how very sweet she looked, working away with her colored pencils. Many asked if she was a new employee, a quip that was always followed by much laughter.

Shortly before lunch, Charles was needed for a brief meeting downstairs. He told Violet that she must be good, and "help Father work." She knew exactly what he meant, and approached his desk as soon as he left. The poor papers looked so colorless, she thought to herself, and, with the best possible intentions, she sought to remedy this problem.

Coming back to his office twenty minutes later with yet another sheaf of papers, Charles was relieved to find Violet sitting patiently at her desk. "Were you a good girl?" he asked her, giving her a hug.

"Oh, a very good girl, Father!" she assured him.

He sat at his desk and noticed that nothing had been touched. Perhaps bringing his little girl to the office had not been such a bad idea after all. He uttered a small sigh of relief and got back to work. Within a couple of minutes, however, he heard a loud gasp emanating from the hallway. Mr. Daniels came storming into his office, waving a handful of papers in Charles's face.

"Just *look* at what your child has done!" he thundered. Violet shrank into her chair, trying to make herself invisible. She had only tried to help Father by decorating Mr. Daniels's papers, but he didn't seem to value her hard work.

"The clients are on their way upstairs, and *this* is what we have to present to them?" And with that, Mr. Daniels stormed out of the office. Charles asked Violet why she had done such a thing, and, upon hearing her explanation, could only chuckle softly.

"Your desire to help may cost me my job, but I appreciate your efforts," he told the frightened girl as she came and sat on his lap.

While recalling this event for his wife that evening, Charles was all smiles. It turned out that the clients found the small, colorful drawings in the corner of the contract's pages charming, and even asked to meet the young artist.

As Violet grew up, she developed a sense of joyfulness that attracted attention everywhere she went. Her parents saw to it that all their girls were educated at the best schools, and Violet found that she was good at most everything she undertook. There wasn't a subject at which she didn't excel; she even held the position of president of her student body during her junior year. She and her sisters sang, often in church, and around the piano in the family parlor. Violet also had a natural ability to play music on stringed instruments, especially the guitar and ukulele. The entire family enjoyed the evening musicales they spontaneously presented, at times inviting in neighbors and friends for an impromptu concert, culminating in ice-cold lemonade and Mary's special spice cake.

It was no surprise, therefore, that the music-loving family jumped at the chance to see a vaudeville show in Seattle. Just the opportunity to watch these exciting performers was irresistible. So the Williams clan decided to make a weekend of it, traveling to Washington and seeing a big-time show.

The date: October 17, 1915. Their destination: The Orpheum Theatre at Third Avenue and Madison Street. As they approached the theatre, Violet gazed with wonder at the decorative wrought-iron canopy which extended from the Orpheum box office to the curb. The interior was no less impressive. Pulling from classical Greek and Italian architecture, the lavishly decorated main foyer was awash in marble, onyx, and glass. The actual auditorium of the Orpheum was as ornate as the foyer, with murals depicting both classical and mythological themes decorating the walls and ceilings. Selections included scenes from *The Iliad* and *The Odyssey*, Aesop telling his fables, and the twelve Muses. The main floor of the auditorium had a thousand seats, yet the venue could have easily been equipped with more—theatre manager John Considine boasted that fewer seats were installed to provide wider aisles and more legroom for patrons. Six individual boxes (with six seats each) lined the sides of the auditorium. Violet's father paid top price—fifty cents per person—to get the very best seats in the house.

Their experience of enjoying this true vaudeville show was like that of many theatregoers of the day. A typical big-time, eight-act show might run as follows:

1. Acrobat (dumb act)
2. Singer or minor comedy act
3. Tab show or flash act
4. Good comedy team or a top singing act
5. Knockabout or tab show (depending on what is slotted in the 3 spot)
    Intermission
6. A solid dancing team
7. The headliner—the star of the bill
8. Closing, animal act, juggler

The night Violet got her first taste of "the show business" would feature Dainty Marie (Marie Meeker), a singer and dancer who dressed in white tights and performed living recreations of Rodin's statues; Robert Dailey and Company, who performed the farcical skit "Our Bob"; Mabelle Lewis, a petite woman who impersonated young children in songs; The Bison City Four, who sang and performed character comedy dressed, respectively, as an Irish policeman, an Italian fruit vendor, an American bartender, and a nondescript tramp; singer Elsie Fay; and the Novelty Clintons, a popular acrobatic duo well known for their jumping and hopping expertise.

But the big draw that night was already a vaudeville legend: Harry Houdini. Houdini's act began with a seven-minute motion picture featuring the magician in Paris, leaping, handcuffed, into the Seine. At the climax of the film, which showed him escape his bonds, Houdini himself appeared onstage to a rousing ovation. He then donned a straightjacket, from which he soon extricated himself. Next up was what he called "the East Indian Needle Trick." More than fifty needles were given to the magician, along with a thread of silk, all of which he appeared to swallow whole. He would then "regurgitate" the needles, which were now magically threaded together.

The highlight of Houdini's act, however, was yet to come: his famous Chinese Water Torture Cell. A huge, empty tank with glass sides was brought onstage. Selected audience members were allowed to examine it, after which Houdini briefly left the stage to change into his swimsuit while his assistants filled the tank to the brim with water. When he came back on the stage, Houdini lay down and placed his feet in stocks, which were also inspected by various audience members. His feet were then locked into place. Hoisted upward, he was lowered head first into the tank, where the stocks were secured to the top. Velvet drapes were raised around it, and the audience waited for him to escape.

One minute passed, then two. Violet, along with the rest of the audience, was feeling nervous for the famous man. How could anyone hold their breath for this long? He would surely die if he didn't get air soon! An assistant held an axe at the ready, in case of emergency. The orchestra began playing "Asleep in the Deep," and just as the audience began to yell to the assistant to shatter the glass, Houdini emerged from behind the curtains, to thunderous applause. Violet clapped until her hands stung, so enthused was she by the experience.

This encounter with vaudeville left a deep impression on Violet, one that would remain with her for the rest of her days: the reaction from the audience—seeing the joy on the faces of those who attended the show—made her happy, transformed. Excitement hit her in the solar plexus. Simply put, she now became impatient with anything approaching a boring life.

When Violet reached her mid-teens, everyone agreed that her beautiful inner spirit was in equal measure to her outer beauty. She was petite, but always carried herself with perfect posture, an air which made her look much taller than she actually was. She had many beaux, but chose to flirt with several rather than get serious with just one. They all seemed—the worst thing she could say about a person—rather ordinary. Try as they might, no one could receive her full attention, or her heart.

Her best feature (besides her large, expressive walnut-brown eyes and her full, perfectly bowed mouth) was her thick dark brown hair. She wore it long and curled, as was the custom, and people were always taken with its luster. More than a few friends thought it shocking when, in 1923, she determined to get it cut off for her eighteenth birthday. She wanted this not because it was the trend of the times, but because she loved the freedom it seemed to give the wearers. In fact, she eschewed girls who took on all the trappings of the libertine flappers of the day; she would never take up a habit or affectation just because it was mirrored by a crowd. She was what her father wanted most for her to be: a confident, independent thinker who made her own decisions in life. Violet was no prude—she did swear, albeit internally, the only evidence of which was the occasional reddening of her cheeks.

Because the trend of bobbing women's hair wasn't accepted by many salons, barbers became the stylists of necessity for these modern women. Violet, who took Rose along with her to the barber shop for moral support, opted for the bob-and-shingle cut—a short bob haircut with a tapered back and bangs which almost reached the eyebrows—the style that would be popularized by Louise Brooks. She was a bit anxious to view the result, keeping her eyes closed during the entire haircut. When finally opening her eyes, however, she loved the finished look. She felt lighter, breezier, and exactly what she wanted: unencumbered. Rose decided to keep her own locks long, but was very tempted by how cute the style looked on her sister. The one who admired Violet's new look the most, however, was her father, who gave her a huge bear hug when he first saw her.

Violet was also the kind of girl who never backed down from a bet. One Saturday afternoon the three Williams girls decided to attend a variety show at a local theatre. Violet led the way, arranging transportation and procuring tickets. Once ensconced in the second row facing the huge stage, Violet again began to feel that excitement at the thought of the delights to come. After the initial performances, comprised of a barbershop quartet and a trained dog act, a magician came onstage and addressed the audience. He was garbed in black from head to foot, wearing a silk top hat and satin cape. Featured most prominently upon his face was a large mustache, waxed and bent into two great wings.

"Good afternoon, ladies and gentlemen," he said grandly. "I am The Great Grandoli, and today I shall astound and amaze you through my supernatural feats. But, in order to do this, I must first ask for a volunteer from the audience."

Rose turned to Violet, whispering, "Bet you won't volunteer."

That was all it took. "I'll take that bet," she whispered to Rose. Violet then jumped up, waving her hand and shouting, "I'm your volunteer!"

The magician took one look at the beautiful, petite young girl and smiled a broad, toothy smile. "Yes, young lady, please come up and assist The Great Grandoli."

Daisy gave out a short gasp. Rose laughed and looked on as Violet made her way to the side of the stage and up the steps to the center. She joined the magician, who took her by the hand. "What is your name, dear child?"

"I'm Violet Williams," she said in a loud voice with barely a tremor. The lights were brighter than expected, but she felt that maybe it was a good thing she couldn't see the crowded auditorium. She noted that The Great Grandoli wore a tremendous amount of make-up and smelled strongly of bay rum.

"Now, my dear Violet, as pretty as the posy itself, I shall make you disappear from sight! Behold! The Gateway to the Next Dimension!"

The orchestra began playing the dramatic opening chords of Rimsky-Korsakov's *Scheherazade*. As the main curtain slowly parted, a large, ornately painted chest came into view, located in front of a black backdrop. The magician walked to the box, opened the front-facing door with a flourish, and displayed the emptiness of the container. He walked back and forth, whipping his cape as he strode, turning the container around and showing all four solid walls. Returning the chest to the center as it was first presented, he again took Violet's hand.

"And now, my enchanting assistant will enter The Gateway to the Next Dimension!" He moved Violet into the box, and whispered, "Just stay put, kid, and someone will grab your hand."

Closing the door with imposing fanfare, The Great Grandoli proceeded to again walk back and forth on the stage, whipping his cape and tapping on the door as he passed. On the second tap, Violet heard a small door open from the back of the box and felt someone grab her hand. "Squat down and crawl backward," came a whisper. The curtain rose sufficiently for her to slink beneath and out of the box. She rose on the other side, trying to see in the dark, just making out the shape of the small, rotund man who had taken her hand. He closed the door of the box, rearranged the curtain, then turned and smiled at her. He raised a finger to his lips in a gesture to ensure silence. She smiled back, nodding.

The Great Grandoli knocked on the door once more, then stood in front of the prop, facing the audience, holding a hand to his head and appearing to be in a state of great concentration. He suddenly came to and yelled at the top of his voice, "Behold, she is no longer in this realm!" He opened the door and, sure enough, The Gateway had apparently transported the young girl to a different world. The orchestra played a fanfare as the audience rewarded the magician with cheers and applause. Rose laughed out loud, amazed by her sister's daring. Daisy, however, took Rose's hand—just for a bit of reassurance.

After a suitable pause, the performer again addressed the audience. "But beauty such as our Violet's cannot be cast asunder from our earthly sphere. I shall will her back from the depths of time and space!" The orchestra returned to the eerie *Scheherazade*. Once again closing the door, he walked with even greater purpose across the stage. Violet, still looking at the little man, saw him mouth the word, "Okay." He motioned for her to crawl under the curtain, open the small door, and stand, once again, in the box. She did so, soon hearing the door click behind her. She quickly brushed off her skirt and smoothed her hair for the big reveal.

The Great Grandoli stopped pacing and stood in front of the door, once again in an apparent state of great concentration. He suddenly came to and yelled, "She is back with us, ladies and gentlemen.

Behold!" He threw open the door to uncover a squinting Violet. The orchestra again played a fanfare as he took her hand and both walked toward the cheering audience, taking a deep bow. Violet even mimicked the opera singers she had seen by throwing in an extra deep curtsey. As he bent to kiss her hand, the magician whispered, "Good job, kid, you're a natural." Violet made her way back to her seat, flush with excitement and triumph.

"I can't believe that you did that!" Rose exclaimed.

Violet beamed. She was fearless, and perfectly poised to take on these roaring times. After all, the decade of the 1920s was outrageous, loud, and progressive. It was a time of giants—Dempsey, Jones, Tilden, Ruth, who excelled in their given fields and became heroes to kids across the nation. And it was a time of hoodlums—Owney Madden, Dutch Schultz, Al Capone, and Jonny Torrino, who ruled the streets of major cities like New York and Chicago, offering those who didn't comply with the new order a one-way ride in an automobile. Women, who had broken free of the Victorian mold, were bolder, sleeker of form (thanks to bound bosoms), and set about changing the rules and reinventing society.

The decade began with the ratification of the nineteenth amendment in 1920, and no American was more pleased than Charles Williams. He impressed upon his daughters the importance of making oneself heard, in the voting booth and in life in general. One evening, while reading his paper, he could be heard—shouting at the top of his voice.

"Listen to this, Beryl, Violet, Rose, Daisy—come here! Tonight's paper has run the following quote: 'Harvard Medical School professor said higher education damaged a woman's ability to bear children by causing the uterus to atrophy.' This is the kind of ignorance and nonsense you will be up against! Don't let *anyone* tell you that you aren't a man's equal." He paused and looked at his girls, who were calmly standing around him and smiling.

"What is wrong with you?" he asked, perplexed. "Aren't you outraged?"

"Father, you have already prepared us for this sort of thing," Daisy grinned. "Don't you know that you started lecturing us on the importance of running when we could hardly walk?"

He finally relaxed. "I'm proud of all of you. No matter what you do with your lives, just don't let anyone hold you back from what you really want."

In 1924, Violet had decided that what she really wanted was to go into business. She went to the library to do some research on trade schools and found information on the Olympia School for Secretaries located in Washington. There, they trained students for high-grade secretarial and other business positions suitable for progressive women. The proprietress, Katharine Gibbs, wanted to expand the opportunities for women in the workplace and to prepare them to succeed. Violet felt that the business world, with its fast-paced decisions and artful finessing of clients, could be that arena in which she would shine.

So it was off to Olympia, where she would live in a hotel for single young ladies. Violet loved this new environment and quickly settled in. The school boasted an elite image, offering classes not only for typing and stenography, but English, speech, and proper etiquette. A dress code was strictly enforced, and Violet was regularly complimented on her posture and bearing. Gibbs girls were taught to be punctual and organized. Standards for properly written and typed letters were uncompromising: there couldn't be a single mistake. Violet worked doggedly at her assignments, often sporting the bright red flush of hard work when turning them in. She exceeded the expectations of her teachers, once again proving that she could excel at any given task.

In just a short year she graduated at the top of her class. Miss Gibbs approached Violet personally attempting to secure the girl's employment, so impressed was she by her charisma and aptitude in the work environment. She told Violet that a new position would be created for her: as an attaché for the company, reaching out to young women in high schools. Traveling across the country as a recruiter, she would be a shining example of a Gibbs Girl: the perfectly tailored and successful working woman in the America of 1925.

Violet considered this proposal, thinking about what her new life would entail. She felt that, whereas it did propose some of what she believed would be fulfilling, there was still something lacking. Simply put: excitement didn't hit her in the solar plexus. Thanking Miss Gibbs profusely but politely turning down the offer, the ever-more confused Violet went back to Portland, to her parents, and to her endless-possibilities future.

This pivotal year of 1925, which caused Violet consternation, brought Rose bliss. She turned eighteen and became engaged to Thaddeus J. Proctor IV, a man who was actually more pretentious than his name, if such a thing were even possible. But Rose was extremely happy and, most enviable of all, she knew what she wanted for her life: to be married and gift the world with little Proctors. Her father was thrilled that his middle daughter had found her calling. Violet was extremely happy for Rose, and the three girls talked long into the night about the forthcoming wedding. Daisy, ever the romantic of the era when her favorite Jane Austen books were written, found the prospect of a wedding particularly exciting. She was already obsessed with the notion, the idea of a perfect love. Violet didn't believe in perfect love, although seeing first-hand evidence to the contrary through her parents' devoted union. She somehow got it into her head that love was a jagged path to be traversed, comprised of great sacrifices one must make to gain the gift of all-consuming adoration. Perhaps this would be a prescient view.

One evening Charles and Beryl called Violet into the study. This was more or less Charles's office at home, but the whole family used it, or specifically the large oak desk, for projects. The room was the most Victorian in the house, utilizing furniture which Beryl inherited when her mother passed away. Along with a large aubergine-and-gold Queen Anne sofa and matching chair, the room featured dark wood paneling, Byzantium-colored curtains, and bookshelves lined with the classics in special, leather-bound editions. Violet spent many hours in this room as a child, curled up in the chair with one of the fascinating books that put her directly into the most deliciously exciting situations imaginable.

Now she sat in the same chair, but with no book into which she could escape. Violet looked at her mother, seated on the sofa, and father, in his chair behind the desk, and knew what they were about to say. She was well aware that she needed to find a calling that would make her feel fulfilled. This feeling less-than (less than happy, less than confident, less than satisfied) wasn't like her at all. Her normal joyfulness had to be manufactured, which she certainly could do. But she wanted the real thing. She wanted to make something of her life, and give of herself, and experience love, and embrace joy, and realize her true possibilities.

"Violet, dear," her father began, "we heard from Miss Gibbs, who told us about the offer she made to you regarding a post with her firm."

"Yes, Father, she did make me an offer," Violet answered unenthusiastically.

"Why didn't you take it?" her mother asked quietly.

"I don't know—I just couldn't." She looked down at a crease in her skirt, and began working the fold with her fingers. "I don't believe that it is the right, well, the right fit for me."

Charles stood and walked around the desk, sitting on the end. "Well, Violet, you seem at odds with yourself these days. Is there something you feel would fit you more?"

"That's just it," Violet said, looking at her father. "I don't know what I want, and I don't mean to be ungrateful for the time and money you have spent on me, but I just don't know. I *do* know that I want to make people joyful in their lives."

"You have to be joyful to bring joy to others," her mother wisely observed.

"I *know!*" Violet affirmed. "Life, well, it seemed so easy when I was little. Do you remember the thrill we all felt going to the vaudeville show in Washington? Everyone was so happy, and it was so exciting."

Beryl suddenly knew what must happen, but she needed to have a heart-to-heart talk with Charles first. "Violet, honey, why don't you go upstairs and lie down and we can continue this conversation later." She walked over to the girl and kissed her lovingly on the top of her head.

Violet took her leave and went upstairs. Beryl walked over to Charles and took his hands in hers. "I think we need to give our girl some direction, and I have an idea which could prove beneficial to her. You know Patrick's work in New York; what if she were to take a post in his office? That way, she would either be interested in the office machinations or the theatrical end."

"New York is such a big city," Charles murmured, feeling a sudden rush of protective feelings toward his eldest daughter.

"Yes, my love, it is. But that may be just what she needs. I think that it would be good for her to experience it. And I have no doubt that she can take care of herself."

Charles looked pensive, and then nodded. "You are right, of course, my dear. I think it's a splendid idea. Why not give Patrick a call and see if he can use another office worker."

And so it soon came to Violet's attention that an opportunity had arisen to work in Uncle Patrick's agency in the heart of New York City's theatre district. She saw it as an omen. Just being around show people, she believed, would be thrilling, and she thought that the excitement of the huge metropolis might add a new dimension: life painted in vivid colors with broad, confident strokes.

Her parents smiled at the gleam which reappeared in her eyes, and knew that they had made the correct decision for their daughter.

Violet bought a light blue traveling suit with a white silk blouse, thinking it would be ideal for the warm summer weather. She was packed in no time, excited, even, at the idea of the long train ride, which, her father assured her, would be first-class all the way. He also pulled her aside and put $500 into her hand, insisting she tuck it into her handbag; it would be a necessity in the city, for everything costs dearly in Manhattan. "I don't know how long it will last you, but if you need more I can wire it. Patrick will be paying you a pittance, nothing to live on, but we both know why you are doing this, and it is not for the money! Am I right?"

"You are. Thank you, Father," Violet said, kissing him gently on the cheek.

Her family saw her off with hopeful cheers as she boarded the North Coast Limited, which she caught in Seattle. First-class it may have been, but the train ride was anything but comfortable. The windows were open because of the July heat, and the soot and smoke from the steam locomotive made its way into her seat, her clothes, and her eyes, bringing with it a horrible, burnt stench. The noise was deafening: from the *clickety-clack* of the wheels to the ear-splitting whistles and the ceaseless conversation of fellow passengers. She did have a berth for sleeping, but found it stiflingly hot and cramped, so she spent most of her time sitting in the open-air cars. By the time she arrived in Chicago, to take another train to New York, Violet's excitement, just like her traveling suit, was a bit wilted.

But this brave young lady was not one to let an uncomfortable few days get her down. After journeying for several more hours, there appeared a city whose skyline left her transfixed. She stared in amazement at the skyscrapers that were so tall they made her dizzy. As the train pulled into the station, she looked with astonishment at all the people. Crowds of them, which she would come to find was the normal state of affairs in New York. She stood and walked off the train, and into the packed terminal.

And so it was that Uncle Patrick and Aunt Mavis first saw their pretty young niece: suit rumpled and covered in soot, white gloves and face darkly smudged with smoke, hat askew atop tangled hair. But all they could see was her ebullient smile.

Her journey had begun.

CHAPTER THREE

THE ENCOUNTER

August 1925

Patrick M. Goodman, Theatrical Agent. The name gleamed on its brass doorplate. Danny O'Brien walked into the office suite at 1270 Sixth Avenue and looked around at the assortment of vaudevillians and stage actors sitting in the small anteroom. Most he recognized; some he had yet to meet. All he could charm into seemingly close friendships while simultaneously keeping everyone at a safe distance. Smiling and greeting those individuals he knew by name, he slowly made his way to the front desk and the petite receptionist sitting behind the mahogany behemoth. Her head was buried in a drawer from which she was attempting to extricate her nail file.

"Helen, you just get prettier every week." He flashed his professional full-wattage smile.

Helen jolted up, bumping her head against the drawer. "Well, *Danny!*" she cooed, returning his smile in full measure, subtly rubbing her sore scalp. "If I had known *you* were coming in today, I'd have dressed up." She self-consciously patted her hair and rearranged the long strands of beads around her neck.

"Oh, honey, you don't have to do a thing. You're as pretty as a sunrise over Central Park."

Helen blushed with pleasure.

A couple of office girls who were working at typing machines paused just to look at the handsome performer. A small, unison sigh could be heard. He nodded toward them and they quickly bowed their heads, finding shelter in the *tap-tap-tapping* of the machines.

"Now, honey," Danny said, returning his full attention to the awaiting Helen. "Can you get me in to see Patrick? Tell him I only need five minutes."

"Let me see what I can do," the receptionist said, quickly standing. "I'll be right back!" She attempted an even broader grin, swiftly turned, and banged her hip against the desk. Smile still intact, she attempted a recovery and strode with a self-conscious gait down the hallway towards the agent's office.

As he turned from the desk, Danny's expression returned to the all-too-familiar serious set of late. He walked over to get a drink from the fountain, looking around this familiar locale. The Goodman office was a huge structure which housed several smaller rooms flanking the reception desk. The largest room, naturally, was occupied by the chieftain. Other offices were used at various times by performers to write, work out contracts, and even rehearse—Patrick attempted to meet the needs of his clients as best he could. Danny felt as if he had grown up between these walls, remembering earlier days when he had been left to read in the waiting room while his parents discussed business.

Danny glanced into a small filing cabinet-filled office just off the reception area, a dark room with just one beam of light breaking through the shuttered windows and casting an amber glow. He saw the back of a girl who appeared to be wrestling with a stack of files, trying to get them to fit into an obstinate cabinet. After some contortioned manipulations she finally gave up and unceremoniously shoved the lot of them into the bottom drawer, slamming it shut with her foot.

"Stupid files," he heard her mutter under her breath. Danny chuckled quietly. Having finished her task, she brushed off her skirt, smoothed her hair, and slowly turned to face the door—and him.

Their eyes locked.

Time, always attempting to scurry away like a leaf in the breeze, chose this moment to stand perfectly still. Two old souls recognized each other and exchanged a lifetime in a split-second. The air became too heavy to breathe; the world around them absented itself, leaving only these two people.

Danny swallowed, then moved a few steps towards her. "Have we met?"

"I—I'm not sure. I'm Violet, Patrick's niece."

"Oh," Danny paused, not knowing what to say; feeling lost without his normal glibness, forgetting to change his expression into his patented killer smile so consumed was he by her large brown eyes.

"Danny? Mr. Goodman is ready for you now," Helen said in a louder voice than was necessary. He nodded to Violet, taking just one more second to try to figure exactly what it was about her, then turned, collected himself, and walked into Patrick's office.

"Pat, you old dog, how are you?" Danny smiled broadly as he shook his manager's hand in a firm grip. Just being in this familiar office always made him feel confident, like he could take on Hamlet and win. And today he surely needed all the confidence he could muster.

Patrick shook Danny's hand, finding it hard not to be taken in by his highly prized client's exuberant attack on life. His thin lips almost formed a smile, but thought better of it and remained in a firm line. He was one of the most valuable gifts Danny inherited from his parents. The young man knew that the agent was always working to get him the best, and most favorable, routes. Patrick knew that Danny understood the ropes and was the ultimate professional. And he headlined regularly, bringing in a steady stream of revenue for the Goodman Talent Agency. The inverse pair had forged a strong bond over the years.

"I'm fine, Daniel, how are you?" he asked with his signature formality.

"I feel like a million. I've got what I think is a great idea for a new act, and I want you to hear me out."

"What are you talking about? You're doing well on the circuit. Has Albee said anything to you about changing your act?"

"No."

"Then it's out of the question." Patrick strode to his chair behind the desk and sat down resolutely, being prepared not to give Danny an inch in this fight.

Danny sat down slowly and took a moment to plan out his strategy. He looked around the room and wondered how many times he had sat here, talking across the wide, mahogany desk with Patrick. The office was flooded with natural light, exposing tall pieces of outdated furniture that stuck out willy-nilly. Papers were stacked upon every surface imaginable, some already taking on the yellow hue of age. Dust motes played tag in the sunlight that poured through the tall windows.

"No one has said anything to me about my act," he began by assuaging Patrick's fear, sounding so unfamiliarly serious that he actually put more concern in Patrick's breast. "I don't think *anyone* notices it anymore. I've been thinking about my image, and, frankly, I am sick and tired of the whole thing."

"But you are headlining, need I remind you? You don't just up and change a successful act."

"Yes, I know, but I want to take a stab at making people laugh."

"*Laugh?*" Patrick spluttered, skepticism written all over his dour features. "What type of act do you have in mind? Daniel, you worked hard on your songs, your image. And you've only been doing it for, what, eight years?"

"Pat," Danny said persuasively, feeling frustrated that he couldn't communicate his intent. "I want to try comedy—I really think I could be great at it."

"Again, I repeat: it's out of the question."

"Damn it, Patrick," Danny growled, abruptly standing, then pacing the floor, his hand rubbing the back of his neck. "This singing routine was not my idea. You know, it was Mother and Albee and you, but I didn't get a vote. Well, now I have one, and I want to do something different."

"I see," Patrick said quietly, comprehending just how serious the young man was, and realized that he would have to change his approach. He put the tips of his long fingers together and listened. "Go ahead."

Danny sat down, finally having the man's attention, prepared to make his case. "Look at it this way. In no time my act will be completely out of date, and I will be forced to come up with something new. Now, I want to appeal to people my own age, the modern audience, and what they consider funny. I'm thinking about doing a flirtation act—perhaps a sketch involving a delivery boy wooing a receptionist. She keeps turning him down, you know, putting him in his place. It will be a strong role for the girl, and that's all the rage these days. This woman is not just playing straight for the comedian. She is what every woman wants to be today. Intelligent. Glib. Beautiful. And I've come up with a hook—I turn to the audience and say, as a catch phrase, 'Will *she* love me!'"

Patrick seemed to be running the concept through his inner files, trying to recall if anybody else had done anything that was similar. "Hmm," he said, "not bad. Simple enough setup, and it *would* appeal to a younger crowd, which is becoming a larger percentage of the audience; you are right about that."

Danny was pleased. "It'll be colossal!"

"It just might, but are you sure this is what you really want, Daniel? Are you just going through some dissatisfaction with your life in general? Changing an act like this is a serious move, and I don't want you to regret it. What you've got right now you can bank on for at least five, maybe ten more years."

"I know." Danny sat back and thought for a moment. "But, Patrick, I need to change this. I really want to—" He was going to say "to *be* someone else," but stopped short. "—to try using this talent I *know* I have. I can make it work. I'm afraid that if I keep doing this singing act I will get to the point where I walk away from vaudeville entirely. And that's something I don't want to do."

"No, I don't want that either," Patrick said as he rose from his seat and walked toward one of the tall windows. He thought for a few minutes, and then moved over to the young man, putting his hand on Danny's shoulder in a fatherly fashion. "Alright, Daniel, but I want you to have a full treatment on my desk in a couple of weeks. And it had better be good, or I'll pull the plug on this nonsense."

"Pat, you'll love it. I promise. And I'll talk with Albee about this change myself. He'll go for it—I just know it."

Patrick looked at Danny with uncertainty. He knew the close bond Danny had with the vaudeville impresario who alienated most performers in his employ. If Patrick had tried to go to Albee with this request himself he would have been shown the door faster than a traveling salesman. But Patrick knew that if anybody could talk the businessman out of one of his most high-profile acts and into an untried commodity—that would be Danny. Such was the extent of their relationship.

Danny rose, and Patrick walked him out to the reception room.

"Oh," Danny said casually to Patrick when he was halfway out the door, "and I know the girl I want in the sketch."

"You do?" Patrick knew most of the young girls in comedy these days, and was interested to hear just who Danny thought would be strong enough to star against him. "Who?"

"Your niece. Violet."

And with that, Danny quickly made his way out onto the street, seeing neither the livid expression in Patrick's eyes, nor the flabbergasted expression in Violet's.

"You are not to get any ideas, young lady," Patrick turned, shaking a long, thin finger at Violet. "This is absurd." He turned and strode defiantly into his office, slamming the door for emphasis. He was responsible for Violet as long as she was on the East Coast, and he didn't completely trust Danny. He had seen the boy go through more women than is respectable, and he just couldn't face Violet's parents if he allowed this to happen to her. His sister told him to acquaint the girl with the business world, and that didn't mean monkey business. And Danny may decide that he didn't want to change his act after a while, and then Violet … well, no sir.

Danny ran as if the devil himself were chasing him. After a few blocks he slowed down, breathing deeply. He took out a Camel, lit it, and took a long drag. After holding the burning smoke in his throat for several seconds, he slowly exhaled. *What just happened?* What made him say something to Patrick which he knew would make him angry? He paced on, gripping the cigarette for dear life. *And that girl.* She was … well, he didn't know what. But, after being around hundreds of girls in and out of show business, he knew when a girl had "It." And boy, did she have It in spades! He wanted to get to know her. He wanted, no *needed*, to spend some time with her and see just what made her tick.

Violet didn't know what to make of Uncle Patrick's strong reaction to the young man who breezed into the office and turned up everyone's volume. What an amazing man, with all the energy of a freight train and the looks of a movie star. His voice was that rare combination of silky smoothness with a raw edge: the kind of voice which, when uttering your name, turned it into something intimate. Something Violet wanted to hear. The way he stared at her unnerved her at first, then made her feel, well—just made her *feel*. How exciting life could be with someone like that! She hauled up the next batch of paper-jammed files to be sorted in the long-term file cabinets and walked toward the little room.

"Don't take it personally," Helen said, idly filing her nails, then looking up and shooting daggers at Violet. "I mean the Danny thing. You're nothing special—he flirts with *all* the girls just like that."

"Yeah, no, I wouldn't," Violet said mindlessly, walking into the room. But she *did* take it personally. He wanted *her* for his act? Being in a vaudeville show—she had never considered it for herself as she didn't think she had any real performing talent. Then she thought of the thrill of being the magician's assistant. She also thought about the idea of being on a stage with someone like Danny. Then she felt it. Excitement hit her in the solar plexus, and she knew that she had to give it a try. But she wondered: Was the excitement about being on the stage, or working with Danny? She didn't know and, frankly, she didn't care. She only knew that she didn't like Uncle Patrick ending the conversation before it began. Then again, she knew how to get around him …

⤙⧫⧫ ⧫⧫⤚

"Hi, Father, how are you and Mother?" Violet stood in the back hallway of Uncle Patrick and Aunt Mavis's home, talking on their telephone. They lived in a pre–Civil War brownstone row house in Brooklyn Heights, most recently known as Brooklyn Village. This location was perfect for the couple: Patrick loved the drive over the Brooklyn Bridge to work, and Mavis loved the access to the city. Their home had all the quaint ambience of the Victorian era: The walls were painted bold and dusky colors of amber, scarlet, and peacock blue. It was brimming over with ornate furniture, textiles, knickknacks, and gilt-framed paintings. Violet's room, with its pale blue walls, white furniture, and richly flowered counterpane, was the simplest, and the one in which she felt the most at home.

She stood a moment, staring at the wall-mounted phone and figuring out her plan of attack.

"Just fine, dear," her father answered. "How is the business world treating you?"

"Well, alright, I guess. The work is rather dreary, Father. I guess I had expected more."

"I should have a talk with Patrick about him being able to utilize your skills to their fullest," Charles sighed. "But perhaps you should handle that yourself."

"That's just it, Father. You see, a—situation, an opportunity, I'm not sure what—has come along, and I would like to see where it takes me. The only problem is …" Here Violet paused for emphasis, "is that Uncle Patrick seems to think he can make the decision for me."

"Nonsense. He should know by now that we expect you to make such decisions for yourself. Does this 'opportunity' involve your working for a different firm?"

Violet took a deep breath. "No, it involves working in an entirely different setting. I have been asked to be in a vaudeville sketch—with an entertainer with many years of experience," she hastened to add.

Charles paused. "Oh, I see." He thought of how wise his wife had been to suggest this particular arrangement. But he had to be careful about just how this situation was handled.

"Uncle Patrick told me flat-out 'No'—that I shouldn't even think of this … opportunity. I didn't want to make a scene in the office, so I thought that, well, maybe you or Mother could have a quiet word with him and … set things right. I think that he feels that you both have a much narrower idea of what my future should be, and that you only authorized me to do office work."

"I understand the problem," he said matter-of-factly. "I will speak with your mother about this, and we will put in a long-distance call to Patrick."

"Oh, thank you, Father!"

"Of course, dear." And, after general questions regarding family matters, they rang off.

Violet stood by the phone and stared down the darkly paneled hallway. What was she getting herself into? She smiled the answer.

⋆�⟩⟩ ⟨⟨þ⋆

"And, did she tell Charles the nature of the act?" Patrick asked sternly into the telephone receiver.

He realized he was throwing, or attempting to throw, gasoline on a fire, but he wanted the full story made known. He sat down behind his desk, making sure that his office door was closed.

"Charles didn't tell me that Violet said anything about the nature of the act," Beryl said, sounding like she was ten thousand miles away. "Is it a singing group? Because she has a lovely voice, you know." Beryl was happy when Charles brought this situation to her, and knew her daughter well enough to give her approval to any project she wanted to undertake. But she had to have some fun with her brother.

"No, Beryl, it is not a singing group. It is a comedy act—with a boy."

"And who is this fellow?" she questioned.

Patrick thought about how to portray Danny, and be fair. "He is an upstanding young man, I believe he is around twenty-eight now, and has been in vaudeville all of his life. He began with his parents, and, for the last seven years has been on his own."

"What is his name?" Beryl asked.

"Danny O'Brien."

"Yes, that rings a bell. I believe our neighbor, Mrs. Shaw, has some sheet music with his picture on it—an Irish song of some sort."

"Yes, that would be he. His current act is as a singer, and he is a headliner. He wants to do a flirtation act."

"Wait, now, Patrick, this act wouldn't be tawdry in any way, would it?" Beryl had to work to keep a laugh out of her voice, as she knew good and well that vaudeville was a clean business.

"Oh, no, *no*," Patrick was quick to reassure his sister. "It is more of the, how do I put this? It's the fellow himself that has me concerned."

Beryl paused, then finally had to ask: "Well?"

"He is a bit of a bounder." There. Patrick had said it, and his conscience could be clear.

"*Bounder*?" she finally had to let go with a full-bodied laugh. "*Bounder*? Oh, Patrick, *really*. Kids these days are different than in our day. They understand the rules, but want to kick up their heels. Have some fun!" She paused, then had to add, "You know, you have always been a bit on the stuffy side."

"I just wanted you to have all the information," Patrick huffed. "And, besides, I am *not* stuffy."

"Oh, so then you *don't* remember the first time you met Charles?" Beryl smiled at the memory of her overprotective older brother.

"Well, how was I to know he was out on the front porch?" Patrick began to chuckle, too, thinking of the time he spoke sharply with his sister about her choice of date—with the timorous fellow standing on the other side of the door overhearing the whole tirade, growing more nervous, and finally making a hasty retreat. Beryl didn't speak to her brother for a full week after that—and then, only after he apologized to Charles.

"So you can consider us warned, dear brother. We do want Violet to decide this issue for herself, so please don't stand in her way. She must gain these kinds of experiences now to enable her to be wiser in her full adulthood. And, besides, I think she would be perfectly marvelous on the stage."

"If you insist," Patrick said with a barely audible sigh. "Now, I really must get back to work."

"Don't let me keep you, Patrick. Oh—and thank you for being such a protective guardian. Charles and I really *do* appreciate it."

Patrick actually felt good about the talk, and could go home and tell Violet that he would arrange a proper meeting with Danny.

By the next afternoon, all three members of this awkward trio—Danny, Violet, and Patrick—were meeting at Lindy's. Located at Fifty-First and Broadway, the four-year-old restaurant had become an important spot for vaudeville and Broadway actors. There was, in fact, already an established hierarchy regarding seating: music people sat to the right of the entrance, small-timers and those who handle the business end of show business sat to the left, headliners held court in the center, and civilians (code for all non-professionals) were relegated to the back. Patrick and Violet arrived first, securing a good table to the left.

When Danny arrived, there were many who greeted him as he strode through the crowded restaurant. But once Danny saw Violet, he quickly made his way to the table. Patrick offered the formal introductions. "Miss Violet Williams, this is Mr. Daniel O'Brien."

Violet put out her hand and offered her best smile. "It is nice to meet you, Mr. O'Brien."

"Danny. Please call me Danny," he said, taking her hand. He was once again bowled over by her ethereal beauty, which seemed at odds with the shaken-champagne-bottle-ready-to-explode spark in her eyes.

Patrick sat, and, reluctantly, Violet and Danny withdrew their hands and sat opposite each other. Patrick had ordered drinks, three root beers, which were soon delivered.

"I want to get right to it," Danny said, not taking his eyes off Violet. "I am in the process of looking for someone to be in a great new sketch with me, which will debut in a couple of months, and I would like you to consider it."

"But, Mr. O'Brien, I haven't any experience in acting, or in comedy. Why would you think that I would be right for this—" and here Violet paused, not knowing the exact terminology, "—*sketch*, did you say?"

"Yes, Vi, you are right. And I don't want the typical actress or comedienne. I want something, and someone, new and fresh."

"Violet. My name is Violet," she corrected.

"We will write the sketch together," Danny continued. "I know you can write. Pat told me that you attended business school. I also have a feeling that you could learn timing and delivery pretty fast." He took a swig of root beer.

"I might be willing to consider your offer, Mr. O'Brien. Where would we work? We would need a place convenient for both of us."

"We have a room in the back of the agency which is currently unused," Patrick said quickly, before Danny could suggest their going to his apartment. "We could set up a table and chairs for you. I did promise your mother that I would supervise this endeavor, after all. And because you will have to work in the morning and later afternoon, around Danny's performances, I will release you from your work with the agency."

"Oh, that sounds perfect, Uncle Patrick!" Violet was happy with this easy solution, and was thrilled to be rid of the mountain of filing that greeted her every morning.

"I'm amenable to anything that makes Vi comfortable," Danny said gallantly.

"*Violet*," she said, glancing around the room imperiously. "Please, Mr. O'Brien, my name is Violet."

"Yes, and I suppose your sister's name is Rose." Danny tossed off, taking another mouthful of his beverage.

"Well, as a matter of fact, it is. And before you say anything else, my other sister's name is Daisy. So there you have it."

"Did your father ever hope to have a little 'Bud'?" Danny ventured.

"Mr. O'Brien, there is not a horticultural reference with which I am unfamiliar. So I will simply say that yes, I am named after the flower, but my mother fancied the color as well, so you could say that I was named after both."

"Do you like it?" Danny asked.

"Do I like *what?*"

"The color? The flower?"

"Neither."

"Wait," Danny leaned forward, obviously amused. "Your name is Violet and you hate violets and the color violet? Don't your beaux always send you that type of flower?"

She looked at Danny with one eyebrow arched, and replied in her staunchest manner: "They wouldn't be my beaux if they did."

Patrick sat up a little straighter in his chair. He was pleased with her tone, and felt that she could certainly take care of herself. Danny's Irish blarney wouldn't sidetrack his niece, he was proud to see.

"I'm just saying," Danny continued, seemingly undeterred. "Sometimes maybe you enjoy a pretty violet."

"No, I can't abide that insipid flower."

"Of course, of course—It's just that, well, every once in a while you throw on a purple dress and go down to the garden to look at that specific variety of blossom." Danny was obviously enjoying himself.

Violet huffed: "You are impertinent, Mr. O'Brien." She picked up her glass to take another sip of the cold soda.

A waiter approached the table with a note. He gave it to Patrick, who read the missive and stood, ready to leave. "You two can stay here and talk things out; I have a call I must make back at the office. Nice to see you again, Daniel."

Danny stood and put out his hand. "Pat, thanks for arranging this today."

Violet stood and gave Patrick a quick peck on the cheek. "Thank you, Uncle. I will see you back at work."

He nodded, and was out the door.

Danny sat down and looked at Violet, who slowly sat and looked right back at him. He didn't quite know what to do. He suddenly felt dry-mouthed and lost, the way he did when they first set eyes on each other. "Would you like a piece of cheesecake? I hear it's very good here."

Violet shook her head slowly, then abruptly gulped the remainder of her root beer, setting the glass back on the table with a decided thud. "Now that Uncle Patrick is gone, I'd rather hear about our exciting new act, Danny," she stated with a wicked grin, the first of the *real* Violet that he would see.

Danny beamed, folding his arms and leaning back in his chair. Oh, but this was going to be fun!

The following day, a box from the local florist was delivered to the Goodman residence. Aunt Mavis excitedly brought it into the living room, and handed the beribboned package to Violet.

"For you," she announced with an air of excitement in her voice. "This is from the best florist on Broadway."

Violet took the box, untied the purple ribbon, and lifted the lid. Inside, nestled between layers of French decorative paper, was a large bouquet of violets staring back at her.

"Well, look at that. How sweet! Is there a card?" Aunt Mavis asked, all smiles.

"No card, but I know who sent them," Violet said, an artificial grin forcing her lips to bend into a curve.

"Well, *who?*"

"Danny."

"Oh," Aunt Mavis said in a swoon, "isn't that sweet of him? And to send you violets, because of your name—how clever! You must thank him for this thoughtful gift!"

"Yes," Violet said, trying to keep the ire out of her voice. "I *must.*"

CHAPTER FOUR

THE INKLING

September 1925

Danny paced around the room like an expectant father in a hospital waiting room. He paused for a moment, looked at Violet, and then resumed his endless trudge.

"It's not that it's bad, I just think it could be a lot better," Violet affirmed. She looked away from Danny, scanning the small back room of the Goodman Talent Agency, which they had claimed as their temporary office. To appease Violet's parents, or at least to do what he thought a proper guardian would in such a circumstance, Patrick had solemnly promised to oversee Danny and Violet's collaboration. Charles and Beryl Williams were more than satisfied, although this arrangement resulted in Patrick poking his pointed nose into the room every half hour, making Danny jumpier than usual.

"So *talk*," Danny said. "Give me solid ideas. We have the Delivery Boy coming in, making a pass at the Secretary, she puts him in his place, he asks what type of guy she goes for, she says something, he goes and changes into that guy, he makes a big entrance, we put in some business, then eventually she is crazy over him for becoming her ideal. She agrees to go out with him. Then maybe a song and dance for the finish."

"It's just too easy. How long should the sketch be?" Violet questioned, toying with the fountain pen and steno pad lying on the table in front of her.

"Fourteen minutes. With any luck we'll start in the four spot; if the act goes over, then we could headline. That means that we need to be able to stretch it out, with extra business and stuff, to seventeen minutes."

"The four spot?"

"The last act before the tab show, you know a flash act with a big set. You've got the audience's full attention, and it's in Two."

"Into what?" she asked.

"No. In Two, t-w-o. The term gets into the amount of area the act takes up on the stage. Ours is two people doing an act in front of a drop, you know, a type of curtain painted to look like an office. All we will need is a desk, a chair, the trunk backstage with the costumes. Simple."

"And then headline? Really?"

"Yes," Danny took out a pack of Doublemint gum, offered a stick to Violet, then took one for himself.

Violet unwrapped the gum, put it into her mouth, and slowly began chewing. "Okay. But this girl, the Secretary, she should really make him work for this date."

Danny sat down across from Violet and looked at her with the seriousness of a lawyer with a guilty client. "Go on."

"Well, how about if she turns the guy down? 'No, thanks,' she says casually. He asks her what her type is, and she says, you know, a different type, like a doctor or a college boy, or something. Then each time he comes in—"

"—she turns him down, until, well, we need a way to get off this train." Danny got up to resume his pacing.

Violet looked pensive, chewing her gum. "I've got it!" she jumped up, jolting Danny in the process. "After making him work for it five or six times, she finally says, 'The Hard-Working Type!' Because, you know, he has changed so many times for her."

"Huh. Not bad," he said, stopping right in front of her. "We can do easy costume changes, you know, coats, hats, things like that, with recognizable characterizations." He paused and thought for a while.

"Then, at the end, she could throw him on the desk and give him a big kiss, with his feet going up in the air. Blackout."

Violet laughed. "That *would* be funny."

"Maybe we should just practice it a few times now," Danny said, grinning and wiggling his eyebrows suggestively.

"Oh, no. We've got work to do. And, besides, wouldn't it be a stage kiss—a fake?"

"Well, technically yes. You would grab me, push me onto the desk, and just bring your head down onto my neck. It would look like a kiss from the audience's perspective. Like this." Danny stepped toward Violet and leaned into her neck. He could smell her fresh scent of carnations and mint. Slowly, he lowered his lips to her neck and could feel her shiver, then giggle. Moving back, he noticed the bright color which crept up her neck, reddening her cheeks. He thought how innocent she was; a refreshing change from the seen-it-all chorus girls he dated … or *had* dated. And that giggle of hers affected him in a way no others' laugh had. He felt it all the way down to his … toes.

Violet turned and sat at the table, pulling the pen and pad close. Danny was always flirting with girls, she thought—she shouldn't take it seriously, and she wouldn't.

"Okay," Danny said, clearing his throat and sitting opposite Violet at the desk. "Let's talk about some of the 'types' she would mention. And, as I said, they all have to be able to be communicated easily to the audience through a simple wardrobe."

"Well, The Rich Type, with a frock coat, top hat, and walking stick," she suggested.

"Good, good. Write that down."

"And," Violet interjected, "a great idea. We have the college boy, you know with the raccoon coat, pennant, and all, and he comes in doing the Charleston. The audience would love that—to see you dancing again. Unless …"

Danny nodded in agreement. "I see what you mean, from the old days. Yes, that would probably—hold it, what do you mean, 'Unless …'?"

"Well," Violet suppressed a grin and looked down, "unless you couldn't *do* the dance. Perhaps after so many years you just couldn't move well enough to do such a complicated step."

Danny jumped up from the table and walked to a clear area in the back of the room. He began humming the tune, "Hmm, hm—hmm, hm," and simultaneously began stepping back, then forward, forward, then back, while rhythmically swinging his arms. After a few more bars, he added foot twists with elbows lifted, and ended with pivoting his knees, opening and closing them as his arms mimicked the motion. It was graceful, professional, and appealing. Violet jumped up and began clapping.

"Oh, you are wonderful!" she cried.

Danny stopped, just a little out of breath, and sat back down. "Anything else I have to prove?" he muttered, while suppressing a smile which indicated his pleasure at her approval.

"Danny," Violet suddenly interjected. "Does this sound like it could be silly? I mean, the whole premise of the skit?"

"It's farce, Vi. 'Nut' comedy. People right now love ridiculous humor. Look at Ed Wynn. He does this monologue, prop based, about his new inventions. At one point he takes out a pair of eyeglasses with windshield wipers attached; he says it's for people who eat grapefruit. *That* is what's filling the seats. So, I don't think *anything* can be too silly today."

"I see what you mean," she said seriously. "Okay, now what else?"

"Umm, how about The Exotic Type, like Valentino—the Sheik," he ventured. "He could wear a—, you know …" Danny motioned around his head.

"I think it's called a *Keffiyeh*, the square scarf headdress with a headband."

"Yeah, and flowing robes, colorful."

"*Bisht*, although I don't know if they are traditionally colorful. I believe they're usually white."

"How do you know that?"

"I read an article about Valentino in *Photoplay*."

"Oh. Okay, white robe, but colorful hat."

Violet laughed. "*Keffiyeh*! And, okay, *that* can be colorful."

"You bet it can be colorful. Red. Passionate." Danny stood arms akimbo and legs apart. He began to speak in an exaggerated, unconvincing Middle Eastern accent: "May I abduct you and convey you to my tent in the Sahara, wherein we will partake of an exotic repast?"

Violet laughed loudly, causing Patrick to come striding into the room.

"You two are being disruptive," he said with a dour expression, removing his pince-nez and using them to point at the culprits for added emphasis. "Please keep your voices down."

"Oh, Danny, do that funny accent for Uncle Patrick," Violet choked out.

Danny complied with her request and repeated the line, adding, "Once we have completed our culinary indulgence, I will shower you with rubies and gift you with perfumes and unguents."

"Unguents," she repeated, slapping the table and doubling over.

Patrick looked at her, then at Danny, giving a brief nod. "Yes, but please, keep your voices down. We are conducting business here." With that, Patrick turned and walked right into Helen, who had hurried into the office to see what was so funny. She stumbled backward, then regained her footing, smiling at Danny the entire time. "Come along, Helen, and get back to work," Patrick huffed. She reluctantly followed, hitting her shoulder on the door frame on her way out.

Danny and Violet exchanged stifled smiles. Still in character, Danny added, "Well, *he* will not be invited to my camel's birthday celebration. It will be held at the Hooch Hump, and because my camel is a dromedary, there will only be one hooch. I couldn't afford the two-hump model."

Violet was laughing so hard her make-up was running. She looked up at the cute, silly man in front of her and felt lost in joy.

He just thought how beautiful she looked.

⊷⊜ ⊜⊶

They worked the better part of four hours, Danny trying on various personas, and discarding those they agreed wouldn't go over. They evaluated the merits of a postal delivery man (hard to get across the outfit in time), a circus strong man (too difficult to come up with a suitable outfit with muscles that could be a quick change), and a cowboy (too complicated a change, what with the chaps, spurs, large ten-gallon hat, etc.). Violet suggested a doctor, an idea Danny loved.

"Perfect. We could use the white coat, and, you know, that thing they wear around their heads with the mirror attached. What's that called?"

"It's a rather technical term," Violet paused, her expression perfectly deadpan. "A head mirror."

Danny laughed. "Okay. So we've got this doctor coming in. What should he say?"

"Well," she thought for a moment, then smiled broadly. "Say, young woman, I have just completed the first transplantation of a human brain into a canary. I happen to have a break between appointments. How about you join me for some lunch?"

"And we could add something, like, 'It's just what the doctor ordered.'" Danny said.

"Yes. And you know how she's always turning him down for lunch? At some point the Delivery Boy should ask her, 'Lady, do you *eat?*'"

"Yeah, write that down. After a few of the character changes, it would take the audience off guard," Danny nodded, pacing the length of the room before stopping right in front of Violet. "We want to build repetition with our catch-phrases, but not make them so predictable they get sick of it before our time is up."

"You are right." Violet made swipes across the page.

"Let me see that," Danny said, pulling away Violet's pad, which was full of squiggles. "What is this? Arabic? Chinese? Sanskrit?"

"No—shorthand. Gregg shorthand, to be exact."

"Wow. Can you read it?" Danny stared at the sheet in complete bewilderment.

"Of course."

"Okay, read back the last thing we said."

Violet took the pad. She cleared her throat and said in a low, mock-serious voice, "Add the line, 'Lady, do you *eat?*' toward end of routine. And I can't believe how talented and intelligent Miss Williams is." She stared at the paper, expecting Danny to chuckle. When he didn't make a sound, she looked up to find him staring at her.

"I really *can't* believe how talented and intelligent you are, Vi," he said, his manner more serious than he had yet been with her. "You are pretty amazing."

"I didn't mean to—I was just—" she blushed.

"I know. But it's true. Now, shall we get back to the canary?"

"Vi, what hidden talents do you possess?" Danny asked as he took a huge bite of the hot dog he was demolishing. "I ask because we need more business for the Secretary."

Violet nodded, thoughtfully chewing her tuna sandwich. She was already used to his name for her—a name no one else had ever called her. Because of that, she really liked it. "Talents? Like what?"

"Well, do you sing? Juggle? Play a musical instrument? Do a sword-swallowing act? Do the 'Dance of the Seven Veils'?"

Violet laughed. "Too bad I left my veils in Portland."

Danny laughed. "Interesting …"

"No. I'm actually pretty wholesome. Nothing exotic. Just—well, everybody can sing and play the ukulele today."

"Great, that will work. We'll take a popular song and have you do it. The song pluggers are always trying to get us to work in one of their new tunes, so that'll be easy. We'll just have to figure a way to work it in. She could be answering the telephone in different ways—or with a different slogan each time."

"Yes," she agreed, putting her sandwich aside to write down ideas as they came. "And we could add a few jokes, you know, like the lawyer firm with three identical names, and the person on the phone asking for each one individually." She paused. "Say, how do we make the phone-ring sound?"

"Good question. I remember one act utilizing a telephone, and someone offstage had a little box they used. I'll look into it."

They brainstormed a dozen slogans, narrowing them down to the best. They also discussed songs the pit band could play to introduce each of Danny's characters.

"We only need about sixteen bars of each," he said. "We'll have to make up a sheet of song cues and supply that to the orchestra leader at each theatre. Oh—we'll also need a theme song. You know, one that fits the act."

"I'll think about it as I go freshen up," Violet said, walking toward the back of the room, putting down her pad and pen and getting her purse. As she was going out the door, she turned and exclaimed, "You be thinking, too!"

"Oh, sure," he mumbled, then noticed a piece of paper that had fallen out of her steno pad. Picking it up, he saw that it had several typewritten lines, and looked like a poem. Curiosity got the better of him and he quickly scanned the lines.

```
She sleeps atop a desk which holds
A coffee cup, a telephone,
And papers bearing scars of folds.
She's small and cold and, all alone,
Gets by unseen.  Her form is slight:
A single sultry limb which twines
About a hollow core.  It might
Be called an oval wreath of lines.
She waits in mute suspense until
They say.  Then fatally she grips
Her prey which forms a molded hill
Around and through her metal lips.
But she knows soon they'll take her keep,
And leave her hungry, cold, to sleep.
```

Danny read it. Twice. A perfectly measured sonnet masquerading as … well, it hinted of … Danny wasn't sure, but while reading it he felt like the kid who could get caught with his hand in the cookie jar. And to think that Violet just called herself *wholesome*! He read the poem once more, then folded the paper and hurriedly put it on the table. No, it hadn't been on the table. He ran over to where he found it on the floor just in time to hear Violet come rushing into the office.

"'Love Me, and the World Is Mine'!" Violet crowed.

"I didn't see anything!" Danny barked.

"Wait, what?" they both said in unison.

"I mean," Danny said, inching away from the paper. "I didn't think of anyone—I mean, I couldn't think of anything. Song. Any song."

"*I* did!" Violet strode toward Danny but, seeing the paper on the floor, bent down and picked it up. She looked at it, then casually took it over to her steno pad and slid it in. "The song 'Love Me, and the World Is Mine.' It was popular only a year or so ago."

"Perfect!" Danny enthused. "It captures the feelings of the Delivery Boy who really falls for this girl, the Secretary."

By the time evening fell they were creatively spent, but very hopeful. They went out to the street, where she locked the front door of the office, setting about to find a cab.

"Thank you, Vi, for working on this. It means a lot to me." Danny gave her a sweet smile, and turned to leave. "Oh," he said turning back, "Did you get my flowers?"

Violet looked at him with an innocent air. "Oh, were those from *you*?"

"Yes," Danny said.

"I thought they were from a stranger. Surely no one *I* know …"

He looked at her, not knowing what she was thinking. She then shook her head slowly, with a tight-lipped grin. He laughed at her reaction. "Good night, Vi."

Danny blithely walked home, feeling more alive than he had in a long time—a very long time. He had to admit that he enjoyed spending time with Violet. Being that comfortable around a girl felt good—

he didn't have to be the Danny O'Brien women saw on the stage. He found the process of working with her on the act from the ground up to be stimulating. And then, to find that poem. Well, there is apparently a lot more to Miss Williams than meets the eye. Danny slid his hands into his coat pockets and began whistling, then stopped short. She was his partner. *His vaudeville partner.* He couldn't think of her as just another girl with whom he could have some sort of flirtation. Not in real life. Besides, a lot was riding on this change in his career, and if they had a falling out (which, if history was any indication, would be inevitable) and she walked out on him *and* the act … it would be his own fault. He began walking again, only with a slower, more purposeful pace. This girl has already earned his friendship and respect; he would gift that back to her in equal measure. No funny stuff.

Violet hailed a cab and relaxed in the back of the beautiful gray taxi. She loved the work and found it incredibly rewarding to come up with just the right word, just the right detail. It was exciting. And then she thought about her partner … how easy it would be to really fall for Danny. He intrigued her; something about him moved something deep within her—and it wasn't just sexual attraction. But, of course, she wouldn't let anything go too far. After all, she was in control. Wasn't she?

Violet looked out the window at the city, with all the lights and the late-night hustle. She contemplated the vast number of people, too many to count—the very people, perhaps, who would be in the audience when they did their routine. Then she felt a stinging twinge of nervousness at the thought of being onstage. Knowing that Danny was a seasoned professional certainly gave her some confidence for the act as a whole.

Hmm.

By the time she got home she determined to get a new look at this partner of hers—from the audience's perspective.

Violet quickly settled into a plush seat toward the rear orchestra of Keith's Bushwick Theatre. She was glad that she didn't know any of the performers or stage hands who worked at this theatre; she didn't want anyone to see her and mention to Danny that she had caught his act. What if he was horrible and she didn't like it? She wouldn't want to have to say anything to him about seeing it. But don't be silly, she reasoned. He'll be wonderful. This was going to give her more information about him as an entertainer—and, perhaps, a bit of confidence for their sketch, too.

She had missed the first several acts, but caught the comedian who was in the number-five spot and thought some of his material was funny. She understood what Danny said about comedy being silly: he crossed his eyes and took several dangerous looking pratfalls—the audience responding big to the even bigger lines. The next act featured a young couple doing a scene from *Romeo and Juliet*. The set was quite elaborate, with beautiful greenery festooning the balcony. The actors did a commendable job and received a hearty round of applause at the conclusion.

A stagehand came out and changed the card on the easel, announcing the headliner:

Danny O'Brien
Singer of Songs of the Old Sod

She found that she was a little anxious. Was *he* nervous right now? How many times had he walked onto a vaudeville stage? Violet knew that he started when he was a child with his parents' act, so it must be counted into the thousands. But now, tonight, what were the thoughts he had? Oh please, dear God, just let him be good. The orchestra struck up his theme song, "Danny Boy." A spotlight hit the left side of the stage and followed Danny, who confidently strode out, looking elegant in his white tux with green waistcoat and bow tie. His hair was slicked back, making it appear darker in color. He acknowledged the applause from the audience with a big smile and a wave of his hand.

When he arrived at center stage he stood like he belonged there. The orchestra began a tune with which she was completely unfamiliar, and after the opening few bars, he began to sing.

Violet sat in awe of his abilities. His voice was superb and he effortlessly found each note the song required. But that wasn't what sold his act: it was the way he interacted with the audience. He gave so much of himself; he seemed to offer this group of strangers everything he had—everything he could ever possess. When the song ended, he bowed, appearing to be surprised that they found it to be worthy. But the ovation told her they believed he was far more than that. He gave them that deep-dimpled smile of his, and they ate it up. Song after song continued in his mesmeric journey. She heard women commenting on how handsome he was—even better-looking than his picture in the lobby. By the time the opening strains of "Danny Boy" sounded, he had made hundreds of conquests, and probably dozens of husbands and boyfriends jealous. When he sang the line, "It's I'll be here in sunshine or in shadow" toward the end of the song, he hit the word *here* with a sustained, clear note that drew its own round of applause. The song finished and Danny took his final bow, putting his hand over his heart with a look of utter sincerity, a gesture of deep appreciation to the audience. To a thundering ovation, he lithely sprinted offstage. Violet felt even more excited than before: this dynamic performer was going to be *her* partner.

The last act up was a magic show, featuring a wonderful magician who did some sleight-of-hand illusions, followed by a regurgitation trick. She felt like the little girl who was watching Houdini. The show finished, and she joined the horde of satisfied customers as they filed out of the auditorium.

On her way home, she thought of how strange this life was; that she could be as close to Danny as they were last evening, then be only a small part of a crowd applauding him tonight. Interesting. Deep down she had to admit that she was looking forward to tomorrow, when she could get him back all to herself.

CHAPTER FIVE

THE CITY

September 1925

Violet heard a soft knock on her bedroom door the next morning. She opened one eye and glanced over, looking at the brass alarm clock: 6:30.

"Yes?" she asked.

"Violet, honey," came Aunt Mavis's soft voice. "Danny is on the phone for you."

"Thank you, I'll be right there!" Violet yelled while jumping out of bed and throwing on her robe. It took her all of ten seconds to make herself presentable enough to go downstairs to the hallway phone. She picked up the receiver.

"Hello?" she said, with more pep in her voice than she felt.

"Hi'ya, Vi. I didn't wake you, did I?"

"No, no, I was just upstairs. Reading."

"Great. Well, I was thinking today that you could go with me while I run some errands," Danny said casually. "I'd like to show you more of New York, *my* New York anyway."

"Yes, that would be fun. How was your evening?" she asked, wondering if he would relate the huge success of the night before. He had to be proud of his great accomplishment.

"Fine. Why don't you swing by my place at nine o'clock. I live at the Osborne. Take a cab. I'll introduce you to my roommate."

"Great. But, didn't you have a show last night?" Violet probed.

"Sure. Why?"

"Just wondering how it went, that's all."

"It went okay—like it should have gone. I sang, they clapped, you know, the usual," Danny answered in a matter-of-fact tone.

"And that's *it?*"

"Yes—say, Vi, what are you getting at?"

"I was *there*. Last night. In the theatre," Violet said in a quiet voice.

"You were at—well, why didn't you come backstage and say hello?" Danny sounded surprised.

"I didn't want you to know I was there. But, well, your act seemed to go over more than just 'okay,' I mean, the clapping. I thought it would never stop."

Danny smiled and couldn't resist teasing her. "Yes. They really loved me, didn't they. Wasn't I just the monkey's eyebrows?"

"Well, the regurgitator didn't seem to think so," Violet retorted quickly. "See you at nine." And with that, she rang off.

With a half-smile Danny slowly replaced the receiver. She was becoming more interesting all the time.

Violet showed up exactly at nine. Not knowing what was on the docket for the day, she had taken quite a while to decide what to wear. She finally settled on a butter yellow sleeveless dress with a matching cloche hat. When Danny opened the door he looked more like himself; his hair was tousled and blond again, and he looked very casual in a collar-less shirt and linen trousers. "Hi, come on in. Just getting a few things together and we can be off." Danny went into the kitchen and began putting some items into a wicker hamper.

She stepped into the small but airy apartment and saw the effort Danny had put into making it look clean. The stuccoed walls were a creamy white. There was a long green horsehair sofa against the far wall, above which hung a beautiful painting of a Tahitian sunset. A chair that matched the sofa stood steadfastly by a table; this served as a stand for a Victrola. From the hardwood floor, which looked freshly swept but in need of a good polish, grew oak bookcases that held dozens of old volumes and just as many 78 records. The apartment smelled faintly of cigarette smoke, but more of a deep woodsy, leather, and vanilla scent—just like Danny. She inhaled deeply.

"Is your roommate here today?" she asked.

"Yes, he's here—somewhere. Maybe in the back bedroom."

As if on cue, the blanket on the sofa began to move, slowly giving birth to Murray. He yawned, stretched, then ambled slowly toward the visitor.

"Well, hello, handsome!" Violet said with an obvious smile in her voice. She knelt down and moved her hand slowly toward the cat, who immediately began purring as she petted him. "What's his name?"

"Murray, meet Vi. Vi, Murray."

"Well, hi, Murray. Very nice to meet you!" She picked him up and he was soon rubbing his muzzle against her cheek. "Boy, you work *fast!*"

Danny walked into the living room, hamper in hand, and took in the scene. "Disgusting," he said, shaking his head. "I thought we talked about appropriate behavior toward young ladies, old man." But Murray couldn't be bothered; he was enjoying the attention far too much to pay any consideration to his roommate.

"Say, Danny, what kind of aftershave do you use?" She couldn't help but ask.

"Jicky. Why? Does it offend you?" he asked seriously.

"No, as a matter of fact, I like it," she said shyly.

Danny grinned. "Okay, then. We can be off."

When Violet reluctantly placed Murray on the ground, he looked at her as if she didn't realize he had been enjoying her affections. "Goodbye—hope to see you again soon," Violet said as Murray swished his tail. He wandered back to the sofa, jumping up by the blanket's edge, then slowly slinked beneath its warm folds.

"Does he have a limp? His right-rear leg?" Violet asked, concerned.

"Yeah, he's had that since he was a kitten. Long story," Danny said as he picked up the hamper. "Shall we?" he asked as he opened the door.

At the end of the hall, they got in the elevator and went down to the richly decorated lobby. Just as when she had walked in, she noticed the stuccoed walls and the floors that mixed tile mosaics and slabs of varicolored Italian marble. Danny pointed out the complementary marble which was used for the wainscoting and carved recesses with benches. Mosaics and glazed terracotta "Della Robbia" panels covered the walls and ceilings in rich hues of red, blue, and gold leaf. Danny noticed her looking around, and told her that the great sculptor of the American Renaissance, Augustus Saint-Gaudens, the muralist John La Farge, and French designer Jacob Adolphus Holzer all had a hand in creating the Osborne's distinctive look. He also pointed out the glass by the Tiffany studio.

"It's beautiful," she said, taking it all in.

"This is the first of two buildings you're going to see today which, to me, say the most about New York."

"How long have you lived here?" Violet asked.

"At the Osborne? About eight years now. I got this apartment shortly after my father died, after I had been out on my own a while."

"And your mother?"

"She lives with her brother, upstate, near Ithaca. And, before you ask, I am an only child."

Walking out to the street, Danny hailed a black-and-white cab. "The Dakota, please," he said politely to the driver. They got in the taxi and were soon on their way to the west side of town.

"I've heard of that building. It is an odd name—why is it called the Dakota?"

"Apparently," Danny said, settling into the worn upholstered seat, "somebody said to the man who built it that it was so far north and so far west of civilization that he may as well be building in Dakota. The guy thought that was funny, so it became the building's name."

Violet laughed. *What a town,* she thought. As they approached the building, she gazed in wonder at the magnificent architecture, so different from the Osborne's solemn brownstone front. The outside was of light yellow brick, covered with carved stone friezes and mullions. The succession of turrets, pyramids, towers, peaks, chimneys, finials, and gables were trimmed with copper. Windows gleamed in the sun, and were a multitude of shapes and sizes. From this mammoth building grew intricate ledges, balconies, decorative iron railings and tall columns of bay windows climbing nine stories high. A massive, iron-gated archway, flanked by iron planter urns, provided the main entrance from the Seventy-Second Street side of the building. This led into an H-shaped interior courtyard, in the center of which stood two stone fountains, each spouting a dozen iron calla lilies. The musical splashing water could be heard from the street, which added to the otherworldly ambience of the Dakota.

Violet got out of the cab, followed by Danny who carted the heavy hamper. He paid the driver, apparently giving him a big tip as the fellow thanked him enthusiastically. "I don't care what they say," he said before taking off, "you show people are alright."

As they made their way into the lobby, Violet noticed that the building was as beautiful inside as out. There were carved plaster ceilings. Walls were paneled with oak and mahogany. Marble made an appearance in the floors, and wrought-iron traced the path of the stairways. After speaking with a woman at a front desk whom Danny seemed to know, he escorted Violet to an elevator, only one of several they would take to get to their destination: the ninth floor. The elevators were gorgeous, with elegant, open cages of carved, spindled wood, set in fanlike patterns.

The minute the last elevator opened, Violet felt as if she had entered a different building. The Dakota, apparently, had many personalities. Here, the corridor was dark, and scented with spicy Italian and Portuguese cooking aromas. Women wearing kerchiefs and aprons carried pots of steaming stews from one area on the floor to another. Danny made his way down a large, winding hallway, greeting individuals by name as he walked. He stopped in front of one door and put the basket down, away from the entrance. Pulling out what looked like two boxes of candy, he knocked loudly. The heavy door was soon opened by a pretty woman with long blonde ringlets.

"Good marnin', Miss Browning." Danny said with a huge smile. "And how would ya be doin' this foin day?" Violet was amused to hear the thick Irish brogue Danny used to address this woman, and knew there had to be a back-story.

The resident squealed and clapped her hands together. "Oh, Danny, how wonderful to see you! Adele, Danny is here!" she added, calling to someone in the apartment. In no time another woman of about the same age, probably early thirties, appeared.

"Hi, Danny, how are you?" she asked, her eyes shining with joy.

"Great! I'd like ya both to be meetin' Miss Violet Williams. She and I are workin' on a sketch."

"Hi," Violet said engagingly, smiling at the two in the doorway.

The two muttered something unintelligible, barely taking the time to look away from Danny to acknowledge her. Facing Danny, they asked, "Won't you come in?"

"Not today, unfortunately. We have more stops we need to be makin'." He handed them the boxes, which they took with obvious delight.

"Thank you, Danny. You are always so sweet to remember us!"

"I'll be back. 'Twas a pleasure to see ya," he said as he backed away, making ready to leave.

"Goodbye," they said in unison, their bright smiles dimming as they closed the door.

Danny grabbed the hamper and continued down the corridor, walking briskly and filling Violet in on the women she had just met. "They were born in this building in 1890 and were about my age when my parents and I used to drop by. My folks knew many residents, so we would be here for several hours at a time. The girls and I would come up here, to the forgotten areas of the building, and run up and down the halls, bouncing a ball and singing."

"That is extraordinary," Violet said, running to keep up with Danny. "And, I might regret asking, but why did you speak with them using the brogue?"

"Air ye daft, woman. I dunna ken what yer talking 'bout," he teased. Then, in a more serious tone: "You see, they loved my father, and he spoke with a heavy brogue, as did his father. So I just fell into it when I was around them, and now I don't have the heart to change. And then, to make matters worse, when I was just starting out on my own they came to see my act—Danny the Irish Wonder Dog—and they really went on."

Violet hit his arm. "That is for putting yourself down. Remember, just last night I was privy to—"

"Last night you were in a privy? Please, Miss Williams, spare me the details!"

"Danny!" Violet hit his arm again.

"And stop beating me," he demanded, but couldn't take the laugh out of his voice.

They continued through the labyrinth of the ninth floor, next paying a call to a man with a glass eye. Danny explained that he was an actor who had been injured while working for Florenz Ziegfeld, when a piece of flying scenery hit him in the face. To him, Danny gave an envelope she suspected contained money. The man seemed very grateful indeed. Next up was a fragile yet lovely woman, Mrs. Denton Barclay, to whom he gave a couple of bottles of cough syrup and some fresh fruit. Danny later explained to Violet that this lady was often ill and was in need of such fare. She just rarely went out to get fresh food for herself. They spent the entire morning making these calls, with Danny methodically emptying the hamper. The final stop was to an elderly woman on the second floor. Danny told Violet that this fascinating lady had moved into the Dakota with her parents when the building first opened.

"Danny! Why, what a lovely surprise!" the small, delicately featured woman said as she opened the door. "Now, you must come in for just a moment. And who is this pretty girl you have with you?"

"Miss Cordelia Deal, please meet Miss Violet Williams. She and I are working on a new routine together." Danny could be very formal when he wanted to, Violet noticed with a smile. When addressing Miss Deal, Danny spoke loudly and enunciated more clearly.

"It is such a pleasure to meet you, Miss Deal," Violet said, mimicking Danny's style. She extended her hand and took Miss Deal's birdlike claw.

"Oh, this is wonderful," Miss Deal said, pulling Violet into the huge apartment. Immediately, Violet was overwhelmed with the scent of lavender. "She is perfect for you, Danny. Now come along. Dear, did you know that when Danny was little he would come and visit me? He would sing the most beautiful ballads to me—he had such a lovely voice. Clear as a bell. His mother and I were the dearest of friends, which some of the residents here found rather shocking. Many of them didn't approve of show people, you know."

Miss Deal continued until they came to a large drawing room containing massive furniture that dwarfed the small woman, and a huge fireplace with a marble mantle. The elaborate ceilings must have been eighteen feet high, Violet deduced, and every foot of wall space was covered with paintings. Some looked like landscapes hanging in museums painted by the masters, and Violet could only wonder what marvels she was actually viewing.

"Please, sit. Would you like tea, my dear?" she asked Danny.

"No, thank you, we can't stay very long. But, Vi, Miss Deal remembers New York long before I was born. Would you tell us some of your early memories?"

"Yes, Miss Deal," Violet added encouragingly. She faced the small woman who had been devoured by the enormous chair in which she sat. There was a large window behind her, the encroaching light giving her thin puff of gray hair a halo effect. She was dressed in an old-fashioned day dress of periwinkle-blue chiffon, and folded her hands in her lap like a small child sitting in church. Violet was intrigued by her. "What *was* New York like when you were growing up here?"

"I'll tell you. People were politer then, it seems to me. Mothers went for tea at Sherry's, and the children had hot chocolate. Young men sent young ladies candy from Sherry's. It came in lovely lavender tin boxes, and you saved the boxes to keep your toiletries and love letters and other treasures in. There was so much more service then. The manicurist came to our house. The hairdresser came once a week to wash my mother's hair. If she were going to a ball, the girl came to dress her hair. The chiropodist came to the house. The dressmaker came to the house. The maids were Irish or German, and the coachmen were usually Scots, for some reason."

Danny looked at Violet, who was smiling and nodding at Miss Deal. *I could get used to this,* he thought. He appreciated her deportment being that of a proper young lady, with sweetness and genuine caring radiating from her. His Vi. She seemed to actually be enjoying the conversation with the older woman. He couldn't help but think of how it would be, just sitting and looking at her adorable face for a lifetime.

"Don't you think, Danny?" Miss Deal's loud words caused him to come out of his dreamlike state. He noticed that Vi was looking at him in a curious way, as if wondering what he was thinking. "Well, *don't* you?" the older woman queried.

"Of course," Danny replied hastily, "but only on Wednesdays."

"*Harrumph.*" Miss Deal turned back to Violet. "It is true, my dear, nobody talked about crime. Nobody talked about security. Here at the Dakota no one bothered to lock their apartment doors. There was some talk about bribery and corruption in the city government, particularly during the Boss Tweed period. I remember that Mother and her friends would have tea and talk about men and their—" she looked at Danny, who was looking down at his hands, then whispered to Violet "*mistresses.*" This hesitance, for some reason, made Violet blush.

"How very sweet," Miss Deal observed. "There are not many girls around today who have the decency to blush. When are you two planning to be married, Danny?"

Danny was completely taken off guard. "I—oh, I really, I mean," he swallowed hard. "What I'm trying to say is that we're not, well, you know. Miss Deal, we're *vaudeville* partners."

"Pish tosh. She is *perfect* for you." Miss Deal was emphatic.

Violet's blush became an inferno.

Mercifully, Danny was able to steer the rest of the conversation into other, less personal, directions. When they rose to leave, Miss Deal put her thin arm around Violet.

"Now, sweetheart, you keep this boy in line. I like you, and I will expect to be invited to the wedding."

"Believe me, you'll be the first we invite," Violet said brightly, holding back a laugh. "Thank you for your hospitality, Miss Deal. Goodbye." She kissed the old woman on her cheek.

"Goodbye, dear; goodbye, Danny. Come back anytime."

"Thank you, Miss Deal," Danny said after also planting a kiss on the woman's withered cheek.

They strolled back to the elevator, rode up to the ninth floor, then walked the length of it, ducking into a stairway off the side.

Halfway up the stairs, Violet stopped. Danny turned and looked at her. "Why didn't you bring Miss Deal anything, Danny?" she had to ask.

"Because she is as rich as Croesus and doesn't need anything—except someone to hear her stories. And that someone is me—well, sometimes." He turned and continued the long climb. They finally emerged into a room which served as an attic, storing random furniture covered with gigantic white cloths. Danny went to a large window which ran from the floor to the ceiling of the room. The dust and grime, formed through decades of neglect, was embedded in the glass, serving to soften the bright sun shining into the room. Danny set the hamper on the carpet just in front of it, then motioned for Violet to join him. He lovingly pointed out some New York landmarks which could be seen from this vantage point: Central Park's picturesque Belvedere Castle and lake, as well as Long Island Sound and the hills of Brooklyn, just visible through buildings which rose majestically throughout the landscape. After the rooftop tour, he opened the basket and brought out a multi-colored blanket, which he spread on the dark wood floor. Sitting down, he patted the spot next to him.

"Will you join me for a picnic, Miss Williams?" he asked invitingly.

"Why, I'd love to, Mr. O'Brien," Violet said as she joined him.

He then produced a veritable feast from the basket. Cold fried chicken, carrot salad with bits of fresh pineapple and raisins, thick slices of fresh bread with a pot of butter, and a couple of bottles of Coca-Cola. And for dessert they had chocolate cookies. Danny had also packed plates, forks, knives, and napkins, and even remembered the bottle opener for the Cokes.

"Oh, this is perfect!" Violet said appreciatively, "It's been a long time since I have been on a picnic!" She felt like a kid, and loved the adventurous feeling of the afternoon.

"Well, everything is from Katz's, a great deli by me. I eat there often."

"Was your mother a good cook?" Violet asked.

"No," Danny answered, picking up a chicken leg. "She was in show business. We always ate at the boarding houses or hotels, you know; it was easy to catch a bite here and there. They never really put much stock in more formal meals, per se."

Throughout the picnic they talked about family. Violet spoke with great pride about her parents' role in the suffragette movement, which Danny found most interesting. After asking about Murray's history and getting the whole story, she asked some details about Danny's upbringing.

"I guess you could say that my mom was—what's the right word?—too 'preoccupied' to take on the mother role very often. She was a professional and kept pretty busy with the act. But she did her best, and I love her dearly," he added. Violet suddenly saw him as a small, lost boy, and immediately wanted to take care of him.

"I bet you were proud of them, of your parents' work ethic," she ventured.

"Oh, yes, I was—and am. They were troupers, and giving me that approach to this profession was a real gift; something that a lot of performers today don't understand."

Violet smiled and grabbed a cookie.

"So," Danny said, also seizing a cookie, "you've seen my New York— describe your Oregon to me."

"Hmm, I guess the first thing that comes to mind is green. Wet, gorgeous, wide expanses of grass and fir trees—quieter than New York, to be sure, and so many fewer people! The air smells like the trees and flowers. And rain, which is the best scent in the world, especially in the summer when it hits the warm ground. In general, there is a calmer feeling, definitely slower paced, which is both good and bad. I love the fast-paced feeling of New York."

"I don't know," Danny said, looking down, "I think Oregon sounds pretty wonderful." He looked up at Violet with a small, wistful smile, an expression that Violet had never seen Danny wear, and it gave her a look at the man in a new, intimate way.

After the food was consumed and the drinks polished off, they lay back on the blanket and stared at the high plaster ceiling. A stain from a long-ago leak formed a dark blob.

"A cow, lying down, wearing a straw hat," Danny announced.

"Wh-what?" Violet stammered.

"The stain. It looks just like a cow wearing a straw hat. Look, its head is pointing toward the window."

Violet squinted at the mark. "Yeah, I think I see what you mean. Holstein?"

"No, Catholic," Danny said dryly.

 Violet giggled.

"So," Danny began, "tell me something no one knows about you."

"What? A secret even my *sisters* don't know?"

"Yup."

Violet hesitated, wondering what would be interesting enough, but not too embarrassing. She really had to weigh her answer, that was apparently taking too long because Danny began to snore loudly.

"I'm *thinking!*" she said exasperatedly. "Well, okay, I do one thing, or I should say I *have* done one thing, but only a couple of times."

Danny looked over at Violet, his curiosity clearly piqued.

"I eat sweetened condensed milk straight out of the tin. With a spoon."

Danny looked mock-appalled, sitting up. "*Well.* If I had known that you were *that* kind of girl, I would never have begun our association, Miss Williams! To eat an entire can of—*(gasp)*—sweetened con—"

"Stop it," Violet laughed, "And it wasn't a whole can. Just a little."

"Oh, no you don't. No backpedaling. You opened your can; now you must eat it." The more umbrage Danny displayed, the more Violet laughed. She hit him a few times, but it didn't help.

"I thought, well," Danny began, changing his tone, "I thought maybe you were going to tell me something about writing suggestive poetry."

"What?" Now Violet sat up. "Whatever do you mean?"

"I saw it, the poem you had—or have—in your steno pad."

"Oh, that. I considered having it published. It's an ode to—wait, what do *you* think the poem is about?"

Danny began picking at some imaginary thread on the blanket. "Well, you are the one who wrote about sultry limbs twining and molded hills around her lips."

"Metal lips, and it is an ode to a *paper clip*, you dirty man!"

"*A paper clip?*" he asked, incredulously. He quickly ran the poem through his mind. "Okay. Say, that's good!"

"Thank you, and I wrote it while I was at school. Business school, while surrounded by the things." She lay back, and said, "Okay, Mr. Worldly-Wise, you tell me something that no one knows about *you!*"

Danny thought for a minute and rolled onto his side, facing her. "A truth?" he asked.

Violet rolled onto her side, facing him. "Yes. I am owed it."

"I love paper clips," he said, giving her a wink. Usually Violet didn't respond to winks, sometimes even finding them tawdry. But Danny had a way of making that small gesture seem very personal—and made her toes curl.

She laughed. "No, really, Danny. You have to play fair."

"Okay. Well, you mentioned the show last night."

"Yes." Violet thought back to the huge ovation Danny earned, and received.

"I hate it." It was all he said. She looked at him and saw a person who was deeply unhappy, in the middle of a war with himself. He saw in her a dawning expression of great compassion which shone through her eyes. "I know that sounds harsh," he continued, "and I should be so grateful, and I am. I don't take my good fortune for granted, believe me. But I'm, I don't know, it's so mind-numbingly routine for me. I feel like I'm always lying to people, to audiences. My heart's just not in it. I know my father could do the same act for his lifetime, but to me, I don't know, it—"

"—it feels artificial," Violet finished.

"Yes! Exactly. I was beginning to feel as if nothing was real anymore, and I was just going through the motions. I haven't been excited about anything until …" and here Danny paused for a moment, running his hand over his face then through his hair, turning just a bit red. "Until we started working together. I haven't been this happy in years, Vi. And now I am telling you this, and why, for the life of me, I don't know." Danny laughed self-consciously.

"You trust me," Violet said, the warmth in her voice nurturing his fallow heart.

"I trust you," Danny said, looking up, and taking her hand. They threaded their fingers together for just a moment, then let go.

They both rolled over, lying on their backs, looking up at the ceiling. Through the enormous windows they could hear the traffic sounds of the street below. They could smell the mustiness of the old furniture. And each was more content than they had perhaps ever been.

"Paper clip," Danny muttered, and they both laughed.

This would be a memory of a lifetime.

⭑⭢═◉　◉═⭠⭑

They entered the Goodman Talent Agency precisely at 7:00 PM—the time Uncle Patrick had set up for them to use the typing machines. Danny was "laying off" for a week since finishing his run at the Bushwick, so they decided to take advantage of the evening and get their routine finalized. Violet sat at one of the office tables, put down the stack of handwritten papers that was their sketch, and carefully removed the machine's cloth covering. The Underwood Standard she exposed was a fairly new model, one with which she was very familiar. Uncle Patrick acquired, and maintained, good equipment for the girls to use. She checked the ribbon, which was fine.

"How many carbons do you want?" she asked the now-pacing Danny.

"What?" Danny stopped and faced her, looking extremely distracted.

"How many carbon copies do we need for the script?" she answered.

"Oh, well, let's see—you and I should each have one, and Pat, and one to file with the Registry, and one for the Keith office, so *five*? Would that be alright?"

"Sure," Violet answered, reaching into the desk drawer to remove typing paper and a thin box containing carbon paper. She opened the box and removed the top carbons which bore the type strikes from past correspondences and contracts. She reached down to the fresh, unused papers, and extracted a small group. "That will be one original and four copies."

"Yeah." Danny stopped moving and leaned against a desk. Removing the pack of Camels and matches from his shirt, he withdrew one and lit it.

"Do you have to smoke? I'm sorry, but I hate the smell," Violet said apologetically.

"Oh, sure," Danny replied, stubbing out his cigarette and sitting on the edge of one of the desks.

Violet took five pieces of typing paper and four pieces of carbon paper and alternately stacked them, making sure that the carbons faced in the proper direction between each sheet of white. She carefully loaded the bundle into the machine, rotating the roller so that the paper was comfortably in the carriage, and then snapped the bar into place. On her right she arranged the stack of handwritten papers and looked at the top of the first page.

"So, do I just center the title then—wait, I think I saw a typed routine on Uncle Patrick's desk. Let me get it." She hopped up and ran into his office, returning in no time with a bundle of clipped papers. "Is this the form?"

Danny scanned the papers. "You know, I've never actually produced one of these. But this looks good, so let's go with it."

"Okay." Violet sat down and looked at the papers in front of her. She noticed that the name of the sketch was centered at the top. She tabbed the carriage to the center, then counted the spaces for the title: "Will She Love Me!"

"What are you doing?" Danny asked, looking over her shoulder.

"Centering the title. You count all the letters, spaces, and punctuation marks and divide by two. Then you backspace that many spaces. Watch."

She counted nineteen, so she backspaced ten times, then typed the title. Perfect! She then set the spacing lever on 2. Now she was ready to type the script.

As her hands flew over the keys, her right hand rising up after each bell ring to return the carriage, Danny couldn't help but be amazed. She sat ramrod straight, shoulders back, arms comfortably by her side. And she was typing so fast! He couldn't think of hearing anyone type with such speed. He watched her for a while, then began walking around again.

From the corner of her eye, Violet was aware of Danny pacing. She noticed him pick up an object from one desk, go to another and snatch something else, then look around for a third item. Upon finding what looked like a paperweight, he began tossing the items into the air, juggling them at an increasing pace. She stopped typing and watched him, until he noticed the lack of sound in the room and turned to face her. He was manipulating the items when he began walking toward her. She shook her head and got back to work. Danny walked right up to her desk, juggling the items closer and closer to her face.

"Stop it!" she laughed.

"What?" he asked with a serious tone.

"Stop doing *that*."

"Doing *what*?"

"Juggling, or whatever you call it."

"I don't know what you're talking about," he replied, not missing a beat. "I'm certainly not juggling or whatever you call it."

She stopped typing and leaned back, arms in back of her head. "Well, if you're on a break, so am I."

That stopped him. "You win," he said looking at her with a smile as she got back to work. He examined one of the paperweights in his hand, trying to make out just which building was represented.

"You should juggle," Violet said, not looking up.

"I thought you just told me to stop." He looked at her, confused, putting down the paperweight.

"No, in the sketch. You should juggle as part of a character in the routine." She stopped typing and thought for a moment. "You know how we have 'The Fun Type'? Well, how would it be if you were to come on the stage juggling, wearing a silly wig or something?"

"That would actually be a great visual bit. Then I could leave the—we'll use beanbags as they're easier to work with—beanbags on your desk. After I leave, for the bit you do, *you* can juggle." He felt that sense of elation creep over him again, just as it had on those days when they worked on the sketch. Just as it did every time they were together.

"I could learn, certainly. After all, how hard could it be if *you* can do it?" she asked with a twinkle in her eye.

He grabbed his chest. "*Ugh*, you got me, Miss Williams."

She laughed and continued on, putting in the new information where they had made changes, discussing possible substitutions for awkward words or phrases, and generally smoothed out the skit until it was as polished as they could make it.

When she had finished, they separated the paper into five equal scripts. They then began reading their sketch from beginning to end, checking for mistakes and anything which needed to be changed.

"There is a small mistake on page two," Danny said, moving to Violet's side. "Here, where it says, 'Mr. Hoffensteader is on a meeting,' it should read '*in* a meeting.'"

"No problem," Violet said as she opened a drawer in the desk and got out a fountain pen and a stick with an odd eraser attached to one end. "This little eraser is tougher than the normal one for pencil lead," she said. Setting to work on the copies, she erased the errant "o" and filled the blank in with a handwritten "i," carefully matching other like vowels on the page.

"You, Miss Williams, are an artist," Danny said, bending over her work. "I wouldn't know that there had been a mistake if I didn't know!"

"Well, being an artist for a minute sure beats retyping the whole page!" Violet laughed.

They went over the remaining script and, finding no further mistakes, carefully laid three copies on Patrick's desk, with a cover note from Danny.

"And now," he turned to Violet, his eyes flashing bright blue, "it seems to me that you are in need of a juggling lesson. We also need to begin blocking this out and learning the lines. Why don't we meet here tomorrow morning and get to work?"

"I can't wait!" Violet answered. They called it quits for the day, each feeling that they had given their best.

The next morning Danny and Violet had a quick conference with Patrick regarding their act, and presented him with the finished script. While Patrick was reading, Danny was pacing. Violet sat quietly, the only indication of her nerves being the ever-so-slight wiggling of one foot.

"Good job," Patrick said with an almost-smile when he had read the last page. "It should time out to just fourteen minutes, and there is plenty of room to stretch to seventeen in the headline spot. I think, with proper staging, lighting, props, wardrobe, and such, it could be an excellent routine."

"Great," Danny said.

"I'll get this to Mr. Casey at the Vaudeville Managers Protective Association to register the act, and a copy to the Keith office for approval; probably Albee will want to see this himself," Patrick said, shifting the papers on his desk and making notes at the top of each. He retrieved some paper clips from a drawer to form each set, the sight of which caused Danny to grin and Violet to blush ever so slightly. Patrick then pulled out two large envelopes and, stuffing a complete copy into each, wrote out the needed information on the front. "The girls can take care of getting this to the currier. I will make sure the other set is filed with our office," he mumbled to himself, then to the couple: "I will come up with contracts for both of you. Good job."

After thanking Patrick, they went out into the hallway, closing his office door behind them. After taking a few steps, Danny did a bell kick. "And that is great praise from our Patrick. I couldn't be happier!"

Violet was thrilled, determined to put her all into this new phase of her life. They went into their little office and Danny removed his jacket.

"And now, for the serious business of clowning," he said. From his coat pocket he removed three small burlap bags filled with beans and held them up. "The basics of juggling."

Danny started her off tossing two of the bags back and forth, which she found to be easy. But it took her a while to get the rhythm of the three-bag toss-and-throw pattern. Violet realized that juggling was harder to pick up than she had hoped, and she was getting tense. But Danny was patience personified, which allowed her to relax and, after a while, start looking like a real juggler. She was feeling pretty confident by the time they had to break so he could get home to feed Murray.

"Now," Danny said as he put on his jacket, "when I get back, let's start blocking the routine and do a run-through. Is that okay with you?"

"Sure is," she beamed.

Danny walked out of the room, leaving Violet alone with the little burlap bags. She picked them up and began to juggle, only to have one troublemaker go flying across the room. She threw the other two at the first, and stuck her tongue out at the pile. Then, struck by inspiration, she grabbed her purse and ran after the guy with the cat.

⋆⊷══⊶　⊷══⊶⋆

Finding time over the next week to rehearse the sketch was fairly easy, until Danny had to do a jump out of town for a few days. During that forced time-off Violet really missed him, and decided to make the moments count. She learned from Uncle Patrick the best place to secure the wardrobe and props for the act, and he gave her the sizes to order for Danny. He also gave her a purchase order, allowing the cost of the costumes to be absorbed by the Goodman Talent Agency. Soon, she was in a cab headed toward 151 West Forty-Sixth Street.

Advertised as "The World's Largest Rental Costumers," Eaves Costume Company began its existence in 1863. Violet walked through the front door and was amazed at the vastness of the place. There, Elizabethan ball gowns cavorted with caveman loincloths, nurses from the Great War stood side by side with caped vampires, and an armored Sir Lancelot (lance included) kept a watchful eye on Cleopatra (asp not included).

"Hello, I would like to speak with Mike," Violet said when a short man in shirtsleeves approached her. He had a tape measure around his thick neck, and wore dark, horn-rimmed glasses which reduced his eyes to two dark, unblinking specks. A large cigar protruded from his mouth, and his short, dark hair was sharply parted on the side, then forcefully slicked back into a helmet. His overall demeanor was that of someone who did not suffer fools, or anyone who would dare to waste a minute of his precious time.

"Yah, I'm Mike," the man stated, his attitude pairing both disappointment and boredom; his strong Bowery accent wielding a warning. "Whattyawant?"

"I'm Violet Williams, Patrick Goodman's niece."

"What does Goodman want now?"

Violet cleared her throat. "I need to order some costumes and props for our new act. It takes place in an office setting and—"

"Look, lady," he interrupted. "We're busier 'n hell right now. Why don't you come back next week?"

She made up her mind to try one more tactic. "Well, that would be fine, Mike, but my *partner* was hoping that we could get these items as soon as possible."

"*Partner*?" Mike repeated as if the mere word was a transgression. "And exactly *who* is this impatient partner?"

"Danny O'Brien."

"Danny O'Bri—why the devil didn't you say so in the first place? Come back here where we can get to work." And with that, the newly energized Mike led Violet into a small room which had stacks of catalogues and paper hiding a table and chairs.

"Sit. Coffee? Tea? I think I have some cookies around here someplace," the busy man said in a decidedly friendlier tone.

"No, thank you. But here is the list of costumes we will need." She handed him the list she had typed out:

```
CLOTHING:
Collarless shirt, medium, white
Plus-fours, size w. 30, black-and-white
    houndstooth pattern
Men's stockings, black
Men's short boots, black, size 10
Men's vest, black, medium
Rifle frock coat, full length, black, large
Bisht (long)
Doctor's white coat, ¾ length, tight
    fitting, large
Camel hair polo coat, natural, full
    length, large (with full skirt)
Raccoon coat, full length, large
```

HATS and WIGS: (hat size 7 ⅜)
Newsie cap
Top hat, black
Dark brown bowler
Porkpie hat, tan, dark brown goose-grain
    ribbon band
Keffiyeh, red
Multi-colored wig (clown)

PROPS:
Candlestick desk phone
Red nose (clown)
Head mirror (doctor)
Ukulele
Monocle
Walking stick
Juggling beanbags (two sets of three)
College pennant on a stick
Large mustache, dark brown

"Hmm, let me see what I can do," Mike said, looking over the list. "For Danny, we can have this in just a few days, including the props."

"He will be so pleased," Violet assured him. She was learning the ropes slowly, but surely.

Mike got Violet's information and the purchase order, and she was out the door in no time.

Her next step was to procure the perfect dress for her own costume. She hailed a cab, and was off for Broadway and Twentieth Street, the location of Lord & Taylor. She made her way to the women's section and found a salesgirl who could show her several different selections. Some dresses were too severe for her Secretary, who was, after all, a fun-loving girl of the '20s. Others were simply too casual. This out-fit had to be colorful and special—it wasn't really an everyday office dress, but a stage costume. It had to strike the right balance. When the girl brought out one particular ensemble, however, she knew *this* was the one. The salesgirl read in a stilted voice from a card:

Strikingly smart and very new is the gaily colored futurist print that adorns the blouse of this attractive two-piece frock. Material is soft, lustrous all silk crepe de chine, the skirt being of solid tone that matches the background of the print. The skirt also has a lower border of matching rich colors. It comes attached to a soiesette bodice lining. $14.98.

The girl looked up to find a smiling Violet. "I'll take two!"

CHAPTER SIX

THE SCRIPT

"Will <u>She</u> Love Me!"
Flirtation Act in One Scene
O'Brien & Williams

CHARACTERS: Delivery Boy and Secretary

SETTING: an office in Two (special drop)

STAGE: (left) desk topped with nail file,
telephone; chair; trash can and ukulele on
left of desk; overturned metal trash can
topped with telephone-ring box on right of
desk

LIGHTING: two follow-spots

<u>Music cue</u>: "Love Me, and the World Is Mine"

Delivery Boy: (enters, stage right, carrying
package) Package for Mr. Hoffensteader.

Secretary: (taking package, barely making eye
contact with Delivery Boy) Thank you.

Delivery Boy: (doing an exaggerated take looking at Secretary) Say, you're alright!

Secretary: (rolls eyes and files nails, doesn't reply)

Delivery Boy: (turns to audience and preens, using exaggerated gestures; then turns to address Secretary) So, honey, how about you and I go grab some grub?

Secretary: (not looking at Boy) No, thanks.

Delivery Boy: Say, what type of fella do you go for?

Secretary: (pause while putting the file to her mouth, then says with conviction) The Rich Type.

Delivery Boy: (looks at the audience, rubs his hands together and flashes a big smile) Will she love me! (Boy exits with exaggerated movements, stage right)

Secretary: (phone rings) Hoffensteader, Hoffensteader, and Hoffensteader, Attorneys at Law—Your pain is our gain. (pause) I'm sorry, Mr. Hoffensteader is out. (pause) No, Mr. Hoffensteader is in a meeting. (pause) What? Why, Mr. Hoffensteader died last week! (pause) Oh, no problem! Call anytime. Goodbye!

Music cue: "Feather Your Nest"

Delivery Boy: (flies back onstage, only to slow down and take on Rich Type character,

strutting like a swell. Approaches Secretary
and begins speaking in a phony British accent)
Good afternoon, young woman. Would you be
at all interested in accompanying me in my
Duesenberg limousine to a fine establishment
for the purpose of taking nourishment? Money
is no object; we can partake of fish and chips
anywhere in the city. My vast fortune of
(pauses, puts hand in pants pocket, extracts
coins, counts them, returns them to his
pocket) seventy-eight cents shall be at your
disposal. Shall we take our leave?

Secretary: (looks up, sizing up The Rich Type,
then looks back at her nails) No, thanks.

Delivery Boy (looks surprised, but quickly
recovers, he speaks still using a British
accent) Well, what type of chap do you go for?

Secretary: (pause while putting file to her
mouth, then says with conviction) The Fun
Type.

Delivery Boy: (looks at the audience, rubs
his hands together and flashes a big smile)
Will she love me! (Boy exits with exaggerated
movements, stage right)

Secretary: (phone rings) Hoffensteader,
Hoffensteader, and Hoffensteader, Attorneys
at Law—Let a smile be your umbrella, unless
you're wearing silk. How may I help you?
(pause) Oh, hi, Mabel. (pause) No, I'm not
particularly busy—what's up? (pause) A double
date … with you and Freddy? Hmm, that sounds
like a lot of fun, but I don't have a date.

(pause, then perks up) Wait a minute, there is this cute delivery boy who might just fill the bill … providing he's the right type. And am I ever going to have fun with him! (pause, then laughs) I'll explain later, Mabel. Bye!

Music cue: "Ain't We Got Fun"

Delivery Boy: (flies back onstage doing a little dance while juggling three beanbags and whistling) Hey there, cutes, even though I have several things up in the air, I think I could juggle one more item this afternoon—how's about lunch with me? Why, you'll forget your worries while I entertain you. Don't be a Mrs. Grundy—come and join me for a memorable afternoon. I guarantee you'll laugh so hard your tummy will Shimmy and your tonsils will do the Charleston. (pause) So, how about it, are we on?

Secretary: (sizes him up, then looks back at her nails) No, thanks.

Delivery Boy (crestfallen, he stops juggling and plops the beanbags on the desk) Well, what type of fella do you go for?

Secretary: (pause while putting the file to her mouth, then stands and says with conviction, looking off as in a hypnotized daze toward the audience) The Exotic Type.

Delivery Boy: (looks at the audience, rubs his hands together and flashes a big smile) Will she love me! (he exits with exaggerated movements, stage right)

Secretary: (laughs, then looks at the beanbags on the desk) How hard can it be? (Secretary picks up the beanbags and begins juggling them, walking out in front of the desk. After juggling for a time, she begins behind-the-back juggling. She returns to regular juggling, sending the bags high up in the air, then plops the bags one at a time into the waste basket. She curtsies to the audience and returns to her seat behind the desk)

Music cue: "Sheik of Araby"

Delivery Boy: (flies back onstage, adjusting his robes, only to slow down and take on Exotic Type character. He swaggers up to the Secretary, utilizing a lowered voice and a bad Arabic accent) Hello, woman. May I abduct you and convey you to my tent in the Sahara, wherein we will partake of an exotic repast of quail beaks, camel hoofs, and goat's milk? (pause) Once we have completed our culinary indulgence, I will shower you with rubies, gift you with perfumes and unguents, and I will gaze longingly at you 'neath the stars. All the sand of the desert shall be yours, or in your shoes. (pause) Will you join me?

Secretary: (looking The Exotic Type up and down) No, thanks.

Delivery Boy: (crestfallen and beginning to show some frustration, he now speaks in his usual voice) Oh, applesauce. Well, what type do you go for?

Secretary: (pause while putting the file to her mouth, then answers in a swoon) The Professional Type.

Delivery Boy: (looks at the audience, rubs his hands together and flashes a big smile) Will <u>she</u> love me! (Boy exits with exaggerated movements, stage right)

Secretary: (phone rings) Hoffensteader, Hoffensteader, and Hoffensteader, Attorneys at Law—We fix speeding tickets, lawsuits, and juries. How may I help you? (pause) What? (pause) What's the difference between a lawyer and a herd of buffalo? Oh, that's easy! The lawyer charges more! (longer pause) What's the difference between a jellyfish and a lawyer? (pause) I'll tell you. One's a spineless blob, and the other is a form of sea life. (longer pause) What do lawyers wear to work? (pause) Why, lawsuits, of course! (longer pause) You're welcome, Mr. Hoffensteader. Goodbye. (pause, then does a double-take at the phone, saying with surprise) MR. HOFFENSTEADER?

<u>Music cue</u>: "I Don't Want a Doctor—All I Want is a Beautiful Girl"

Delivery Boy: (walks onstage with a fast, deliberate gait, as the Doctor character) Say, young woman, I have just completed the first transplantation of a human brain into a canary. Now the canary will be able to sing "Show Me the Way to Go Home" and not only know all the words, but be able to point in the right direction. (pause) This afternoon I shall attempt my most daring surgery to date:

I will endeavor to implant a conscience into a politician. (pause) But, before that dangerous feat, how 'bout you join me for some lunch? It's just what the doctor ordered.

Secretary: (sizes up the doctor, then looks back at her nails) No, thanks.

Delivery Boy (crestfallen, showing irritation, he looks at audience in wonder, shakes his head, then addresses the Secretary directly) Lady, do you eat?

Secretary: Why, sure!

Delivery Boy: Well, then, and I hate to ask (pause), but what type of fella do you go for?

Secretary: (pause while putting the file to her mouth, then answers in a matter-of-fact fashion) The Strong Silent Type.

Delivery Boy: (looks at the audience, rubs his hands together and flashes a big smile) Will she love me! (Boy exits with exaggerated movements, stage right)

Secretary: (phone rings) Hoffensteader, Hoffensteader, and Hoffensteader, doctor's office—I mean, Attorneys at Law. (pause) Oh, hi again, Mabel. (pause) Current events? Oh, sure, I'm up on current events. Why, I just heard about a woman who sat next to President Coolidge at a dinner party. She turned to him and said, "You MUST talk to me, Mr. President. I made a bet today that I could get more than two words out of you." Well, Coolidge

looked at the woman and replied, "You lose."
(pause, laughing) Now, HE'S the strong, silent
type! (pause) What about my date? Well, let's
just say the Delivery Boy is getting on the
trolley! (pause) Talk with you later, Mabel.
Bye.

Music cue: "Old Pal, Why Don't You Answer Me?"

Delivery Boy: (flies back onstage, only to slow
down and take on Strong Silent Type character.
He moves in an awkward, overly masculine
fashion. He approaches Secretary and, without
a word, hands her a card)

Secretary: (takes proffered card and reads
aloud in a slow, stilted manner) "Hello, young
lady, if you would be at all interested in
going to dinner with me, I would love to …"
(Secretary looks up at Boy)

Delivery Boy: (quickly hands her second card)

Secretary: (reads aloud second card) "…
take you out tonight?" (pause for a moment,
thinking) No, thanks.

Delivery Boy: (Crestfallen, he hands her a
third card)

Secretary: (reads aloud third card in same
slow, stilted manner) "Well, for Pete's sake,
girlie girl, what type of fella do you go
for?" (pause, then smiles) The College Type.

Delivery Boy: (looks at the audience, rubs
his hands together and flashes a big smile. He

pulls a large card from the back of his coat
and holds it up for the audience to read: "WILL
SHE LOVE ME!" He throws down the card and exits
with exaggerated movements, stage right)

Secretary: (phone rings) Hoffensteader,
Hoffensteader, and Hoffensteader, Attorneys
at Law. Good afternoon, Mr. Hoffensteader!
(pause) The company talent show? Why yes, I
have a little something I can do! (pause)
Right now? Well, okay. (sets down phone at
the edge of the desk, picks up a ukulele,
sits on the desk by the telephone, then sings
a fast-paced rendition of "Let Me Call You
Sweetheart." [Number of choruses dependent on
length of time needed.] Picks up phone) Did
you get that? (pause) Thank you, and goodbye.
(hops off and stands behind desk)

Music cue: "Ten Thousand Men of Harvard"
(Fight Song)

Delivery Boy: (flies back onstage, only to slow
down and take on College Type; he does a few
steps of the Charleston and waves a pennant)
Hey—YOU'RE the berries! The cat's pajamas! The
bee's knees! How's about we jump in my fliv-
ver, doll, and go to a joint and get some giggle water? If you get a wiggle we can fly in my
breezer! Now, don't give me the bum's rush.
Whaddya say?

Secretary: (slowly sizes up The College Type)
No, thanks.

Delivery Boy (now completely exasperated, he
throws down pennant, coat, hat) Look, lady,

<u>please just tell me</u>, for the last time, WHAT TYPE OF FELLA DO YOU GO FOR?

Secretary: (smiling, she grabs the Delivery Boy by the shirt) The Hard-Working Type. (Secretary throws him down on the desk and gives him a big kiss. His legs go up in the air; freeze pose)

LIGHTING: (blackout)

<u>Music cue (faster tempo than opening)</u>: "Love Me, and the World Is Mine"

LIGHTING: one spot on each performer, following them

(take bows. She exits stage left; he goes right. He turns around, seeing that she has gone left, and quickly follows her)

The End.

CHAPTER SEVEN

THE TRYOUT

October 1925

D anny got back into town on October 2, having successfully performed his final show as a headline singer on the previous evening. Not that the audience knew of the auspicious event they
were witnessing; but Danny knew, and earnestly gave his final rendition of "Danny Boy" a fitting send-off.

Violet was ready for his return, having all the costumes and props
arranged in their makeshift office, and sat waiting for him at 9:00 sharp.
Not two minutes later Danny bounded in, carrying a box, looking tired
but happy to see her. In fact, he couldn't take his eyes off her, which
conveyed to her that he had missed her as much as she missed him.

"Look!" she said waving her arms toward the piles of neatly folded clothes.

Danny's gaze broke away from her long enough to take in the
scene. "Wow!" he exclaimed. "Did you do all this?"

"Yes, and Mike says to tell you 'hello.'"

"Mike is such a great guy. His wife makes the best rugelach I have
ever tasted."

"Well," Violet said as she walked to his side, smiling, "for some
reason he thinks the world of you."

Danny gazed down at Violet, wanting to touch that beautiful face
he had been dreaming about for over a week now—in fact, well over

a week. "You gotta question that guy's taste," he whispered. When she turned her attention to the clothes, Danny reluctantly followed.

"Try on these coats. Let's see if the measurements Uncle Patrick gave me work." Violet went over to the camel hair and held it up. Danny, after divesting himself of the coat he had been wearing, slid his arms into the sleeves and easily glided it over his frame. It was a perfect fit. Violet ran her hands over the coat's shoulders and sleeves—his shoulders and arms—ostensibly to smooth out the fabric. She kept up the charade as long as she could, finally resting her inquisitive hands on his back. She began breathing shallowly, feeling that specific spark she got whenever she was near him; hoping this moment would never end, knowing that it would all too soon.

He looked in the mirror, trying to concentrate on the coat. But his sense of sight was usurped by the feel of her touch. He craved her nearness, her hands on him; he stopped breathing for fear she would withdraw. He had to wonder: Could she be feeling the same electricity he was experiencing? After what seemed like a second to him but was undoubtedly far too long a time, she stood aside and tilted her head.

"I think this looks great," she said at last. "It will work perfectly, don't you agree? Oh, and the hat—" She walked to the table, picked up the brown bowler, and put it on top of his head, "well, it's perfect, too! Oh, Danny, I'm *so* excited!"

"Me too, Vi. And look what I found," Danny proudly exclaimed as he opened the package he had brought with him. He withdrew a small metal box with a large button on top. He set it on the table and held down the knob. Immediately the sound of a ringing telephone filled the small office.

"Oh, that's ideal!" Violet exclaimed.

"We can set it over to the side of the desk, and you can press it just before lifting the receiver."

Violet walked over to the box and looked at it. "How 'bout if we put it on a tall metal, um—like an overturned metal waste can. We could keep it almost entirely out of the view of the audience, and I could press the button with my right hand."

She took the box to their desk, and overturned the waste can which sat by its side. She placed the box on top, then nonchalantly pressed the button a couple of times. "Perfect, no?"

He smiled. To Danny, *everything* looked perfect.

They practiced the routine from beginning to end that day, and Danny was very impressed by Violet's ease with her role. He worked with her on timing the telephone conversations so that it would appear realistic enough but not slow the momentum of the routine. Danny had laughed when she pointed out a specific prop on the table: a package, *the* package which she had wrapped in brown paper—the package which would bring the Delivery Boy into the Secretary's world. She also pointed out, with great pride, a large sign emblazoned with their catchphrase, "WILL SHE LOVE ME!" to be used for the Strong Silent Type.

"Wow, they did a great job on this card for us," Danny said, looking at the card.

"What do you mean *they*?" Violet questioned. "It is *she*."

"She who?"

"She me!"

"She you? Wait, *you* did the lettering on this card?" Danny was intrigued. Looking more closely at it, he marveled at the perfectly drawn letters.

"Yes, I have always loved to draw, and this was easy."

"Incredible. Oh, and speaking of this bit," Danny said, sitting down on the edge of the desk and reaching for his Camels, but thinking better of it, "one thing we must work out is this business of pulling the card out of nowhere for the audience. I've been thinking, and I can't quite figure it out." He looked pensive.

"I have that solved." She looked around the room, finally finding a small paper clip, and held it up. "Does this look familiar?"

He sonorously chuckled before saying, "Oh, yes. But for the purpose of the coat it won't work, my dear. I'm afraid it's far too small to hold that card."

"True," Violet began, "but I spoke with Mr. Denison of the Cushman & Denison Company; they've manufactured these for years and years. I told him what we were doing, and asked if they could make us a dozen bigger, stronger versions of this clip. I could sew them into the back of the coat, and we could carefully clip the big card to them, then you could just pull it loose when you need it. We could experiment with the number of clips and find out how many would be just right."

"That is ingenious! You've stopped amazing me, though. Now I am not at all surprised that you could think of something this, well, marvelous." Danny just sat and looked at her, causing her to flush with victory—and pride.

They continued on, dissecting certain parts of the routine, working out the parts that still didn't seem completely smooth. He handed her the ukulele and had her sing "Let Me Call You Sweetheart," finding her voice to be unique: sweet yet strong, and her accompaniment on the ukulele to be more than adequate.

"Great! Now wait just a minute," Danny said as he left the room. He reemerged a short time later with a make-shift audience comprised of performers stolen from the anteroom and office employees. "Now, Vi, I want you to sing while sitting on the end of the desk, like you'll do during the sketch."

Violet did as Danny directed, and when she finished, the small audience broke into enthusiastic applause. The group then crowded around Violet, telling her how good she was and that she would be a natural on the stage. This, Danny knew, would give her more confidence than all the words he alone could say. Even Helen told her that she was just wonderful. Violet hugged her, then watched as she almost made it safely out of the office.

"Your voice is really good," Danny told Violet when they were again alone, "but I do need to teach you some techniques to help you project for the stage."

He spent the next couple of hours going over the basics of proper diaphragmatic breathing and vocal utilization. Violet readily picked up the techniques and promised to practice them on a regular basis.

Before leaving the agency that day, Patrick pulled them both into his office and sat them down in front of two small stacks of papers. "These are the contracts for your act—standard contracts. Danny, it's just like the one you signed a few years ago. Violet, I want you to read it over and ask me any questions you might have."

Danny and Violet both took a few moments to read over the terms of the agreement.

"Uncle Patrick, I see this orders a fifty-fifty split; shouldn't Danny get more? He's the headliner, after all."

"I'll field this one if you don't mind, Pat," Danny said. "Vi, the half and half was my idea. Normally, a comedy team splits sixty-forty: sixty for the straight man; forty for the comic. In our act there is no straight man, we both handle the comedy. So, fifty-fifty seemed fair to me."

"I tried to argue him out of this, Violet dear," Patrick sighed. "Like you said, Danny *is* a headliner, with many years of experience; his name on the marquee brings in the customers, which will assure that your act eventually will get a good spot. But he felt—"

"What I *felt*," Danny interrupted, "was that you and I, Vi, are a team, and that's that. Besides," he said in a decidedly lighter tone, "what do I need with more money? I'm a bachelor with a cat."

Violet and Patrick realized that there would be no use arguing this.

"Thank you, Danny; that's very generous of you," Violet said, her brown eyes downcast, then looking at her uncle, "Um—if you don't mind my asking, Uncle Patrick, how much will we be making, approximately?"

"Well, the Keith-Albee office reviewed the routine and agreed that, with Danny's star power, it could headline. At that point the team will get twenty-six hundred a week, so, thirteen hundred for each of you, approximately. Until then, you can expect around sixteen hundred a week; eight hundred a piece."

"Holy cow!" Violet declared, genuinely stunned. "If I had taken that job with the secretarial company I would be making $120 per *month*—and I thought *that* was a well-paying job!"

"Considering how much most people are paid for their jobs, it *is*," Patrick noted. "For instance, a public school teacher makes around $900 per year. *Per year*! And medical workers make around $1,100 per year."

Violet felt very blessed, indeed.

"And, of course," Danny added, "our man Patrick here will deduct his customary ten percent."

"Oh, of course," Violet added, hastily.

Patrick flushed self-consciously. Finances were not usually discussed in mixed company, and certainly not with family members. This was difficult for him, but it was part of his job. "If the rest looks up to snuff, then we'll sign."

Danny and Violet took turns writing their names at the bottom of the contract with Patrick's fountain pen. When they were done, Danny handed the papers to their agent, who used his ink blotter on the signatures to dry them. After securing the documents, Patrick, quite out of character, jokingly took on an ecclesiastical tone: "By the power vested in me by the Keith-Albee Vaudeville Exchange, I now pronounce you O'Brien & Williams."

Danny inwardly grimaced at the wedding implication, but he had to admit that he was glad they were officially a team.

The next couple of weeks found the duo rehearsing daily, quickly getting to the point where each felt comfortable with their respective lines. The clips for the camel hair coat came in and, after Violet sewed eight of them to the inside of the garment (making sure to not just use the thin lining, but have the stitches catch the thick outer material as well), they tried the trick. At first, Danny couldn't easily pull the card out, so they decided to slide the card between every other clip. This proved to work, and they both felt secure with the mechanics of the gag. The large card didn't even look as awkward hanging inside the coat as Violet feared it would.

Danny asked Patrick to reserve a couple of hours in a theatre so they could practice on a real stage. In no time it was duly arranged that they would have access to the Bushwick Theatre in Brooklyn, at the corner of Broadway and Howard, the very theatre in which they would be breaking in their act. Because this was a "big-time" vaudeville house on the Keith-Albee circuit, featuring only two shows a day, it would be available in the mornings. Violet couldn't wait to take the next step.

The following morning found vaudeville's newest team parked in a taxi directly in front of the Bushwick. Danny asked the cabbie to carry in their trunk, which he was glad to do for the generous tip Danny slipped him. Violet took in the grandeur of the theatre's façade: it soared high above the street, a veritable cathedral of the arts—a stone-and-mortar tribute to vaudeville. Seeing his partner's awed expression, Danny pointed out the detailed stonework surrounding some trumpeting cherubs, as well as the "B" in Bushwick, which was festooned with musical instruments. He suddenly realized that he was admiring these details for the first time, despite having played this theatre often over the years. How refreshing it was to view the world through Violet's eyes.

Ducking through the stage door, they walked past a bulletin board on which was posted a daily sign-in sheet, information about nearby hotels and restaurants (for those coming in from out of town), and rules particular to the theatre.

"They all have this," he said tapping the list with his index finger. "Make sure you read it and abide by it. A slipup can get us canceled before we even go on."

Violet quickly skimmed the severely worded warning:

```
Don't say "slob" or "son of a gun" or
"hully gee" on the stage unless you want
to be canceled peremptorily. Do not ad-
dress anyone in the audience in any man-
ner. If you do not have the ability to
```

```
entertain Keith-Albee's audience with
risk of offending them, do the best you
can. Lack of talent will be less open
to censure than would be an insult to a
patron. If you are in doubt as to the
character of your act consult the local
manager before you go on stage, for if
you are guilty of uttering anything sac-
rilegious or even suggestive you will be
immediately closed and will never again
be allowed in a Keith-Albee theatre.
```

"Thank you for pointing this out, Mr. O'Brien," she said with mild sarcasm. "I'll also do my best to refrain from chewing tobacco and spitting!"

"That's a relief," Danny said, nodding a "hello" to Pop, the old gentleman who guarded the backstage area. Violet next wanted to see this vaudeville house from the performer's perspective. Passing through the wings and onto the huge, wooden stage, she looked around at the rows of empty seats, noting the boxes which lined the walls. She looked up to find a painted mural spanning the entire orchestra section. She was astonished to see that the ceiling above the backstage area rose over thirty feet. Off to one side there was a tall, thin stand with a bare, caged bulb that glowed in the semi-gloom. She looked at Danny, who answered her unasked question. "No, it's not a stage light. It's a ghost light. All theatres have 'em. Some people say it stays lit throughout the night for safety; others say it's for the theatre ghosts."

A stocky man holding a cheroot walked up to Danny and shook his hand. Danny introduced him to Violet: "This fine fellow," Danny said, "is David Stockton. He is what is commonly referred to in theatrical parlance as the stage manager; his are the shoulders upon which rests our success or failure, for this is the man who makes sure everything is ready when it's time to make our entrance; he's the one who lovingly sees to the proper placement of our props and lighting; he's the one—"

"Okay, okay, that's enough," Stockton said self-consciously. "I know blarney when I hear it; I didn't just get the job yesterday, you know."

"That's true," Danny said. "David here remembers my parents the first time they did their two-act, back in 1891." He turned to Stockton and asked, "Did you receive a copy of our routine from Mr. Goodman's office?"

"Sure did," he said. "I've got the office desk and chair you requested—and a wastepaper basket. You're doing this in Two, right?"

"Yeah," Danny averred. "But not in front of the curtain—"

"I know," Stockton stopped him. "You want the office drop. So we're done here?" he asked, already walking away.

"We're done," Danny answered, then turned his attention to their now-opened trunk and began sorting through its contents, checking each item in the order of its use. The old theatrical trunk, which Danny had used for twenty years and bore the travel tags on the worn leather to prove it, had been sectioned off into shelves, drawers (for miscellaneous props), and a hanging space. The clothes for his quick changes, therefore, could be neatly arranged, allowing him to hit all of his marks on time. He squatted down and placed a card on top of the trunk that listed every costume change, for easy reference during the performance.

And then it hit him. He was completely overwhelmed. This new act. What if it completely flopped? He would become a laughing stock. What if their ideas didn't translate to the audience? *They* would become a laughing stock. What if audiences didn't accept him as a comedian? *Oh, God.*

He put his head in his hands. His heart pounded. His head throbbed.

Violet came up behind him quietly, seeing that he was in distress. "Can I do anything?" she asked softly.

"It's just my head—I'm getting one of my headaches," he replied, barely above a whisper. He knew he had a bottle of aspirin in the trunk somewhere, but couldn't move to fish it out.

"Here, let me help," she said as she slowly drew his head back and put her cool, steady hands on his temples. She began to gently massage them, gradually placing both hands on his scalp, weaving her fingers through his hair, making small circles, and communicating serene competence. Danny took in a deep breath along with her equanimity. He couldn't—*wouldn't*—let this girl down. He had been so sure that he knew what he was doing. Well, now was the time to make it happen: it would be a great routine, even if they had to revamp parts of it. They would hone it, like countless vaudevillians before them, into a perfect act. He would be able to give her that, and his confidence, which he felt washing over him once again.

"Vi, thanks," Danny said, as Violet slowly removed her fingers and combed his hair in place. He took her hands and raised his eyes to hers. "Your touch is a tonic to me. My head feels much better. Thank you. Now, let's have a run-through, just take it slowly and let's make sure that everything works."

The run-through was extremely beneficial, and showed each where they would have to speed up or slow down their respective parts. "Remember one thing," Danny said. "No matter how many times we practice, it's not the same until you get up in front of that audience. They will teach us—timing, how to finesse the routine to maximize the laughs."

"So, we'll keep making changes while we work?" Violet asked, still juggling while she listened to him.

Danny watched her juggle the beanbags and stopped her before she finished. "Yes, and you know what we need, for your bit—we need you to do something fancier, harder to do than the straight juggling my character does. A trick, you know? Here, let me show you." Danny took the beanbags from Violet and began tossing them into the air for a time in the regular rhythm, then performed an over-the-shoulder toss. After a while, he slowed the motion and explained exactly what he was doing, how high he was throwing the bag from the back to the front, and how he was catching them. He handed the props back to her and she slowly began, dropping several in a row.

"You can do this," Danny said encouragingly. "Concentrate on the pattern."

She nodded and tried again, this time actually doing a successful pass before dropping them to the floor. "Well, I know how I will be spending my evenings."

Danny beamed. He knew he had a partner who was willing to put in the time to make this sketch work. "Oh, and I have another thing to teach you—we can do a simple trick where you throw the bags way up high. It's a great visual. And, also, juggling them into the waste can."

"Maybe *that* is where they belong from the beginning," offered Violet, a self-conscious grin playing around her lips.

"Why, you're doing splendidly, Miss Williams," Danny said, giving her a confident smile and adding two dimples.

"Now, I've got to go talk with the lighting director and check in with the orchestra leader. I'll make sure they have our cues. So you … just keep at it!"

And keep at it she did. She juggled on the stage during rehearsals. She juggled in her bedroom every night. She juggled in the living room in the mornings. She began finding her hands seeking out the small burlap bags whenever she was idle. Her arms ached and her hands blistered from the burnishing of the rough material. Danny took one look at them and frowned. "Self-mutilation is not part of this act, Vi. Wear gloves next time you practice. Your hands are far too beautiful to have such horrible blisters."

Violet took his advice, and his compliment, with pleasure. At home that night she washed her hands, and then got the bottle of Purex iodine from the medicine cabinet. She applied this stinging solution to her wounds and bound them with some gauze and tape. Within just a couple of days her hands felt much better, so she took up the bags to practice—only this time wearing gloves and watching how long she worked.

Thwack, thwack, buzz. The giant carbon arc lamps came on, flooding the desk with hot white light. When Violet stared into the spotlight, she remembered her magician's assistant turn onstage, but didn't remember the lights being quite *so* bright. She thought she would go blind. As she squinted and covered her eyes, Danny, knowing just how suffocating the light felt for the uninitiated, walked across the stage and leaned over the desk.

"I know the light is bad, but it has to be that bright."

"But I can't see a thing, not a thing!" Violet uttered, wondering if she could ever get used to the hot beam.

"And that's good," Danny replied with conviction. "You don't need to see the audience; it will help with your nerves at the beginning. Just take a minute and get used to it. Then we can go through the routine."

By the time Patrick watched his niece and most important client do their new sketch later that day, she was already feeling more comfortable. Patrick was amazed by the timing and sense of comedy Violet lent their act; and how joyfully Danny got into each character. The boy's energy was thrilling, in fact, and Patrick knew this new act would be a hit. He made a few notes which he would give to the lighting man, and a reminder to the stage manager. When the routine finished, Danny and Violet approached him in his seat.

"Well, Pat," Danny said, just slightly out of breath. "What say ye?"

"Well done, you two! Well done!" Patrick was on his feet, hugging his jubilant niece and slapping a surprised Danny on the back. "It's very good. *Very* good. Now, I believe the photographer has the proofs of your lobby photos ready. And I'll also be dropping in at the stationers for your business cards. I chose blue ink; I hope that's all right."

"Any color other than green," Danny said with shudder. "Although perhaps Miss Williams wanted violet?"

"Oh, no, I hate that color. Anything close to—" Only then did she notice his infinitesimal smile which began to spread like poison oak at a summer camp. Violet rolled her eyes and shook her head.

"I'm going to check in with the lighting director and make sure he gets the timing on the blackout and final tracking for you, Danny, and I need a quick word with David Stockton," Patrick said before taking his leave. "Then I'm going back to the office. Again, great job, both of you."

Patrick made his way down the center aisle toward the theatre's entrance. Danny and Violet watched him leave, and remained standing completely still in the middle of the empty house. Just as the door shut behind him, they burst out laughing at the same time, releasing the tension they had felt, as well as the joy. Danny pulled Violet to him and gave her a big hug. After a while they stopped laughing, simply experiencing the sensation of being in each other's arms. Violet closed her eyes and wound her arms tighter around Danny's waist.

"You folks done for the day?" a stagehand yelled from the wings.

"Yes," Danny said tearing himself away from her, giving her shoulder a little squeeze as he did so. He sprinted up to the stage, extending his hand to the fellow in overalls. "I'm Danny."

"George," the man said unenthusiastically.

"Well, George, we sure appreciate all you folks do," and, with that, Danny took something out of his pocket and handed it to the man. The fellow looked at it, and then smiled.

"We'll take care of you, Danny." Saying which, he turned and left.

Violet approached Danny, who was already organizing the clothes back into the trunk. "What did you give him?" she whispered.

"A big tip," he whispered back. "If you don't tip the stagehands, props can wind up broken or 'forgotten' right before the show. This helps things go more smoothly."

Violet nodded. There was a lot to learn about this business.

CHAPTER EIGHT

THE VAUDEVILLIANS

October 1925

The next few days went by as fast as a rum runner's speedboat. Violet got progressively more nervous as their opening performance approached, but knew that they had a good sketch, that Danny was an absolute sensation in his role, and that she was certainly capable in her part. She had the over-the-shoulder juggling down pat, and now felt truly ready for anything.

One day Danny suggested that they stay after their rehearsal to see the acts they would be joining. He explained rather disappointedly that they would be in the number-two spot—often referred to as the deuce spot. It was the first act on a bill that most of the audience would pay notice, but not fully. For this reason it was dubbed the "burying ground"—because so many performers "died" there.

After the orchestra struck up the overture, a bored-looking stagehand placed a large card on the easel, reading, "Sally & Co." Sally, it turned out, was a trained seal that could play horns, "count" to ten with her flippers, and dance.

Danny leaned over to Violet and whispered, "The handler is Tommy Anderson; the best, and most humane, animal trainer on the circuit. Not like some of those other bastards."

"There's a star I'd like to meet!" Violet whispered back.

"Tommy?"

"Oh, yes. But I was also thinking of Sally."

"I think that can be arranged."

As the program unfolded, they enjoyed the entertainment which this wonderful showcase offered—especially one singer who took Violet's breath away. Her name was Grace Manning. She was both extremely talented and beautiful, wearing her blonde hair in a stylish finger wave. "Do you know Grace Manning?" she whispered to Danny.

"Yes, and she is a really great kid. I want you to meet her, too."

Violet thought that the petite singer looked so tiny on the large stage, having an almost angelic quality reinforced by her white sequined gown. But her voice filled the room, a strong yet vulnerable sound just made for the new style called torch singing. Grace put her whole heart into each word of "After You've Gone," "All Alone," "Deep In My Heart, Dear," "Honest and Truly," and her signature song, "I'll See You In My Dreams."

After taking in the remaining acts, they left their seats and made their way unobtrusively through the side door, walking around to the backstage area. They approached a large storage room on the ground floor of the theatre, the place where all animal acts were housed. Currently it was being used by a certain diva who was lounging luxuriantly in a tub of water.

"Well, well, well. Danny O," Thomas Anderson said, walking forward and shaking his old friend's hand. "Good to see you again." Then, noticing Violet, he added, "And who's this lovely girl who is willing to be seen with you in public?"

"This," Danny said proudly, "is my partner, Miss Violet Williams, of O'Brien & Williams."

"Pleased to meet you, Miss Williams," Thomas smiled.

"The pleasure is mine," Violet beamed.

Turning to Danny, Thomas asked, "Since when are you doing a 'Two'?"

"Since right now. Violet and I have cooked up a little flirtation act."

"That's wonderful, Danny O!"

Like Danny, Thomas Anderson had been in the business all of his life, something which bonded the two immediately. The son of British music-hall performers, Thomas had realized soon into a career as a song-and-dance man that he could neither sing nor dance. So he took a turn in a comedy two-act as the straight man. Thomas's low monotone voice was a perfect contrast to his partner's high-pitched, frenetic style. Thomas was also prematurely gray at thirty, but had a tall, athletic build, which lent a distinguished air to the act. The team was billed as Anderson & Cahill, the latter being Julien Cahill, a very talented comic who loved performing almost as much as he loved gambling. The team lasted nearly ten years, until Cahill met an early demise by way of a poker dispute.

Around this time Thomas got married, or so the rumor mill reported. The woman wasn't in the business and therefore didn't understand him—not his career, not his unpredictable schedule, not his eccentric friends. Within a couple of months she found a better offer. Luckily, Thomas did as well. He always had a way with animals, and possessed the innate ability to train almost any creature with which he came in contact. Watching a seal act during one vaudeville performance, he decided that this was something he could do, and do well. It turned out that the gent working with Sally wanted out of the business; he mentioned something about being tired of his tuxedo smelling like fish. So Thomas happily became Sally's "& Co."

Even though Thomas was now forty-two, he was in no hurry to settle down. He was a man who finally knew what he wanted in a wife: she would have to understand—even love—vaudeville, and appreciate the ways of a prima donna seal.

Violet liked him immediately. She loved the way his lips were always set in a half grin, looking as if he were waiting for a punch line, constantly amused by the myriad of experiences life threw at him. This, and his sure manner, made up an extremely positive countenance.

"Sally, say hello to our visitors," Thomas said with a small hand gesture. And with that, Sally waved her fin and barked. Danny and Violet laughed.

In the cramped dressing room were Sally's bank of horns, her tub, and the bucket which held her food. The bucket was on display at that very moment, filled with some odiferous concoction. "Sorry about the smell, folks," Thomas added. "It's dinner."

"Just what exactly do you feed her?" Violet asked, wrinkling her nose.

"Oh, a little of this and a little of that. She loves mackerel, anchovies, herring, salmon, and sardines. In a pinch she'll eat squid and octopus, but she loves her anchovies."

"Does she need to be in water whenever she is not onstage?" Violet asked.

"No," he answered. "She can go for quite a time without being in water, but I like to have it available for her after being under the hot lights."

"Not a bad idea," Danny said. "I wouldn't mind a nice, cool tub after being under those cursed lights."

"Chow time!" Thomas announced to an obviously elated Sally.

"Far be it from us to interrupt the star's repast," Danny said with mock formality. "We'll catch up with you later, Tommy."

"Take care, Danny O, and you watch out for this one, Miss Williams," he said with a laugh. "Sally, where are your manners? Wave goodbye to Danny and Miss Williams." Sally, always the consummate hostess, waved her fin at the departing guests.

There were other fellow performers milling about backstage, including Joe Frisco, a clever solo dancer, who was in the number-four spot; the distinguished Broadway actor Richard Bennett, who was up next; and the madcap comedy team of Clayton, Jackson & Durante— they were the headliners on the bill who were featured in the prime spot: next to closing. Violet took a shine to the charming Jimmy Durante, whose nose was particularly large, especially in relation to his small eyes. Danny liked this sweet, funny-looking man, and the feeling was obviously mutual. Jimmy wrapped an arm around Danny's broad shoulders and told Violet that he had known him since the days of The Dancing O'Briens.

"Dis guy'll tek good care o' ya'," he said in his mangled Brooklynese. "An' ya' kin tek dat to da bank!"

She had noticed that Mr. Bennett and Mr. Frisco were both sporting large diamond rings; did this, she asked Danny, have any particular significance? Danny told her that plenty of traveling actors wore expensive rings—they regarded them almost like bank accounts. If they were ever canceled and found themselves stranded in some tank town (a calamity faced by many a vaudevillian during their days in the small-time), they could hock the ring and live on the money until they landed their next booking.

"Danny, I heard you were coming on the bill!" Grace Manning greeted him, shaking his hand enthusiastically.

"Good to see you, Gracie," Danny said, beaming. "And I want you to meet my new partner, Violet Williams."

Grace turned and took Violet's hand. "I'm so happy to meet you!"

"Oh, I think you are just wonderful," Violet said, feeling like more of a fan than a fellow performer. She looked into one of the sweetest faces she had ever seen; Grace was as exquisite as her name. "You have such a gift, and such a lovely voice."

"Thank you. I'm just so happy that Danny has a new act. I always knew he had the chops for comedy, and I hear your act is boffo!"

Danny laughed. "You have always had more confidence in me than most."

From around the dark corner sauntered a large man in a long coat and fedora. He sneered at Danny and grabbed Grace's arm. "Come on, now. Get to your room."

Grace, obviously embarrassed by this display, took the fat man's hand. "Violet, I'd like you to meet my friend Jerome DiMarco." At the end of her sentence Grace hiccupped, and was met by a look of disapproval from the big man.

"Hello, Mr. DiMarco," Violet said quietly.

"Yeah, nice to whatever. Now *go*," he said to Grace. She offered a small smile of apology to both Violet and Danny, and walked away, quietly hiccupping once again. DiMarco gave Violet the once-over, sneered at Danny, and ambled after Grace.

After they left the theatre and got into a cab, Violet had to ask, "Who *was* that guy with Grace?"

"He's a plug-ugly who feels that he owns her, at least for the time being. I keep waiting for him to find another girl and leave Grace alone, but he sticks around like a bad cough 'cause she's his meal ticket. He makes me sick."

Danny told Violet that Grace had been born in Wichita, Kansas, into a working-class family. She had always wanted to sing professionally. Although her parents loved her singing at church pageants and socials, they strongly disapproved of her going into show business. After one particularly noisy row, during which her father slapped her across the face, Grace ran away and swore that she would never return. Traveling to Chicago with only a few dollars and the scarce possessions she had packed into one suitcase, she discovered that she needed to get a job—and fast. She worked as a taxi dancer and found the work to be demoralizing and exhausting. It was in just this setting that she met Jerome DiMarco, who realized that the real money to be made was through her singing. It was DiMarco, in fact, who got her an audition with a representative of the Keith-Albee circuit. Grace had the misfortune of developing hiccups when she was nervous or excited, and found that this got in the way of her singing at first. But she soon became more comfortable in front of a group than in one, and the hiccups were relegated to the stresses of her personal life.

"They loved her, of course, because of her talent," Danny continued, "and, unfortunately, *she* fell in love with DiMarco. Or at least she thinks she is; she's most likely just grateful he got her some bookings. But either way, it's no good."

"So, there's nothing that can be done?" she asked.

"No, I've felt that anything I could do would make life harder for Grace. I talked to her one time and told her to dump him, but she said she loves him and that he is good to her." He was quiet for a moment. "The worst part of it is that she is just such a giving, kind person. There was this kid, a little girl, maybe fourteen, who hung around the stage door. She wanted Grace's autograph, but Grace gave her more than just that. She found out the girl had run away from home and was destitute and in a bad way. Grace took her in, fed her, talked with her for hours. Had the girl call her folks, patch things up—even gave her money to take the train back home. *That* is the kind of person Grace is."

Violet shook her head, a look of true consternation on her face. "We'll think of some way to help her."

Danny looked at Violet and smiled. *And that is the kind of person Violet is,* he thought. "Hey, I've got a great idea," he said suddenly as she got out of the cab in front of the Goodman residence. "Whaddya say tomorrow we take our minds off show business and go to Coney Island for the day!"

Violet loved Danny's enthusiasm more than the idea of a hot, crowded day at an amusement park. But getting away from the theatre might just be a tonic for both of them.

"I'd love to!" she said, almost believing it herself.

Violet was sure that she had never seen so many people in one place in her entire life. From the moment they emerged from the subway and walked through the front gates of Luna Park, they were sandwiched into a mass of humanity. All kinds of people came to Coney Island for a respite from their day-to-day lives. And, apparently, more people needed that respite than ever.

The park was a babel of sounds: from the jostling throng's shouts and squawks, to the barker's ballyhoos and calls, to the *clangs* and *clacks* of the rides. Coney Island was an enormous dragon threatening to deafen anyone entering its lair.

Violet was glad that she had worn her floral sleeveless sundress as it was quite a warm summer day. Danny looked elegant in his white linen suit and boater, and she wasn't at all surprised when he was occasionally recognized and asked for an autograph. He was endlessly gracious to the people who spoke with him, reminding Violet that without an audience they would soon be out of a job.

Turning nostalgic, he began to reminisce about the Coney Island of his childhood. "It was different then. My friends and I would see the fortune teller, and go to the fifty-cent museums where they had human monsters and freakish fish. I saw a bearded lady, a very nice woman who just happened to have a thirteen-inch beard. You don't see that kind of thing anymore."

Violet found the glimpse into the park's history to be interesting, if a bit odd. What they saw now, however, was fascinating. They went through the Eden Musee Wax Museum, renowned for its lifelike wax tableaux of such famous works as "Too Late for the Opera" and "The Electrocution of the Four Gunmen." Also depicted were ex-President William Howard Taft; Gerald Chapman, the infamous Garrote Murderer; Leopold and Loeb, the wealthy college students who, just a year earlier, had committed "the crime of the century"; and Marat in his bathtub, being surprised by a knife-wielding Charlotte Corday. Danny laughed when Violet flinched at the last scene, so realistic were the figures.

They wandered through Brandenburg's Aquarium, then climbed into a boat and experienced the Chutes; a ride that featured a plunge into cold water which sent a spray onto the passengers, guaranteed to cool off even the warmest park guest. They also went on the Loop the Loop: A car accommodating four passengers was pulled by a chain to the apex of the structure and then allowed to zoom down a steep incline leading into the loop. There, the car gradually turned upside down until it emerged right side up on a moderate incline that slowed the car's speed before returning to the starting point. The Loop was advertised as the "Safest and the Greatest Attraction—No Danger Whatsoever," but Violet wasn't convinced. She was happy when the ride was over and Danny helped her out of the car. As they were walking away from the area, she overheard the woman who was seated behind them during the ride tell her friend, "I'm *positive* that's Danny O'Brien! We just saw him a few months ago at the Palace! Wouldn't you love to be with *him*!"

Violet smiled and took Danny's arm on their walk to the next stop, which was the Tumblebug. This fun attraction featured a train of five connected saucers moving around a circular and undulating track, each saucer carrying up to six people who were holding onto a central grip wheel to avoid knocking into their fellow passengers. Violet loved this ride, and Danny was delighted by her peals of laughter.

After passing the Hall of Mirrors, which caused their bodies to distort into grotesque short and squat or tall and thin shapes, they tried the Human Roulette Wheel. Being both polite and modest were disadvantages in this game. A group of park visitors would scramble onto a large steel circle which was domed at the center. As it spun around, people would fly off in all directions. Violet and Danny decided to fly off the circle at the same time, holding hands and laughing as they crashed into the padded wall. Violet had to work fast to keep her undergarments from showing, and Danny gallantly looked away to give her privacy.

They passed one crowded booth called "The Big Prize Toss" which featured merchandise precariously set up on shelves for patrons to hit with baseballs. If they could knock the item off the shelf, they would win the prize. Danny stopped, eyeing the baseballs. "Hey, Vi, I bet you wouldn't go up to that booth and juggle the baseballs."

She paused for only a moment. "I'll take that bet!"

Violet walked up to the huckster who was yelling for people to come and "join in the fun, ladies and gentleman, only two pennies, we're having so much fun here ..."

"I'd like a turn, please!" Violet shouted, inching through the crowd and interrupting the pitch. She withdrew two cents from her purse and gave it to the man who examined the coinage, then put it in his pocket.

"Here you go, kid," he said as he handed the balls to Violet.

She turned her back to the booth and began throwing the balls into the air, slowly at first, then faster and faster. The crowd turned its attention from those individuals throwing the balls at the merchandise to the young lady juggling them. Violet began the behind-the-back juggling trick, and was awarded with a round of applause. She ended by throwing each one in turn at the grand-prize bullseye in the booth, and walked away with the treasure: a large, faded, raggedy stuffed dog that looked as if it had seen far too many Coney Island summers.

"I can get rid of this for you," Danny said, laughing and reaching for the dog.

"Oh, no, I plan to keep Harold as a trophy," Violet glowed. "And, by the way, I take every bet that comes along."

"Hmm, I'll have to remember that," Danny said, grinning.

Throughout the day, the scent of various food preparations greeted them, and they ate to their hearts' content. From homemade clam chowder at the Surf House Restaurant to Nathan's hot dogs, they walked among the hordes of revelers and basked in the sun and their time together. They drank mugs of Hires Root Beer and Coca-Cola, ate succulent crab at the Atlantic Seafood & Co., polished off several cobs of freshly steamed corn slathered in butter, and devoured cotton candy, popcorn balls, and candied apples like greedy kids. By the time evening fell, sending the park into a wonderland of strung lights and illuminations of every kind, they were exhausted. After a packed subway ride, with Harold tucked protectively under Violet's arm, Danny walked her home, strolling along the busy street. He abruptly stopped a distance from the Goodmans' front door, standing with her under a street light.

As people strolled past them, Danny took Violet in his arms, holding her and looking deeply into her eyes. He bent toward her slowly. Was he going to kiss her? Out here—*right on the street*? They had just been tossed and lobbed against greater New York and all points East, and she didn't like the feeling of this moment being so public. Violet felt indignation. This wasn't what she had in mind for their first kiss, not that she had been thinking about it for weeks, which, if the truth be known, she *had*. But, being an emancipated woman, she was going to have to stop him. She looked into his eyes, usually a light aquamarine, but tonight turned into the color of a roiling sea. Her eyes traveled to his mouth at the same time his eyes lowered to hers. His lips looked so soft; she imagined that they would taste like a candied apple, and she hungrily wanted a nibble. *Here it comes,* she thought. Really, she needed to pull away. But instead, Violet closed her eyes and leaned in, smooshing Harold between them. Gently running his thumb across her jaw and over her lower lip, he bent toward her and whispered, "Thank you for a perfect day." And with that he slowly backed away, gave her a wink, turned, and strode off into the balmy night.

Now Violet was *really* indignant.

The morning dawned as any other. The birds chirped their bright melodies from the trees and Aunt Mavis was downstairs singing as she baked a pie for that evening's dessert. Violet opened her eyes and smiled, then felt a dark cloud hovering. Today was the day they were to give their first performance in front of an actual, paying audience. She got out of bed and dressed quickly, spending most of the morning pacing while mindlessly juggling the beanbags. She told herself to calm down; she had nothing to be nervous about—not really. After all, she wasn't going off to war. So why did it feel as if she were about to be deployed?

Violet went downstairs and had a steaming mug of coffee with Aunt Mavis, but soon found the sweet woman's idle chatter getting on her nerves. She picked at the piece of toast in front of her, knowing that if she ate too much she would be in danger of seeing it again. On the stage. In front of hundreds of people. Her nerves spiked to the point that she quickly excused herself and ran upstairs. She sat on her bed, just breathing and trying to calm herself, which only did so much. Although they weren't due until 12:30 for the 2:00 show, she needed to get out of the house. After giving herself a pep talk in the mirror, she grabbed her costume and make-up and high-tailed it to the Bushwick.

She walked through the stage-door entrance like an authentic performer, signing in on the call sheet.

"Say, you're Violet, right? With Danny?" She turned around and saw the stagehand Danny had tipped. What was his name? John? No. Gerald? No.

"*George*, it's so nice to see you again," she said, relieved that her memory was still intact.

"Let me show you up to your dressing room. It's on the second floor."

"I would greatly appreciate that." She walked behind him, looking into dressing rooms one and two. They were nice, but they were reserved for the headliner and the next-most important act. On the second level were rooms three and four, theirs being number three. If it wasn't for Danny's reputation, they most likely would be on the fourth floor, dressing with the stray birds that flew into the theatre.

The room was on the small side, but serviceable. There was a dressing table with plenty of lighting, a small couch and stiff-back chair, and a modesty screen—thank goodness.

"If I can get you anything, just let me know," George said as he took his leave.

"Thank you, you've been so kind."

Violet switched on the lights and noticed a box with an envelope bearing her name resting on the table. Opening it, she read the card inside:

For My Girl—
  Break a Leg.
    Danny O'Brien, of O'Brien & Williams

 She closed her eyes, thinking of the night before. Absentmindedly she ran her thumb over her lower lip. Opening the box, she saw the small nosegay of violets and smiled. She found a glass on the table and took it to the sink, filled it with water, and brought it back to the table. Lovingly, she placed the violets in the water. They weren't such a bad-looking flower after all, she mused.

Violet changed into her costume and sat down at the table to apply her make-up. She opened her kit and removed the *Picture-Play* magazine article she had found, studying the picture of beautiful Viola Dana who sported the perfect look for her character. First, Violet lined and darkened her eyes with kohl eye-shadow powder. After curling her lashes with her Kurlash, she then melted a cube of lash bead, her preferred brand being "Black Cosmetique," in a little pan over a standing candle. As the waxy concoction melted (filling the room with the sickly odor of burning grease), it became the consistency of a thick soup. She scooped it onto a toothpick and applied it to a few lashes at a time, going from the base to the tip where she would create a bead. Once she finished the upper lashes she did the same with the lower ones, working swiftly and carefully. Cooling time for the make-up was critical as Violet had often dealt with the time-consuming mess of getting the goop off of her cheeks. This was a lengthy process and required a steady hand (which Violet had to somehow manufacture on this day), but the result was dazzling: she looked as though she had strung black beads around her eyes. To finish her guise, she painted her lips into a perfect bow using a dark-red lipstick in a pushup tube. After applying a good coat of face powder, and brushing her glossy hair into its perfect bob, she stood back and looked at herself in the mirror. The Secretary had come to life.

The door opened just as Violet had cleared the table. Danny came in carrying his Delivery Boy costume and a leather kit. "Hi, Vi," he said, sounding confident. "George told me you arrived early."

She stood, facing him, and he took in her full look, costume, make-up—the works. "You look—*wow*," he said, words failing him. "That outfit is—*wow*. You look perfect." Gaining his bearings, he asked seriously, "How do you feel?"

"Okay, I guess. Nervous. Oh, thanks so much for the lovely flowers. You're so thoughtful, so pig-headedly thoughtful."

"You'll notice that I signed the card—so you wouldn't think that they were from any of your other admirers," Danny teased.

"Yes, I noticed," Violet giggled.

"Well, I'm going to do my make-up, and then I'll dress," Danny said, hanging his costume on a nail by the screen.

"Mind if I stay and watch—the make-up, that is, not the dressing," Violet said, blushing.

"No, you can see whatever you want," Danny said, comically wiggling his eyebrows.

He walked over to the table and sat, putting down his trusty make-up kit. He pulled out several tubes and a few towels, and arranged the items carefully on the clear surface. He looked like a concert pianist preparing for a performance. Violet immediately walked over and picked up the foundation.

"What exactly *is* greasepaint?" she asked.

"Something I forgot to tell you about. You'll have to get some. Under the harsh lighting an unmade-up face tends to look like death. When you darken the skin color and use this thick base, it shows up as being more natural to the audience. And you can use different colors and add contouring to the face, making it look better, although I don't know how to do that. But I bet Grace would be happy to show you. It also doesn't sweat off like the powder they used to wear. In my parents' day they made greasepaint out of lard and pigments."

Violet made a face. She removed the top and smelled it, reacting to the unusual odor. "It smells like something is rancid."

"You'll get used to it," Danny laughed, putting a towel around his neck. He applied some of the make-up to a sponge, then artfully applied it to his face.

"Say, you're good at this," she said, impressed.

"I've done it once or twice before," he joked, a heavy understatement. "You can get good at just about anything if you do it enough. And it will be easier for you as you don't have to get a close shave before putting this stuff on. Or, wait—"

Danny slowly rose, looking closely at Violet's skin, cupping her chin and moving her head from side to side. She hit his arm playfully. "No, I'm not your bearded-lady friend."

"Just checking." An amused Danny resumed his seat and make-up application.

Violet chuckled, then picked up one of the white towels with a broad blue stripe and saw the words "Pullman Company" in white thread. She held it toward Danny with a questioning look.

"Yeah, that is one of many towels I have, uh, *leased* from the good folks at Pullman. Anytime I'm on a train I slip the porter a few bills and he brings me a stack of 'em. They take off the cream better than anything else. You have to use cold cream." He held up the jar of Pond's. "Believe it or not, they used to use butter to remove the grease-paint. Most of us make use of these towels."

"Now, *that* is a good thing to know. I would have to go home and ruin Uncle Patrick's towels."

Danny flinched. "You can get a stack during our first jump. Until then, use mine."

As Danny continued working, Violet saw, taking shape right before her eyes, a face which wasn't like Danny's, but looked, to her, like a young, naïve boy.

"This will be different from the make-up you wore as yourself, yes?" Violet asked.

"You mean as my 'Danny' character? Yes, it will be darker lining, more comedic, darker eyebrows, so people in the house can see my expressions as I leer over you." He proceeded to use a brush to thickly kohl his eyebrows, then ran the substance heavily around his eyes, bringing out their beautiful light-blue color in the process. Gone was Danny O'Brien; in his place, the Delivery Boy.

When he finished, he looked at her and she smiled. "Boy, you look different!"

"Good different, or bad different?" he asked, looking at himself in the mirror, trying out some broad expressions.

"Just different," Violet laughed, and suddenly realized that she hadn't been thinking, and stewing, about her nerves. Whether or not Danny intended to, he had done a good job of getting her mind off their impending show. But thinking about it now made her almost sick to her stomach.

Danny stopped mugging when he looked at her in the mirror. "You okay? You got kinda green." He stood and walked to her side, motioning for her to sit down on the sofa. He got her a small cup of water, which she took and sipped.

"Yeah, I just got a bad case of the butterflies," she confided.

"That's a good thing; it keeps you on your toes," Danny said casually as he grabbed his costume and walked behind the screen to change. "You know, even seasoned performers get nervous. After a while you just learn how to turn nerves into something that work for you instead of against you."

"Can I have a crash course, please?" she asked with a shaky laugh.

"I wish I could, honey, but that's something that you just have to find out for yourself. Everybody's different. But you'll succeed here, I guarantee it." He walked around the screen. Violet took one look at him and began to feel calmer. He was looking at her with such sincerity, but with that silly make-up and the inane Delivery Boy costume—she just burst out laughing. It only took him a few seconds to see what was going on, so he played it up.

"What, you don't think I look handsome?" he asked, posing in front of the mirror like a swell. "I don't think I've ever looked better. I think, in fact, that I—"

"Five!" The stage manager's voice boomed through the door followed by a quick knock, breaking their mood.

Danny looked at Violet and took her hand. "That's our call, honey. Come on—let's show them how to do a flirtation act."

They ran down to the wings just in time to see Sally and Thomas do their finish. Danny held Violet's other hand and, together, they said a quick prayer. The curtain came down, and next thing Violet knew Sally's props were moved offstage while their desk was being shoved into place. The office drop was lowered with a dull thud.

Her heart leapt into her throat and threatened to render her mute.

"Go on, Vi, get into position," Danny encouraged.

As Violet walked to the desk, Thomas gave her a victory-clasp. She smiled, then sat down on the office chair. The orchestra played the first few bars of their song, "Love Me, and the World is Mine," and the curtain slowly ascended.

⤙⫘ ⫘⤚

If Violet had described in minute detail exactly how she would have wanted their first performance to go, it would have sounded exactly as it went that afternoon. Danny hit every mark, made every costume change, and got every laugh that was in the script—and then some. Violet nailed her song, juggled like a pro, and, most importantly for the sketch, had fun. She perfectly communicated the character, playing every line to perfection. The audience loved her, and she loved them in return. After her last line, when she pulled Danny onto the desk, she buried her face into his neck and squealed with delight. She actually felt the cheers and applause vibrating through the floorboards. Drawing back, she saw him smiling right before the stage went black.

"Come on, let's take our bow," he said as he grabbed her hand and led her to the front of the stage. They took their bow, and then that last little unexpected punch, when he starts to walk off the wrong way but then follows her offstage—well, the audience greeted that with a huge guffaw of appreciation.

They ran back to their dressing room and just collapsed, laughing, on the sofa.

"You see, it *is* worth all the butterflies, isn't it?" he asked, rubbing his hands through his hair.

"Yes—that was *some* experience! I feel elated!" she said stomping her feet on the ground.

And feeling her excitement, Danny realized that, for the first time in half a dozen years, he felt that same way.

They talked with the other performers after the show, all agreeing that it was a great house that afternoon. They spent some time chatting with Thomas, watching Sally cavort in her tub. Grace ran up to Violet and threw her arms around her.

"You were fantastic," Grace whispered in her ear, "and I think that Danny really has it for you!"

"Thank you," was all Violet could manage as the girls hugged.

"And great job to you, too," Grace said as she turned to Danny. Violet noticed that Grace was careful not to touch Danny in any way other than a handshake.

As expected, a dark shadow emerged and grabbed Grace's arm.

"Thank you, Gracie," said Danny as he looked at the girl, who began hiccupping. Violet saw Danny's jaw tighten and his eyes turn cold as they fixed on DiMarco. Grace and the fat man exited with a small wave and a final hiccup.

Danny and Violet ordered sandwiches and ate them sitting on the dressing-room floor. They drank Moxie out of the bottle. They played a couple of rounds of Crazy Eights and several hands of Pinochle with some crew members. They also went to a local theatrical supply shop and Violet bought her very own tubes of greasepaint.

Danny sat at the table to freshen his make-up and noticed Violet's lip print on his neck. He reluctantly wiped it away, hoping that tonight he would get another such memento of their perfect performance.

Violet felt much calmer than she had that afternoon. She took off her powder and had Grace show her how to apply and blend the thick, pungent greasepaint, using one color as her base and a darker color for contouring. She thought she looked like a painted China doll, and joked about it with Danny. She was feeling relaxed even when she heard the knock on the door and the stage manager yelling, "Five!" In fact, all she felt was excitement, to go out and repeat the success of the afternoon.

They walked downstairs, said a quick prayer (as would be their custom before each performance), and she was soon in place behind the desk. The orchestra struck up their theme song and Violet smiled.

But it wouldn't last.

Everything that could go wrong *did* go wrong. Danny couldn't find the bowler and was late on his entrance. Then, when the time came to extract the large card from his coat, he couldn't get it to budge. Violet forgot to ring the phone before answering once, dropped one of the beanbags during her juggling solo, and rushed her song. And, more importantly, the act required an audience's full attention, and that it didn't get from this evening's crowd. Several audience members came straggling in late, talking to their friends and trying to find their seats in the darkened auditorium. This threw off Danny's timing. Consequently, the same lines that were warmly received earlier in the day fell flat. The other performers were kind enough to say it had just been a cold audience, but they knew that wasn't true: Richard Bennett, Joe Frisco, Grace Manning, and especially Clayton, Jackson & Durante were all a smash. Violet and Danny hurriedly removed their make-up and went outside to get a cab. Violet was practically in tears as they rode home that evening, wrapping her arms around herself and leaning forward in the taxi.

Danny tried to be encouraging. "Look, Vi honey, there are times, like this afternoon, when everything just glides. Then there are times when nothing is right." He paused, trying to think of something to say to make her feel better. "You know, you can't be a true vaudevillian until you bomb at least once. So, welcome to the club!"

"It was *awful*," she said in a whisper, not looking at him. "*We* were awful. I'm so embarrassed. But I know we can do better tomorrow. We can win over the audience—tomorrow."

They arrived at the Goodman house and Danny stood outside with her for a moment. "I want you to get a good night's rest. And remember, this afternoon's performance is more indicative of the way it will go than tonight's was." He kissed her on the forehead and watched her slowly walk into the house. Just as she reached the door, she turned and gave him a shaky grin that he would never forget. Smiles are easy to come by when life is good, but that simple expression from a brave soul facing one of life's disappointments is rare—and remarkable. He felt as if a part of his heart shattered, but another part mended. Somehow, right then, he felt whole.

They discussed, understanding what went wrong during that evening's show and made some adjustments. They practiced, Violet repeating the rhythm of the telephone ring and answer. They tinkered, most notably with the camel hair coat trick, which, after repeated attempts, Danny finally mastered (he found that using specific clips in the coat created more dependable results). And, true to Danny's prediction, they did well during both of the next performances. Violet felt that, having experienced both elation and despair over the outcome of a show, she would *always* say they did great—regardless of the audience's response. Danny liked this optimistic view, and thanked her by adopting it himself. (In the past he had been extremely hard on himself if he had a bad night. Now he enjoyed the freedom to be able to put such a show behind him and simply do better for the next show.) They had worked on the timing of the routine, but had to change one part: when Danny said the line "Lady, do you *eat?*" the audience would invariably laugh for much longer than they had anticipated. This surprised them at first, but they adjusted the timing of that part of the routine, and Danny began playing it up. "The audience always tells you what it wants," he said on more than one occasion.

After a few more performances they were indeed moved to the number-four spot. They found that they went over much better in this place on the bill. And, after they had been on the road for a short while, they would definitely be ready to headline.

But mostly, they just enjoyed spending time together. Violet made a habit of going to Danny's apartment a couple of hours before they had to leave for the theatre so that she could spend some quality time with Murray. Always glad to see her, the feline would stretch out on the floor so she could give him a good belly rub, then curl up on her lap, not allowing her to move an inch without getting a pointed look of disapproval.

At Danny's apartment one afternoon, Violet mentioned that she needed to go back to the Goodman house. She wanted to put in a call to her family and fill them in on the whole experience.

"Stay here and use my phone," Danny said quickly, not ready to lose her company. "I rarely make long-distance calls, so please feel free to do so anytime."

"I'll pay you back," Violet assured him as she sat at the kitchen counter.

He waved off the thought. Wanting to give her some privacy, he took his leave, saying, "I'll just drop down to the market for a bottle of milk."

"Why not stay here?" Violet grinned as she picked up the receiver and began dialing. "This won't take long. I just want to let them know I'm still alive."

Violet could hear the connection being made through the receiver, then the muffled, faraway-sounding ringing of the phone. It was quickly picked up at the other end, but a scratchy connection made identifying the recipient difficult.

"*Rose*? Is that *you*?" Violet asked.

"*Violet*?" Rose asked. "Oh, Violet, I'm *so* glad you called. We got your last letter, and I can't believe you are really in vaudeville! And with *Danny O'Brien*! How exciting! But how in heaven's name were you able to walk out on that stage? Weren't you scared to death in front of all those people?"

"Oh, I was scared," she answered honestly. "But after a time you kind of get used to it."

A smiling Danny had picked up Murray and sat down beside Violet, scratching the cat's head.

"Well, you sound just fine," her father chimed in, having taken the receiver from Rose. "Your mother and I are so happy for you. Are *you* happy, honey?"

"Hi, Father, yes, I am happy working on the stage. This seems to be my calling, and I love doing it. I love the theatre and the act. And I love—" She paused. "I love the, well, the whole experience!"

"How is Danny?" Daisy intoned, being the next family member to commandeer the line. "What is he like? He is just *so* handsome." She had become quite the romantic, feeling that life should mirror the Jane Austen novels she continued to consume. Both she and Rose picked up a copy of *Theatre Magazine* that featured an article about Danny, and swooned over the debonair portrait that accompanied the piece. Daisy, in fact, framed the picture and kept it in her bedroom.

"Hi, Daisy," Violet said, feeling a little dizzy from being passed from one family member to another. But she still had plenty of mischief in her. "Danny is not at all handsome in real life. In fact, he's a bit on the homely side, and—"

"Hey, wait a minute!" Danny said, setting Murray on the floor and grabbing the receiver from the giggling Violet.

"To whom am I speaking?" Danny asked in his most theatrical tone.

The other side of the line was silent, save for the sound of static.

Violet snickered. "Come on, Daisy," she yelled into the receiver. "Talk to Danny."

"Hello, Danny," a small voice came through the line. "Oh my, I—I—"

"Well, it is indeed a pleasure speaking with such a fine young lady, my dear." He continued with the hammy voice. "You see, it is only through the support of our fans that we are able to parlay this humble profession into an art form. You, my dearest Daisy, are the reason that I shall tread the boards this evening. You shall be my muse, my Daisy, my flower of joy."

Violet rolled her eyes and took the phone out of his hands. "Ya' big ham," she whispered to Danny.

"Oh, Danny, I love you so!" Daisy's voice poured through the receiver.

"Hold on, girlie girl, it's just me," Violet interrupted in a disgusted tone. Danny sat beside her, chuckling.

"Put Danny back on," Daisy huffed.

"But don't you want to speak with your big sister whom you haven't seen in weeks? *I love you*," Violet said in a sing-song fashion and made loud kissing sounds.

"*Violet!* Put Danny back on the—" Daisy's rant was abruptly cut short by her mother, who took the receiver out of her hands.

"Oh, Daisy, *really*. Hello—Violet? Patrick tells me that you are doing very well. Are you eating regularly? Are you getting enough sleep?"

"Hello, Mother. Yes, I am eating and sleeping and doing very well indeed. You and Father and the girls should come out and see us."

"Yes, we must, sometime. But you know that your birthday is coming up a week from tomorrow. What shall we send you as a gift? What do you need?"

Violet looked surreptitiously at Danny, who appeared to be looking at a hangnail on his thumb. "Oh, I'm fine," was all she said, a little too brightly.

"But, dear, we want to send you something you could use. Can't you think of a thing?"

Violet slyly looked toward Danny, who appeared to be still engrossed with his thumb. "No, no, not a thing ... why, it hasn't rained in weeks," she said with the same exceedingly cheery tone, confusing her poor mother.

"We must have a bad connection, dear," her mother said. "I never even mentioned the weather. What I was asking about was your birth—"

"Thank you, Mother, I will. I love you, too."

"And we love you, too—I mean—oh, never mind. Be good now, honey, and be happy."

Violet hung up.

"Aren't those mutually exclusive?" Danny asked, still looking at his thumb.

"*What?*"

"Being good *and* being happy?"

"Oh, you," Violet huffed. "That was a sweet—wait, you could *hear* that?"

"Yes. I have freakishly good hearing."

"So you heard—*everything?*"

"If you mean that I heard your mother say that your birthday is coming up a week from Wednesday, which means that I am going to have to do something very special for you, no. I didn't hear anything about *that.*"

Violet didn't know if she should giggle or hit him, so she chose to do both.

Danny had been on the lookout for a review of their act in the local papers and the trades. He wanted to make sure that Violet's first taste of this sometimes brutal ritual would be positive. He was used to his fair share of lukewarm appraisals, but he didn't want this kind of intervention to dampen Violet's positive spirit. He worried, however, for naught. The following day he sat with her on the small sofa in their dressing room and presented the *Brooklyn Daily Eagle*, folded open to the theatre section. He took great pleasure in watching her face as she read this, their first review:

"Will She Love Me?"— We Say 'Yes'!

We caught the thrilling new flirtation routine between an over-zealous delivery boy and a provocative office secretary at the Bushwick last night. There isn't an idle moment in this delirious routine, with sustained excitement from the walk-on to the final trick bow. It's chock-full of topical gags, and packed with costume changes and marvelous characters. Danny O'Brien (you remember, the kid with the socko voice who sang Irish honeys) is back doing comedy, and doing a slick job of it. The new face is Violet Williams, who sings, juggles, and lobs the jokes as well as anybody on the stage today. Our office has already overheard someone using the catch phrase, "Lady, do you eat?" It's a darb!

This is just the kind of act your
whole family deserves to see—
imaginative, funny, a delight.

"Oh, Danny, this is wonderful!" Violet exclaimed. She ran her
hand over the paper lovingly, as if trying to absorb the words and remember them forever. "I'm just glad the reviewer caught a good show!"

"We will keep this in the trunk, honey, and when we get the inevitable bad notice, you can reread this."

"Good idea," Violet said, her eyes still skimming the paper. She
then laughed at one line, adding, "I've never thought of myself as being *provocative.*"

Danny bit his lip. "No, *you* wouldn't."

Violet glanced up at his eyes, and into the blue depths which cast
both affection and desire. She took his proffered hand.

"You know, Vi," and here he paused, "I just want to tell you
that—"

Before Danny could say another word, they heard it. *Slap, thump,
thud.* And then a muffled cry from Grace. Danny was on his feet in no
time and out the door. Violet followed just in time to see Danny grab
DiMarco and punch him in the nose. The big man swayed drunkenly
and fell into Grace's dressing-room chair. After shaking his head, he
stood back up and lunged for Danny. The two traded blows, with Di-
Marco clearly the worse for the exchange.

Violet ran to Grace, who lay crumpled in the corner of the room,
her lip bleeding and her face lined with red welts. She held the poor
girl in her arms, smoothing her hair and rocking her back and forth.

After a moment, DiMarco stood back, his hand over his bloodied
nose.

"You'll p—pay for this, On'Brishen," DiMarco slurred. "You'll be
ver—very sorry about th—this."

"Hit her again and I'll kill you!" Danny spat as the fat man stag-
gered out of the room. Danny then turned to Grace. "Are you okay?"
he asked in a gentle tone.

"Yes, I'll be okay," Grace said, her eyes red from tears. She hiccupped loudly, then continued, "But Danny, you shouldn't have hit him. You shouldn't get—"

"Now don't be concerned, Gracie," Danny said. He looked into Violet's worried eyes. "Everything will be just fine. Why don't you help our friend get dressed, Vi?"

"Of course," Violet said, and helped Grace up and onto the sofa. Her cheek was beginning to swell, so Violet got a cold cloth from the sink and held it against her face. She asked Danny to procure some ice, which he managed to do in no time. Violet rinsed out the cloth, tucking the ice into the center, then placed it carefully to the girl's face. Grace looked at Violet with gratitude, hiccupping several times in a row.

"Don't worry," Violet cooed to her. "I'll stay with you as long as you want. Now dry your tears, Grace dear. I'll help you make up your beautiful face."

Violet took some time with her friend, attempting to heal her body and spirit with positive reflections of Grace's inner worth. Violet urged her to recall times in her life when she had shown true strength, and to call upon that courage when she was feeling helpless. Willing Violet's words to fill her heart, she listened to and trusted this strong woman.

Half an hour later, when Violet joined Danny in their dressing room to change and apply her own make-up, she had to ask Danny an important question: "Will that man, that DiMarco, cause you any trouble?"

"No, he's just a local hooligan. It's not like he's a part of the mob. I really don't think he'll try anything, except maybe dumping Gracie, if we're lucky. Now, don't you worry."

Although Danny was confident, Violet had a sense of unease.

CHAPTER NINE

THE MET

November 1925

D are she? She wasn't at all sure.
Standing in the B. Altman & Co. salon and looking in the full-length mirror wasn't making this decision any easier. The department store, located at Fifth Avenue and Thirty-Fourth Street in Midtown Manhattan, had first opened its doors in 1906. At that time the neighborhood was still almost entirely residential, and the design of the new building (to be built on the vacated site of department-store rival A. T. Stewart's grand residence and across the avenue from Mrs. Astor) was planned to fit in with the surrounding palatial mansions. It did, and it was, indeed, as grand as the fashions they featured.

After trying on what felt like a hundred dresses—but in reality was ten—she knew she had to make a choice. She had worn beautiful formal ware before, but this time was different; this was an occasion for which she had to look radiant. No ... stunning. She wanted to be stunning. And this magical creation may just be the thing.

The silk chiffon evening dress had an intricate jet beaded dropped-waist bodice and a partly shear, sequined, scalloped-hem skirt, which gracefully brushed the floor. The sleeveless top was cut daringly low at the neckline and back, and the under-sheath of peachy pink gave the illusion of, well, of nothing underneath.

What would Danny think?

There was also a rectangular shawl made of black satin, which was bordered by the same black beads. The fabric draped over her arms, dipping low in the back to show off her porcelain skin. If the night turned chilly, which was very likely, she would have something to warm her arms.

Although Danny could serve that purpose as well.

The efficacious saleswoman came into the room carrying black twenty-button opera gloves. "Oh, Miss Williams, that fits you beautifully!" she said as she handed the gloves to Violet. "These will complete the look. All you will need now are some black satin pumps and a jeweled comb in your hair."

"It will take me forever to put these on!" Violet said, looking at the long gloves.

"That is why you must allow enough time to properly dress for such an occasion, my dear," the woman said, a tad haughtily. She stood to one side and watched Violet in the mirror, her hands folded obsequiously in front of her.

"This is it. I want this one," Violet said, feeling a sense of relief. She had procrastinated buying an outfit for this special occasion, but now was the time. Danny's birthday gift to her was an evening of *Tosca*, which was the following night. She knew she had enough money to cover the cost of the expensive dress, thanks to her parents' more-than-generous gift she had received the day before. And, after all, a girl doesn't turn twenty every day, she told herself to justify the extravagant $78 price tag.

The sensational new team of O'Brien & Williams had this Wednesday off, taking a short break before they began traveling the eastern circuit. This was the perfect chance to do something she had always wanted to do: see *the* Metropolitan Opera House in person. When Danny had sprung the surprise on her she had to admit that, whereas she was familiar with Puccini's *La Bohème* and had seen a beautiful production of *Madama Butterfly* in Portland, she really didn't know much about the twenty-five-year-old opera *Tosca*.

"So," Violet asked between bites of pizza, a quick dinner prior to their last show at the Bushwick, "what is *Tosca* about?"

"About two hours," Danny retorted.

Violet laughed good naturedly. "*Plot?*"

"Oh, that," Danny said around a mouthful of pepperoni. "Well, Boy meets Girl in Rome of 1800 when Naples' control of Rome is threatened by Napoleon's invasion of Italy. Girl inadvertently leads to the arrest of Boy, who is then tortured. Girl murders torturer, who is trying to have his way with her. Boy is killed by firing squad, and Girl jumps to her death. Just your average happy story."

"It sounds like grand opera," Violet suggested, thoughtfully chewing.

"It actually is known for being compact, fast moving."

"Where did Puccini get the story? Did he make it up?"

"It's based on a Parisian play which was a vehicle for Sarah Bernhardt, who, as you know, was an exponent of the unrestrained school of acting. But Puccini pushed his librettists to play the story up, rather than down, when constructing the opera." Danny stood and walked over to the shelf where he kept his street clothes. Turning around, he became animated. "Now, imagine this. Puccini was a smart guy, and he was able to take all this—this raw drama, and match that intensity with a score featuring crashing dissonant chords that send chills down your spine; lush, heart-tugging cello passages that make you want to cry; and a big church procession against which the antagonist sings that Tosca has made him forget about God!"

"Holy smoke!" Violet was spellbound.

Danny laughed, picking up a package and walking it back to her. "Your first gift—happy birthday." Violet smilingly took the present. Untying the strings and drawing back the brown paper, she found a set of three 78s featuring arias from *Tosca*.

"Now, tomorrow I want you to play these a few times to familiarize yourself with the melodies."

"Yes, sir, and thank you, Danny," Violet said, standing and kissing his cheek. "I will give them my full attention."

And Violet dutifully did just that, the following day in the vacated living room of the Goodman residence. It was evident why he loved this opera so much. She thought the "Recondita armonia" was inspired as sung by Enrico Caruso as Tosca's lover, the artist Mario Cavaradossi. After hearing it just a couple of times it seemed wonderfully familiar and she looked forward to hearing it sung live. She considered Tosca's famous aria "Vissi d'arte" to be performed with great emotion by soprano Emmy Destinn. But it was Tosca's duet with her lover—the aria "Qual'occhio"—which she found to be the most beautiful. The actual disc Danny gave her was from Berlin and sung in German, featuring the amazing Carl Günther and Frida Leider. Entitled "Ach, die Augen," the familiar melody showcased these magnificent voices as they blended exquisitely and, in the crescendo of Puccini's skillful melody, conveyed the passion these characters felt. Violet would have to remember to send a copy of this to Daisy, who would appreciate this audial version of perfect love.

And what was *her* attitude about love these days? She had to admit that her feelings for Danny were complex, more complex than the depictions of love she had heretofore seen; so, perhaps she wasn't *in* love with him. Yes, this could be a different emotion. As she replayed the music, she reclined on the floor by the phonograph and thought about the state of their relationship. She wanted to be a soothing presence for him, to make everything go effortlessly in his world, and to receive comfort from him as well. She loved working with him, developing their routine, and their shared experiences of day-to-day life. That sounded like familial love, between family and friends. *But*, she thought furtively, she also wanted to kiss him—really kiss him—and feel his arms around her. In her mind she saw Eros's arrow sailing through her familial love theory. Well, that was that. At the next possible opportunity she was going to take the lead and give him a kiss he would never forget. Suddenly she sat up. Maybe she *was* in love. She knew that one kiss would yield her answer. And she knew that would be tonight.

She spent the better part of the day listening to the beautiful arias, then decided to start getting ready on the early side. She bathed at leisure, enjoying the carnation-scented bath salts she sprinkled in the water. She styled her hair up, fastening it with pins and her birthday gift from Uncle Patrick and Aunt Mavis: a diamond-and-onyx hair clip, which wound, snakelike, around her coiffure.

She decided to wear her best black hose and black garters, but wasn't quite sure which undergarment to wear. She had a "Miracle Reducing Rubber Brassiere" which, the saleswoman told her, was "scientifically designed without bones or lacings to give the desirable flat lines sought after by young women of today." But she was concerned that it could be seen, as the back of the dress was so low. Taking a deep breath, and wearing only a nude low-cut camiknicker, she shimmied into the beaded dress. Then began the tedium of buttoning all forty buttons on her gloves: a task she finally turned over to Aunt Mavis. When she was finished, the older woman stood back and looked at Violet, not saying a word.

"Well?" Violet queried. "What do you think?"

"I don't think Danny will have his eyes on the opera tonight," was all she said.

A shiny black 1924 Isotta Fraschini limousine pulled up in front of the Osborne precisely at 7:00. The automobile, which looked to be a block long, had the graceful curves and long chrome running board which marked the Italian machine as exclusive—and expensive. The dark gray leather was visible in the open driver's seat; discreetly hidden from view in the enclosed passenger compartment. This was the kind of automobile which made all others appear grossly un-cosmopolitan and unworthy of the '20s elite.

The crisply uniformed chauffeur rose from the driver's seat and waited for his client to appear. In no time, a beautifully dressed young man emerged, wearing top hat, black tux with tails, and gloves. The middle-aged chauffeur smiled. He was glad to see that the youth of today knew how to properly dress for the opera. Rules of proper etiquette were being forgotten so quickly, he contemplated ruefully.

"Good evening, pal, I'm Danny," the young man said, smiling broadly and sticking out his hand.

Well, so much for understanding all the rules, the chauffeur thought with a sniff.

When the limousine drew up to the Goodman house, Danny bounded out and jogged to the front door. He utilized his brightest smile, which he held—until he saw her. His Vi. Standing before him, looking so sophisticated, yet so seductive and gorgeous; she was his ideal personified. As his smile faded he slowly removed his top hat. He really didn't know what to say, so chose the path taken by most men who find themselves at a loss for just the right words: he said nothing.

"You look so handsome, Danny," Violet proffered, trying to break the ice upon which they seemed to be skating.

Still, he said nothing.

"Why is it that nobody pays me a compliment on my dress without being asked?" Violet declared, looking straight into Danny's eyes.

"Of course you look—" Danny began, barely speaking above a whisper. He looked down for a moment, and then continued, finally finding his voice. "I couldn't speak. You took my breath away."

"Good save," Violet laughed. She looked at the car and then back at Danny. "What a glorious automobile!"

She took Danny's arm and they walked to the shiny black vehicle, Danny helping her into the backseat.

"To the opera!" Danny said to no one in particular.

The Metropolitan Opera House celebrated its grand opening on October 22, 1883, with a performance of Gounod's *Faust*. It was located at 1411 Broadway, occupying the whole block between West Thirty-Ninth and West Fortieth Street, on the West Side. Nicknamed "The

Yellow Brick Brewery" for its industrial-looking exterior, the original Metropolitan Opera House was designed by J. Cleveland Cady. On August 27, 1892, the nine-year-old theatre was gutted by fire. The 1892–93 season was canceled while the opera house was rebuilt along its original lines.

In 1903, the interior of the opera house was extensively redesigned by the architects Carrère and Hastings. The familiar golden auditorium with its sunburst chandelier, horseshoe shape, and curved proscenium inscribed with the names of six composers (Gluck, Mozart, Beethoven, Wagner, Gounod, and Verdi) dates from this time. The first of the Met's signature gold damask stage curtains was installed in 1906. While the theatre was noted for its excellent acoustics and elegant interior, it had a decided lack of space for scenery when big productions were presented. In one of the more unusual chapters of New York history, the Met's scenery and sets were a regular sight leaning against the building outside on Thirty-Ninth Street, where they had to be shifted between performances. The Met had a seating capacity of 3,625, with an additional 224 standing-room places.

Just as Danny had gone out of his way to ensure they would have a memorable evening by hiring a special limousine, he had gone to the trouble of purchasing seats that were among his favorite in the house: in the Grand Tier. Violet was awestruck by her surroundings. After Danny checked his hat, they took their places and soon the orchestra was tuning up. The drums were thumping, flutes trilling, and violins humming. Danny got chills.

"Whether it's a small group or a huge orchestra," he said, turning to Violet, "that sound—it's a song in its own right, a promise of what is coming. I know it's silly, but I love that music."

Violet was quiet for a while. "I guess I've never thought about it. That's beautiful."

She looked at him, dressed so elegantly and displaying such dignified gentility on the drive over, and thought that maybe she hadn't given him enough credit for his maturity. They opened their programs and read through the brief synopsis of the opera, the biographical profiles of the leading singers, and the names of the musicians. Danny tapped her on the arm and pointed a gloved finger to one in particular, an oboist by the name of M. Claude Goatrouten.

"You know," Danny leaned in and whispered to Violet, "every orchestra must have a goat routen; it's a very important job. Every theatre needs to routen their goats every six months, no exceptions. You see, I come from a long line of goatists."

And there he was: Danny, tux and all, making a goat joke. She laughed in spite of herself, to the point where she was getting some disapproving looks from those nearby.

"Don't pay any attention to them," Danny whispered. "They hate goats *and* those who routen them."

She elbowed him in the ribs while doing her best to keep from laughing louder than before. He chuckled and turned his attention back to the program.

Before long, the lights went down and the orchestra leader made his entrance. Then, without a prelude, the opera began. The first piece that she recognized was performed shortly into the first act, Mario's "Recondita armonia," which was accompanied by the Sacristan's grumbling counter-melody. This was absent in the recording she heard, and she was enthralled by the sound it created—two opposites threading together to create a glorious resonance. Then came the arrival of Floria Tosca herself, and the wonderful aria the lovers sing together. She felt the same reaction to the romantic quality of the piece, but especially enjoyed the playful flirtation the actors brought to the aria. The first act culminated in dramatic fashion with a juxtaposition of the sacred and profane, as the evil Baron Scarpia's lustful reverie is sung alongside the swelling *Te Deum* chorus. Violet closed her eyes, inviting the music to wash over her, feeling the emotion Puccini ordained. The splendor of the composition touched her soul, and she felt Danny's arm around her, in a brief acknowledgment of the shared experience.

Throughout the rest of the opera Violet sat, entranced. When Cavaradossi cried out while being tortured, she grabbed Danny's hand.

And when the lovers were reunited in the final act, only to have their future cut short, she brushed away tears. The curtain calls were thrilling in themselves, so loved were the artists who gave of themselves that evening.

The weather had turned cold, and Violet wrapped the shawl around her shoulders as they walked from the Met's entrance to the waiting limousine. "Sixty-First Street, off Madison Avenue, please," Danny said to the driver. And to Violet, sitting close to him in the backseat, "I hope you're hungry."

"Yes, I really am. Where are we going?"

"To a place called The Colony."

Danny told Violet all about the checkered history of the restaurant on their ride over. At first, he said, The Colony was known only for its upstairs gambling club where men could meet their mistresses. But after Mrs. William K. Vanderbilt discovered it, the restaurant became *the* fashionable haunt of New York high society. The Colony still served liquor even during prohibition, offering it in china tea cups rather than glasses. They kept their vast array of alcohol in a service elevator where it could easily be moved, though Mayor Walker protected the restaurant from raids. But Danny was uninterested in that extra service as he had not touched a drop of liquor since the days as a kid when he sneaked whiskey from his dad, and it was not because of the Volstead Act. He didn't like the way alcohol looked on a man. Much too often it could look like DiMarco.

After exiting the limo, they walked into the restaurant and immediately were whisked through the cozy dining room, which featured claret-and-gold wallpaper and dark peacock-blue chairs. The pianist began playing "Danny Boy" as they made their way. Danny smiled and acknowledged the smattering of applause that began around them, while at the same time mouthing to Violet a sheepish, "Sorry." They were ensconced at one of the best tables, toward the back of the house, in a quiet little niche. After getting comfortable and ordering some coffee, they settled in to talk about what they had just experienced.

"I loved the singer who played Scarpia, Antonio Scotti, I believe his name is," Violet offered. "He was brilliant. Forceful."

"I agree. You know, he began playing that role in 1901—and in front of Puccini himself!" Danny added. "They say he has lost some of his ability—vocally, but I think he's still great. He brings authority to the role."

"The other two main roles were quite well performed, although I think you spoiled me by having me hear Caruso and Günther first."

Danny was silent for a moment. "The whole story, their downfall, do you think it was because of love?"

"No. Jealousy. Without that, Scarpia would not have found Cavaradossi, and that, as we know, was the beginning of the end. Love, well, it brought hope."

"Have you ever felt jealous, Vi?" Danny asked.

Violet paused, giving the question her full attention. "Not in the romantic sense," she averred. "But I *did* feel jealous of my sister, the one getting married next year. She just seemed to have things all figured out, and, this last summer, I was a bit at sea. I envied her having the answers."

"*You*? I thought you were the business woman who had her life planned down to the last detail," Danny said, genuinely surprised.

"No, I felt, I don't know, *lacking*. That my life was lacking something—and I had no idea what it was! I began working for Uncle Patrick as a way to kill some time until I found an answer."

"And have you found it?" Danny asked while looking down at the napkin he was twisting in his hands, more anxious to hear the response than he knew he should be.

"I think I am closer now than I was then, if that makes sense," Violet answered. She could swear that she saw Danny exhale just a little after she answered, then he nodded. She liked that he seemed to care about how comfortable she was with the progression of her life. And, maybe, that he was waiting to hear how he figured into her future. "So, how about you?" she asked, shaking herself from her thoughts.

"What? *Jealousy*? *Me*? No, never. I haven't a jealous bone in my entire body," he answered candidly.

The waiter arrived to deliver their drinks and take their order. Danny ordered for both of them: tomato bisque soup, steak with piquant sauce, acorn-stuffed squab, and fresh green salad. Then to finish, fresh pears and Camembert. The waiter bowed and took his leave.

"Do you go to the movies?" Violet asked.

"Yes. Some are good; some, a waste of time. But I'm sure that's how people view vaudeville acts, too. What about you?"

"I'm crazy about Buster Keaton. His films are funny—and what that man can't do!"

"Yeah," Danny smiled. "I saw *Sherlock Jr.* when it came out last year. Did you?"

"Yes. Great picture."

"Awfully good and so innovatively made. The movie within the movie idea—that is pure Buster. Groundbreaking. You know he does the stunts for the films himself, like the scene with the motorcycle."

"How do you know that?"

"Well, he told me specifically about the motorcycle scene because we used to joke that—"

"Wait a minute. You *know* Buster Keaton?" Violet asked, her eyes growing wide.

"I do," Danny said nonchalantly.

"You're kidding!" Violet enthused.

"Well," Danny said by way of explanation, "we are the same age, and we both grew up in vaudeville, and had worked on the same bill a few times. We have a lot in common. One time he came over to my place; I think it was 1917, when I was first doing my solo act and he had first gone into pictures, here in New York. We had been sitting around, having a smoke, when I realized it was time to get to the theatre for the evening performance, and I told him to make himself at home. Well, when I got back, there on the floor was my Victrola—in a couple dozen pieces. He was just sitting there, looking at the spring motor, and said, 'Now I get it.' That was it. That is how his mind works. That's what makes him such a great technician."

"Just unbelievable," Violet said, shaking her head.

"No it was alright—he put the Victrola back together for me," Danny said not being able to resist teasing her.

"That's not what I mea—*oh, you*," Violet laughed. She had to admit to herself that she was a little overwhelmed by the small glimpses of Danny's fame. "Say, have you read *Gatsby* yet?" she ventured, pouring cream into her coffee and changing the subject.

"Yes, I have," he confessed, a tone of embarrassment creeping into his voice. "And *you?*"

"Yes. A book is all about the journey. Either you like the path the words have paved, or you don't. And I loved the trip to West Egg, and the parties, and, I guess, the passion of the characters. Fitzgerald has a fresh approach."

"Yeah, I agree," Danny affirmed, deep in thought. "I think that is exactly what I liked about it, too. It takes a lot to break out of the previous generation, you know, the safety of it. And that Scott and Zelda and their group of friends do very well. They are inventive. Generally, though, I don't go in for such populist reading."

"What *do* you like to read," Violet asked.

"Dickens, mostly. I love his characters, of course, and his prose is so beautiful. Rhythmic."

"But wasn't Dickens considered populist in his day?" Violet asked, her brown eyes showing just a hint of a chase.

"Perhaps. Yes. You are correct, Miss Williams. And do *you* usually read Jane Austen?"

"No, that's Daisy's obsession. I love Flaubert, Chekhov, Poe, and—"

"Wait, you like *Poe?* Isn't that a bit dark for our bubbly Vi?"

"Edgar A. is responsible for the most perfect line ever written in the English language: 'And the silken sad uncertain rustling of each purple curtain / Thrilled me—filled me with fantastic terrors never felt before.'"

"'The Raven,'" Danny contributed. "Those are scary birds. And can you imagine encountering a murder of them?"

"An unkindness or a conspiracy."

"What? You've lost me."

"A group of crows is referred to as a *murder*," Violet said, casually sipping her coffee. "A group of ravens is referred to as an *unkindness* or a *conspiracy*."

"Even scarier," Danny joked. "But I'm sure learning a lot from you."

Violet laughed. "Back to Poe. Now, if you want to talk about genuine romance, he is definitely my man." Violet paused for a moment, then began, "'But we loved with a love that was more than love—I and my Annabel Lee—With a love that the wingèd seraphs of Heaven coveted her and me.'" She paused for just a moment, then slowly looked at him, straight into those gorgeous blue eyes. "And that, my friend, is what a girl wants to hear."

"Yes, darling Vi, but Annabelle Lee was dead and the narrator killed himself," Danny replied, his head tilting to one side, a grin playing around his lips.

"Details." Violet brushed her gloved hand through the air in dismissal. "Oh, and another writer I'm passionate over—"

"Hugo," they said simultaneously. They both looked slightly surprised, and then laughed.

The waiter brought their relish tray, and both selected olives.

"Your favorite Hugo?" Violet asked around the olive.

"*L'homme Qui Rit—The Man Who Laughs*. Fitting, don't you think, for a performer?" Danny said with a sardonic look.

"Yes, the unfortunate Gwynplaine," she paused, seeing the revelation in his words. "His face carved into a perpetual smile. That must be the way you always felt, especially as a child in the public eye—like you had to always wear a smiling mask?"

"Yes. To strangers, it wasn't easy; but to the people who knew me, well, it was painful." They paused, the emotional words washing over them, then ebbing away. Rousing himself, Danny inquired, "Tell me, which is your favorite Hugo?"

"I can't say. I love them all, and I love the way he uses words, the unending but perfectly constructed sentences. You get a flow and rhythm from his words that you don't find anywhere else. *The Man Who Laughs* is a good example, as is *Hunchback*, and of course *Les Misérables*."

"Well, there's a light little read," Danny said with a laugh. "Say, we played a game a few weeks ago, about telling the other something nobody else knows. So, dear Vi, tell me something *else* you wouldn't tell anyone—under penalty of torture."

"Oh!" Violet cried, chuckling at the reference to the opera. "Okay. Now I have to think. How about you. Why don't you go first this time?"

Danny thought for a while, weighing his answer. Then he looked at Violet, his expression becoming dark and somber. "I saw my father hit my mother. Actually, he did it a few times, when I was very young."

Violet saw the hurt that dulled his eyes. "Oh, Danny, I'm so sorry."

"Sorry for the serious outpouring tonight. I don't know what would make me think of that, but it has been on my mind of late."

"Grace." It was all Violet had to say, and Danny nodded in agreement. He then looked at her with something akin to fear in his eyes.

"*You* would never take that from a man, would you?"

"No, I'd hit back. I'd like to think that women are different today than they were twenty years ago, but then I think of Grace, and know that life is complicated. Relationships are complicated. But now I certainly see why you are so protective of her."

He gave her a genuine smile. "Well, she'll be alright now. Okay, your turn, 'fess up, and this had better be good."

Violet suddenly felt like pouring her heart out to Danny, telling him that she thought she was falling in love with him; perhaps hoping to hear the sentiment returned. "I'm afraid that I—that is, I think that maybe I'm—" The waiter cleared his throat, interrupting her with the first course. He proceeded to take quite a long while with the elegantly presented bisque laced with cream and topped with buttery croutons. When he left she had changed her mind, feeling that perhaps telling Danny about these feelings right now would be foolhardy.

"Now," Danny asked, sitting forward, "what were you saying?"

"Well, I think that this may be the best birthday I have ever had. Thank you." She then looked down and lifted her soupspoon to her lips.

Danny, too, looked down, the merest hint of disappointment flickering quickly across his face, then disappearing just as quickly into a ready smile. "That means the world to me, Vi."

They talked through dinner, about everything and nothing. Danny paid the $2.80 tab for the superb meal and left a $5 tip. The ride home was beautiful. He put his arm around her and held her while they marveled at this stunning metropolis shimmering in the moonlight. All too soon the limousine stopped at the Goodman house, and Danny saw her to the door.

"Thank you for spending your special day with me," he said.

"You have really been remarkable, and I want to thank you for sharing so much with me tonight."

"Oh," Danny said, a little embarrassed and immediately sad, "the thing about my father."

"No, actually, I was thinking about your revelation of being from a long line of goatists," Violet said, perfectly deadpan.

Danny laughed while taking her gloved hands in his, then spontaneously kissed them. "Thank you, and goodnight, my dear Vi. See you at the train station tomorrow morning at nine o'clock sharp." He gave her hands a squeeze, let them go, and took a step back.

"Goodnight, and see you at nine," she said, and turned to open the door. But she paused for an instant, thinking about her resolve to kiss Danny.

Just then she heard him whisper in her ear, "Bet you won't kiss me goodnight."

She turned around and looked into his darkened eyes, understanding the need they expressed. "I'll take that bet," she said in a voice so husky it was unrecognizable even to her.

Taking her face in his hands, he slowly lowered his mouth to hers. The kiss was gentle and warm, then deepening to try to fill the hunger they felt for each other. Once again, as when they first met, the world fell away. She kissed him back; holding onto him and showing him how much she cared—showing him that she indeed loved him.

He pulled back and smiled, then just held her to him, feeling her heartbeat against his, smelling her sweet scent of carnations. His Vi. He dropped his head to kiss her beautiful slender neck, pressed his lips to hers for one more lingering kiss, then turning, walked to the waiting limo.

She hurried into the house. Tiptoeing up the stairs so as not to wake anyone, she went into her bedroom and closed the door. Leaning against it, she thought about the evening, which became a mad rush of sights, sounds, tastes, scents, and emotions roiling around her. She put her hand to her lips and smiled.

Yeah. She was in love. And so was he.

Danny gave himself a talking-to on the ride home. *You idiot,* he thought. *You've lost all self-control when it comes to this girl.* He knew that he should have just taken her home and wished her a happy birthday, but then he had to go and kiss her. That kiss was … what *was* that kiss? Danny unconsciously ran his thumb over his lips, still feeling the urgency in hers. No, it wasn't a mistake. He knew that what he was feeling was a lot more than anything he had felt before, no matter how intimate he had been with a girl. He was going to have to sort out these damned emotions with a cooler head than he possessed at the moment. But, he thought, even if he wanted to stop feeling the way he did about her, *could* he?

He pondered this most important question as he exited the limousine.

"Thank you for the wonderful service tonight," he said as he paid the driver.

"Thank *you*, sir," the driver intoned when he saw the more-than-ample payment.

Making his way to the front steps of the Osborne, Danny was deep in thought when he heard a man's voice behind him: "Hey, O'Brien."

Oh, brother, probably some jealous boyfriend. He had suffered a few near-misses with this hot-headed type before, but thought those days were behind him. Danny turned and saw two large figures silhouetted against the street light. "May I help you?"

"Yeah. We have a message from Mr. DiMarco. He said that you can keep the girl. And here is a parting gift."

With that, one of the men stepped forward and punched Danny in the stomach, hard—so hard that he doubled over. So hard, in fact, that he couldn't see the brass knuckles coming out from under the massive coat to hit him in the face. So hard, too, that he couldn't hear the kick which broke several ribs. In fact, the only thing of which Danny was aware was how cold and hard the cement sidewalk felt. When he opened his eyes, he saw only blood. Then, mercifully, he blacked out.

CHAPTER TEN

THE CIRCUIT

November 1925

vaudevillian's trunk is his life. It is his home, his security, his turtle shell that provides safety against the real world. It can house his whole act, and with it his livelihood, and was, therefore, considered indispensable to the traveling entertainer. Manufactured by the firm of Herkert and Meisel, it was typically equipped with hanger space on one side and drawers on the other. And, of course, on the outside was the performer's history: cities, countries, and all ports of call on small papers which were pasted onto the leather. These would allow the chest to be taken directly to the theatre where the performers were appearing or to the hotel or boarding house where they were staying.

Violet reread the note which showed up with the trunk late last night while she and Danny were at the opera:

> *Dearest Vi,*
> *Now that you are a real vaudevil-*
> *lian, you should travel as one. Here is*
> *an H&M all your own. Whatever you*
> *do, don't make the damned thing so*
> *heavy I can't carry it!*

Here's to O'Brien & Williams' many adventures on the road.

Yours,
Danny

Violet looked inside the trunk, at the beautiful leather-lined shelves, drawers on the left side, and the hanging rod on the right. It measured 41" standing, by 22" wide, by 15" deep. Why, a person could practically live out of this, she thought. She began filling the luggage, but kept in mind Danny's caveat to keep the trunk on the light side.

After quickly dressing, she made her way downstairs to an awaiting Aunt Mavis and Uncle Patrick.

"My dear," Aunt Mavis said, "you are going to have such a wonderful time. Good luck, and we look forward to having you return to us next January."

"Yes, and I appreciate all you have done for me, I just can't thank you enough," Violet said, hugging her.

"Come along now," Patrick said devoid of sentimentality, "you mustn't be late for the train." He had booked the team into some of the best theatres in the Keith-Albee dynasty. They would be playing Syracuse, Buffalo, Boston, Erie, Cleveland, Columbus, Detroit, and Chicago, then back home to New York where they would do a week at the Palace as the headliners. Patrick put her in the cab, paying the driver ahead of time to assist with her trunk. "Let me know if anything is amiss," was all he said. She gave him a quick peck on the cheek and the cab took off, quickly melding into traffic.

Violet arrived at the train station in good time. After making sure her trunk was safely in the baggage car, she boarded the Pullman. She knew that most of the vaudevillians with whom they would share the bill had taken an earlier train; she and Danny had stayed a day longer to enjoy the opera. Speaking of Danny, she thought, he should already be onboard. She looked around everywhere, expecting to see his handsome face. But she couldn't find him. She began swearing—internally, of course—as she couldn't believe he would take the chance of missing the train by being so late. Annoyance turned to apprehension when she heard the conductor shout, "Last call for boarding!" She went up to the uniformed gentleman and, after giving a quick description of her partner, asked if he had seen him. The conductor was unsure, but thought that he would remember had Danny boarded, as the train was only half full. She made a hasty exit from the train and ran through the terminal, but still did not see any sign of him. Suddenly realizing that something was very wrong, she hailed a taxi and ordered the cabbie to take her to the Osborne as fast as he could get there.

When she arrived at Danny's front door she knocked, then instinctively checked to see if it was locked. As it wasn't, she opened it and began calling for him. The apartment was dark as all the blinds were closed. She heard Murray meowing from the bedroom.

"Where are you?" she whispered to the cat. She slowly made her way into the dark room and saw Murray sitting on the bed next to a crumpled mass of clothing. She opened the curtains and heard a groan. The mass, she soon discovered, was Danny, disheveled and bleeding.

"Danny, what—?" was all she could say. She went to his side and saw that he had a black eye which was swollen shut, a gash on his forehead, several nasty scratches on his cheek, and a split lip.

"Violet?" he whispered. "Could you get me some ice?"

"Of course." She flew into action, getting ice and a washcloth for his face, then slowly helping him out of his tuxedo coat and untying his bloodied tie. He winced when he moved his torso, and Violet deduced that some of his ribs had been broken.

"DiMarco's henchmen," he said. "I—I thought … that he might … send his men out to do something … the coward, so I shouldn't … be too surprised."

"Oh, Danny, when Grace hears of this she will be sick."

"Well, you aren't … going … to tell her. Th—The good news … is that he said he's … through with her." Suddenly Danny sat up straighter, concern washing over him, along with a new jolt of pain. "Wait, the train—"

"I was on it, and when you didn't show I came looking for you. I'll call Uncle Patrick and tell him what happened."

"I can … go on tonight if … wait … I'm not just singing … I will have to get myself—" He winced in pain.

"Shhh, lie back." She helped him get situated, realizing that he was mentally foggy. He had no idea how injured he really was. "Keep the ice on your eye and forehead. I'll be right back."

Going to the telephone in the kitchen, she first put in a call to have a doctor come by. The next call she placed was to Uncle Patrick.

"If, in a week, Daniel is up to it," Patrick said calmly in spite of the circumstances, "you two can meet the troupe in Buffalo. I'll call the house manager in Syracuse and let him know you won't be there; he'll have just enough time to book a 'disappointment' act. I'll send word to the train station to re-route your trunk to Buffalo." He then added, with something approaching tenderness: "This is a real shame; I'm truly sorry. If there is anything you need—anything Daniel needs—just let me know."

"Thank you, Uncle Patrick. I will."

In spite of Danny's admonition, she next placed a call to Grace, who was already in Syracuse at the boarding house where they were expected. Violet thought the girl would be somewhat heartbroken over being dumped by DiMarco, but found an unusual reserve of strength coming from the other end of the line.

"I finally feel like I'm better off without the creep," Grace said, her voice steady. "You know, I have you to thank. Your listening to me, your encouragement, just your support has meant so much to me."

Violet knew that gossip spread throughout the vaudeville world faster than a woman's hair salon, and that if she told her about Danny, she could soften the blow. "Honey, I need to tell you something. Apparently, DiMarco sent some men to rough Danny up. Now—"

"Oh, God, no!" Grace cried into the phone. "Is he okay?"

"He'll be fine," Violet said, tears forming in her own eyes, forcing her voice to sound stronger than she felt. "We are just going to skip Syracuse and meet you in Buffalo. But he's going to be fine."

The two talked a little longer, with Violet promising to update Grace on Danny's recovery. No sooner had they rung off when there was a knock at the door, signaling the arrival of medical help.

While the doctor bound Danny's ribs and put some iodine on his cuts, Violet located a pair of pajamas that the doctor could help Danny into while she and Murray left the room. The doctor had to stitch up the cut on Danny's forehead, which, although he didn't make a sound, Violet knew had to be painful. The doctor left the bedroom and told Violet that Danny would need bedrest for several days, after which he should continue to take it easy for a while. He told her to keep ice, or better yet a cold steak, on his swollen eye, and gave her a vial of small white pills. She could give Danny one if the pain became bad; the doctor had given the patient a shot that would knock him out for several hours. After paying the doctor, she made sure that Danny was comfortable and that the room was as dark as possible.

"Come on, old man," she said to Murray, who had followed her back to the bedroom. "Let's get you fed." He shadowed Violet into the kitchen, where she found the cans of Spratt's. After opening one, she served the hungry cat his belated breakfast.

Violet looked around the apartment, opening curtains and tidying up the living room. She began brushing tears off her cheeks and realized that the emotion of the morning was catching up with her. Those thugs could have *killed* Danny. She went to check on him, just to make sure he was sleeping. He looked slightly better after the doctor had cleaned him up, although the stitches in his forehead puckered the red cut. Lying there asleep, he looked like a little boy who had been in a bad fight. She could protect him, she thought as she made her way back to the living room. And she *would* protect him.

She sat on the sofa, her mind abuzz with everything she had to do. Murray looked at her as he walked by, giving her a silent meow, letting her know that whereas he was grateful for the swell meal she made him, he was going to join Danny.

"You go and take care of the patient, old man," she said, nodding toward the bedroom. Walking to the large sofa, she stretched out and was suddenly hit with a greater sense of exhaustion than she could ever remember feeling. Sleep quickly overtook her.

From the deep recesses of her sleeping mind she heard Danny's voice whispering to her:

"Violet."

At first she thought they were in their dressing room at the Bushwick; then standing in front of the Goodman door entwined in each other's arms, he murmuring her name; then on the train heading for Syracuse. But gradually she began to remember the morning's discovery of Danny, broken and bleeding.

"Violet?"

The voice didn't come from the bedroom as it should have. Instead, it quaveringly hovered above her, sounding immediate and real. She opened her eyes to see him standing over her, in his pajamas, swaying ever so slightly back and forth.

"Why aren't you in bed?" she asked as she sat up.

"I needed to get up to use the bathroom. I think my head is clearer. I'm doing better, honestly." He sat down beside her, wincing as he did so. "You don't need to stay around and experience me at my worst. Go."

"Think again," she said, resting her hand gently on his back. "Oh, Danny, I'm so sorry this happened to you."

"I'll be right as rain in no time," he said, but had to follow with, "and why is rain so right, anyway?"

"It means that you need to get back in bed, mister," she said, standing to walk him back to the bedroom.

"You need to call Patrick—" he began with a sudden sense of urgency.

"Two steps ahead of you. Everything is already taken care of, and we will meet the troupe in Buffalo—if you are up to it, that is."

"Oh, that's more than enough time." He gave her his two hands and carefully stood, beginning a slow walk back to the bedroom. "I wish right now I could do the 'Black Bottom Stomp' to prove it, but I think I'd only make matters worse."

"Come on," Violet said, smiling for the first time all day. "I just want you to get *your* bottom into that bed. I see that I'm going to have to watch your every step. Let me get you a pill and some water."

"No. Violet, you need to go home. I don't want anyone taking care of me. I can do for myself."

"Young man," she finally said, "I'm going to start taking this personally! I sure hope you weren't this bad a patient for your poor mother when you were little!"

"I took care of myself if something happened," he snapped at her.

That line gave Violet all the insight she needed. She thought of her own mother, who worked at times outside the house and was not at her most comfortable in the kitchen. But Violet had always felt that specific form of comfort and support that only a mother could offer, especially when she was ill, and realized that was something of which Danny had been deprived as a child. She needed to change her tack.

"Danny, after I get you water AND a pill, I will take my leave for a time, but I'll be back to make you dinner. After all, I need you to get better as fast as possible so that we can rejoin the circuit. And if you were left alone, you would go downhill faster than a snowball chasing another snowball."

Although still muttering about not needing her to take care of him, he dutifully got into bed, grimacing with each move.

After getting Danny arranged and checking on a few things in the apartment, Violet made yet another telephone call. She was going to have to cook for Danny, and that was completely out of her bailiwick.

"Hello, Mother," she spoke quietly into the phone.

"Violet, what's wrong? Why are you whispering?"

"Well, nothing is really wrong—"

"Then speak up, dear. I can hardly hear you."

Violet ran and closed the bedroom door, then, picking up the receiver, she turned her back to the hallway and spoke carefully into the telephone. "Danny is sick … nothing all that bad, just a head cold. But I need to cook for him, and I was wondering if you have ever made chicken soup?"

"I'm sorry Danny is ill. Be sure he gets a lot of bedrest and liquids. Lots of juice from oranges and lemons. Perhaps even a mustard plaster would be a good idea. I'm not sure about making chicken soup, but I'll go get Mary and she'll tell you."

"No, Mother, that won't be neces—" was all Violet could get out before Beryl left the telephone in search of Mary, their eccentric cook. Violet didn't relish the idea of trying to converse with the woman, even though she had known her all her life. She had never heard Mary utter more than six words at any one time. And, to make matters worse, Violet's patience was as thin as a flapper's eyebrows.

In about four minutes, the small voice of Mary came over the phone. Violet could picture her: eyes wide, hair wound tight around her head, mouth in that perpetual "O." She was probably approaching the phone like it was a snake. "H–Hello?"

"Hello, Mary. How are you?"

There was a long pause. Then came the well-thought-out reply: "Fine."

Violet decided to forge ahead. "Mary, I need to make chicken soup, and I was wondering if you could tell me how that is done."

There commenced an even longer pause than before, and then: "Well, you get a chicken."

Violet waited, in vain, to have the woman elaborate. "Yes," she said impatiently after what she thought to be a lengthy wait, "but, Mary dear, don't you also need carrots and celery, and other ingredients?"

This time Mary was quicker to respond: "You have to wring its neck first."

Violet almost hit the receiver against the wall, and she internally swore up a blue streak. Getting herself together, she ventured on. "Surely markets have chickens already, err, dressed, do they not?"

Here the longest pause yet ensued. "I get a chicken and wring its neck."

Violet couldn't take it anymore. "Thank you, Mary, you have been a great help."

The pause was so long this time Violet didn't know if the slow-witted cook was still on the line. But just as she was replacing the receiver on the hook she heard a tiny voice utter, "You're welcome."

Violet took a cab to the Goodman home. She told Aunt Mavis all she knew about what happened, and that Danny would be just fine. She bathed, changed, and went to the deli (where all modern women who can't be bothered with chickens' necks go) and ordered matzo ball soup, a loaf of fresh bread, cold cuts for sandwiches, and a pre-cooked pot roast. She also stopped by a market to get some oranges and lemons, as well as some fresh milk for Murray. Violet then headed back to Danny's apartment, which would become her command center—whether Danny liked it or not.

The days which made up the next week were quite a change from the hectic pace the team had previously kept. Danny improved greatly under Violet's care, and seemed to enjoy the simple, familiar meals she gave him. Much to her frustration, however, he continued to insist that he could take care of himself. The only change was that the protestations were beginning to sound half-hearted.

Still, she was determined to win him over completely. Violet was the kind of girl who knew how to get around most people—for their own good, of course. Then she had an inspired idea: the way to his heart (and past his stubborn head) was through his funny bone. One afternoon she walked into his bedroom holding something behind her back.

"Whatcha got there?" he asked, sitting up and looking more alert than he had in days. Violet knew that his complete and utter boredom was in her favor.

"It's my idea for a new character in our sketch. The Pirate Type." She brought her hand around and showed him the prop: an eye patch made of a small piece of steak, with a ribbon tied on both sides.

He laughed for the first time since their date, grimacing and grabbing his ribs as he did so.

"Oh, I'm sorry," Violet said as she witnessed his pain.

"No, it's fine. I want my eyepatch." And wear it he did, making pirate sounds and bad puns all the while. From that moment on he let her stay without protest. Also, on a positive note, wearing the cold beefsteak (Violet made a new patch every few hours) actually helped the swelling recede and made his face look less war-torn. The only downside to his new accoutrement was Murray's interest in examining it, and since climbing up Danny's ribs to get closer to the enticement was out of the question, the cat had to be banished from the bedroom while it was in use.

After a point Danny stubbornly refused to take the pain medication, and he was insistent about going to Buffalo and getting back to work. Violet had the doctor make a house call the day before they were scheduled to leave. The medico checked the stitches on his forehead, warning Danny that he must be careful with the wound. Danny spoke candidly with the professional about applying make-up over the stitches, and, after giving the matter some thought, the doctor retrieved a roll of surgical tape from his bag and presented it to Danny. He was to cover the wound with the thin tape, then apply make-up over it. The doctor also checked Danny's ribcage and the other cuts and bruises, and said that he was coming along very well. Violet packed Danny's personal trunk according to the list he had made, and readied their prop- and costume-filled theatrical trunk. She commented on a handsome leather grip with mesh on both sides which Danny had opened and put next to his trunk. "That is for the old man," he said. With just a hand motion toward the carrier, it was soon filled with the feline.

And so, with Danny's ribs re-bound, they were able to board the Empire State Express for the seven-hour, six-minute journey to Buffalo. Several times Violet had offered to carry Murray's grip, and just as often was turned down. Taking their seats, Danny heaved a sigh of relief when he was finally able to put the carrier on the seat between them.

"I think the old man has put on some weight," Danny said, smiling at Violet. "But he'll sleep most of the way." He took her hand and kissed it, then slid down into the seat and closed his eyes, keeping a firm hold on her hand. He was appreciative of her nursing skills, and, in fact, had never experienced such tender care. He knew how lucky he was to have her, but he couldn't allow himself to wholly trust the situation. After all, vaudeville partners had a way of taking off with little or no notice, and she might tire of him. But he would have to work out the emotional part of his life at a different time. At the moment, he just needed sleep.

They were lucky to have good weather—in the low forties—throughout the whole journey. Violet had only been on a train a few times in her life, and she silently dreaded the trip. The last time she traveled—from Seattle to Chicago to New York—the experience had been difficult. But this time out she knew things would be different. It was November, so, even with the mild weather they were experiencing, the windows would be closed, preventing the soot and smoke from coming into the train itself. It was cold inside the train car, but that only gave her a reason to snuggle up, albeit gingerly, to Danny. They sipped wonderful hot chocolate and ate delicious ham-and-butter sandwiches in the dining car. And the deafening noise of the wheels and whistles was merely a privacy curtain for their personal conversations.

They arrived in Buffalo on time and had no trouble at all locating their luggage, and in short order their theatrical trunk was on its way to Keith's Grand Theatre. They took a moonlight-blue Ford taxi to the boarding house where they would spend the next five days when not at the theatre. Danny assured her that this was the best place in the vicinity that catered specifically to vaudevillians.

"The problem is that a lot of people—even in big cities—still view show people as social pariahs. So we can't always stay at the best places. This one is clean, at least. One place where I stayed had an ant problem that was so bad each bedpost was placed in a dish of oxalic acid to keep them off you at night!"

"Oh, that's horrible!" Violet cringed.

They drew up to a nice-looking large house with a sign out front: The Cloverhouse Room & Board. They had the cabbie deliver Danny's trunk to the lobby. A thin, unsmiling woman checked them in. Her hair was pulled so tightly back into a small bun that it threatened to vanish entirely into her high collar, and her face was the sort of plain which caused all others using that adjective to be considered comely. She wore a dark dress of a long-past era, folding her arms in front of her sagging bosom while cross-examining the latest guests with a reproachful air. "What're yer names?" she asked tersely.

"Danny O'Brien, ma'am. And this is my partner, Miss Violet Williams."

The proprietress gave Danny's bruised face a hard look, and then glanced at Violet. "So you ain't married, eh? Shame. I have a nice, big room—but for a *married* couple. Even has a bath."

"That's fine, thank you—we'll take two smaller rooms," Danny said. He paid the woman ten dollars up front.

"I'm Mrs. Main. Got any troubles, just let me know," she said, her expression softening as she looked at Danny—and the cash.

"Thank you, you are very kind," Danny said, flashing his dimples. "And, I want to be honest, I have a cat. But he will cause neither you nor your house any harm. I guarantee it."

"I have a friend, Mrs. Kruckshank, runs a boarding house. She told me about a feller with a cat. Said he was okay. Big tipper. You him?"

"Yes, I remember Mrs. Kruckshank. I enjoyed staying at her place."

"Well, it's okay with me," she said, smiling and holding out her palm. Danny placed two more bills in it. "And the trunk for your party arrived this morning."

"Thank you. If someone could help us get my trunk up to my room, I would be most grateful."

"Vinnie!" the woman turned and yelled, "Luggage!"

They made their way to the second floor where their rooms had been prepared. As Danny had promised, Violet's room was neat and clean. And, more importantly, her trunk stood off to one side. She was extremely grateful for Uncle Patrick's ability to get things done.

"Dinner will be at five o'clock sharp," Danny said. "That will give us just enough time afterward to get to the theatre and sign in."

"Great. I'll be downstairs at five," Violet said.

Danny smiled and went into his room, a smaller one right next door. A short, put-upon-seeming man—Vinnie, he presumed— brought up the trunk, and, upon receiving a tip, merely grunted.

Danny's next priority was to get Murray settled, then he would arrange his trunk. Murray, who had been released from his travel- ing case, had already found a spot on a chair that was getting full sunshine. Danny opened his trunk, cringing with the stabbing pain in his sides, and examined the contents. He traveled with very few changes of clothes and accessories, but had one of the heaviest trunks on the circuit. The reason was the ball of fluff now sleeping on the sun-soaked chair. Danny carefully removed the bowls he used for cat food and liquid refreshment, a few cans of Spratt's (over a dozen of which he could keep in one drawer), a 12" x 18" graniteware enamel baking pan, a kitchen frying strainer, and a small sack of sand. He also removed several sheets of blank newsprint and put them in a corner of the room. On top of that he placed the pan, which he then slowly filled with sand. At home, he had a fellow who made a special deliv- ery to Danny's place with bags of sand. On the road, however, he brought enough to start out, and then had to forage through the towns for more. He knew other pet owners used dirt, shredded newsprint, sawdust, and fireplace ashes, the last of which he couldn't even imag- ine. But the sand worked well for both. He filled one bowl with water (not having milk handy), and the other with Murray's dinner. And then—completely exhausted by that brief bit of work—Danny finally lay down and closed his eyes, attempting to catch up on some much- needed sleep.

Violet moved her trunk to one side of her room, opening it and deciding that it was best to live out of it rather than unpack anything into the lone bureau which stood against the far wall. The bed looked comfortable, and Violet sat on it for a time, and then stretched out. It would be just fine. She looked around the room and noticed, quite prominently on the wall to her right, a huge photograph in an ornate frame. The photo was old; taken probably thirty years earlier, of a careworn woman. The old lady glowered down at Violet, who suddenly felt very small in the bed. Clad all in black, with a black cap of intricate lace atop a head of thinning gray hair, this severe-looking individual appeared as though she had just had a disagreement with someone and won the fight but carried the aftereffects as deep fissures on her angular face. Violet glanced around the room again and thought about Danny, hoping that he was asleep and comfortable in his room. She looked back at the old woman and wondered exactly who she had been (for it was doubtful that she could still be counted among the living) and, more importantly, if her silk night robe could completely cover that dreadful picture.

They joined the other boarders, and their hosts, for dinner. Violet took one look at Mr. Main and recognized the likeness to the apparent relative taking up wall space in her room—if he had been wearing a black lace head cap he could have passed for that bitter old woman. He looked up from his place-setting, scowled at Violet who offered a small smile in return, and proceeded to spear the food on his plate. The only time Mr. Main changed expression was when one of the guests spilled hot coffee in her lap: his almost-toothless grin followed by an unsettling, bronchitic laugh made Violet shudder. The meal—such as it was—featured dry meatloaf, flavorless mashed potatoes, and overly sweetened, mushy carrots. Violet could hardly choke down a few bites, but Danny cleaned his plate with ease. He knew that, whether the food was superb or awful, it was important to show your gratitude by eating anything and everything that was placed before you. Vaudevillians had a bad enough reputation—some troupes were known to condemn the food they were given and disappear under cover of night, so as to avoid paying their tab. Granted, this practice was limited to a few small-timers and hack melodrama companies, but boarding house proprietors had long memories, and were none too quick to forgive. Danny, being from a long line of traveling minstrels, was on a one-man campaign to shine up that tarnished image for every civilian with whom he came in contact. He was proud of his heritage, and this was his way of demonstrating that pride.

With the repast now consumed (the meal's end was signaled by the serving of a burnt, yet somehow undercooked, apple pie), Violet took Danny aside.

"How could you eat that?" she whispered hoarsely. "It was *dreadful!*"

"I've had worse," he said with a shrug.

They walked outside, finding a small garden out back.

"So you've never stayed here before?" Violet asked.

"No," he said, shaking his head. "The place I had always stayed in Buffalo was Mrs. Kruckshank's. She decided that she would no longer cater to show people. Apparently, she could get more money from the regular tourists, who would gladly plunk down four bits to see an actor on the stage, but didn't want to sleep under the same roof with one. I would love that perception to change."

"Well," Violet interjected, "I know Mrs. Main really appreciated your appetite!"

"I also smuggled some of the meatloaf up to Murray. He liked it."

"That," Violet said, "explains a lot."

From the parlor emanated the sounds of piano music, with those gathered there giving voice to the sweet old tune "The End of a Perfect Day." Violet and Danny strolled around the grounds arm in arm, enjoying the colorful autumnal flowers, the delicate scents of nature, and the setting sun of the soft twilight.

⋅→⫘ ⫘←⋅

When they got to Keith's Grand Theatre they went immediately to the stage-door entrance and signed in. They heard a commotion in front of the dressing-room area and saw a couple of old friends: Sally and Thomas. Sally came lumbering up to them, barking and carrying on.

"Hiya, girl! How's the house?" Violet asked as she saw Thomas following along, looking rather irritated.

"She's in a mood tonight. It's always the—" Thomas stopped when he saw his friend's battered face. "Gee, Danny, are you okay?"

"I'm fine—Vi didn't like my delivery last night, and this was her review," Danny said, quickly trying to divert attention away from himself. After a small wink to Violet, who understood, he continued. "Now, what were you saying?"

"Just that I got Madam out of her tub earlier than she wanted, and she's been giving me a hard time all during practice. I don't know how she will do tonight."

"Oh, come on, Tommy," Danny said. "You know she's a pro. When the curtain goes up she'll be great as always."

"I know," Thomas said with a sigh. "She just likes to give me fits. I think I'm getting ulcers."

Violet smiled sympathetically. She addressed Sally: "I understand, girl, but we have to be *nice* to our co-stars every once in a while."

Sally looked at Violet, then put a flipper over one eye. This made everybody laugh—especially Thomas and Danny.

"See you around," Danny said to Thomas, then took Violet's hand.

They found their trunk and got out the first costumes they needed, then took them up to the dressing room. They had devised a plan of attack: Violet would do her make-up first, while Danny conferred with the stage manager, after which he would change into his costume. Then Violet would change while Danny did his make-up. They found, not surprisingly, that they shared a wonderful camaraderie during this before-show time. This helped Violet get her nervousness under control, allowing her to look forward to each performance. Danny knew from experience that a relaxed performer is a much better performer.

After slowly dressing, Danny sat at the make-up table, opened his kit, and withdrew the roll of surgical tape the doctor had given him. He cut a two-inch-long piece, placed it carefully over the stitches, and tapped it down securely. He then began to sponge greasepaint over the top and to his bruises and cuts, applying a thicker layer of paint than usual, and working the area more gently. Danny knew that he could make his face presentable; it was his ability to move that worried him. Violet, knowing what was going through Danny's mind, came up with an idea.

"You know, you could make your entrances more slowly than we had before, I'll fill in longer, and, instead of pulling you onto the desk, I could just pull you close by your lapels."

"Good ideas. I'll just go out and do the best I can."

Violet looked into the mirror at Danny as he completed his make-up. She was amazed at the job he did covering the wounds.

"My word, you almost look like *Danny*," she said with a smile.

"I wish I felt like him," he said as he stood, grimacing and walked to the door.

Because of Danny's slowness, the timing of their routine simply wasn't on the mark. Luckily, Violet saved the sketch by filling in with extra business to give Danny more time to change: She juggled for a longer time. She took more chances with lengthening her bits and went for more laughs. She added a couple of pre-planned lines of dialogue to her conversations with Mabel on the telephone and, luckily, the audience was a receptive one. Violet had gained even more confidence from this impromptu situation, and her timing was sharper; her singing, stronger. She loved this life, and it showed in her jubilant approach to her character. Danny was incredibly grateful for his partner's ability to handle the majority of the sketch, and tried as hard as he could to hide his flinches whenever he twisted his torso.

The bill for this week included a new performer, one well known to Danny. Violet was honored to meet Harry E. Humphrey, who gave a melodramatic reading of Frank Deprez's poem of Western romance, *Lasca*. He was charming, and explained to Violet his choice of material in that both Western themes and dramatic recitations were currently enjoying great popularity on the vaudeville stage. She complimented him on his stirring performance, and he, in turn, told her she had a winning way with the audience.

They also made a point of going to Grace Manning's dressing room on the third floor.

"Oh, Danny, are you alright?" she asked, tears ready to spring from her red eyes, a quiet hiccup forming.

"Sure, honey, I'm none the worse. Don't worry a bit about me."

Violet hugged her and asked how she was doing.

"Actually, I feel much better this week," Grace said, a genuine smile forming on her lips. "I haven't heard from Jerry lately, and that suits me." Grace took both Danny and Violet's hands. "You two have been just swell to me. I couldn't have had the strength to go through this without your understanding and support. Thanks."

"Oh, honey, that's what a show business family is for," Danny said.

After talking about each other's upcoming plans, Violet and Danny left.

When they arrived back at the boarding house, Violet told Danny that he should go straight to bed and sleep as much as possible, a command, he said, he was more than happy to follow. She then thought of the sacrifice he had made that evening to perform their act. Turning to him by her doorway, she added, "And, you know, I think you are amazing. To even attempt what you did tonight—that takes real courage."

"What? *This* bag of broken bones?" Danny asked with a tired smile.

"The exact one," Violet said. "Now, goodnight," and saying that, she leaned toward him, her lips just brushing his.

In no time they had completed their run in Buffalo and were Boston bound. The morning they were to board the train found Danny slowly moving about his room trying to pack his trunk, feeling a bit tired as a result of pushing himself to reach at least his C-game. Knowing that he needed some assistance, Danny knocked on Violet's door. She opened it, looking as fresh as if she were on vacation.

"Could you help me with my trunk? I seem—" Danny began, then stopped when he saw the robe-draped photograph on the wall. "What is *that*?"

"Oh, I almost forgot!" Violet said, swiftly going to the frame and removing the robe. When Danny saw the glaring old woman he looked at Violet who grimaced a bit, then at the robe in her hands, then back to the austere painting, then finally back to the girl who appeared embarrassed for getting caught. Between the feeling of the photograph and Violet's expression lay one of the funniest situations Danny had ever seen. He began to chuckle, then gave way to a full-bodied laugh. He laughed harder than he had in a couple of weeks, holding his tender ribs, tears running down his cheeks. At one point he even grimaced a bit, but the laughter continued.

"Serves you right for laughing at me," Violet huffed. She, however, had to admit that she loved seeing him acting more like Danny than he had in a long time. "Come on, let's get you packed."

Boston turned out to be an even friendlier town toward vaudevillians than Buffalo, and Danny was healing quickly. They stayed in a hotel at which he had lodged many times. The manager rolled out the proverbial red carpet for Danny and Murray, and Violet was gratified to see this wonderful reception.

The food that was offered in restaurants close to their hotel was exceptional, especially compared to their previous fare. They particularly enjoyed succulent Irish stew at the Green Dragon Tavern.

Arriving at the theatre early, Danny slipped in a side door while Violet decided to see Keith's New Theatre from the outside-in. Like many vaudeville houses, this one adapted the excessive and opulent architectural styles of Southern European palaces to create an atmosphere with few precedents in American cities. The front of the theatre featured a wealth of decorative detail. Wrought-iron railings, stained-glass windows, incandescent lighting, a Moorish dome, sculpted gargoyles, arches, and marble pillars bespoke gentility, elegance, and success to all passersby.

"Excuse me, ma'am, are you the woman working with Danny O'Brien?" came a small voice behind her. Violet turned around to find a cadre of young girls. "From the skit, you are, aren't you, working with Danny?" the girl asked again.

"Yes, I am. Have you girls seen the show?" Violet asked.

"No, but we will tonight! We recognized you from a picture in *Theatre Magazine*." All of the girls seemed to be in the same kind of outfit, a sort of uniform of young girls: loose, dropped-waist dresses in bright colors, and cloche hats with rich, unusual trimmings. One girl's hat was clustered with ornamental red cherries which dipped to her shoulder, matching her dark lipstick perfectly. They appeared to Violet like a colorful flock of canaries.

"Wonderful!" Violet enthused. "I really hope you enjoy it—I think you will!"

"What is he like?" a dreamy-eyed canary queried, her hands reaching out to Violet in a plea for information.

"*Danny?*" Violet asked.

"Yes!" they chorused.

"Well, he is very kind and sweet, and, well, just marvelous!"

You'd have thought that Violet had just given each girl a hundred-dollar bill. They chirruped and tittered, sighing and moving closer to the receding Violet.

"Would you sign our books?" pleaded one canary.

"Of course," Violet said, cheerfully. This was her first experience dealing with fans close up, and she was pleased. To think someone wanted *her* autograph! She was almost giddy.

"Put down that you are the one working with Danny," the first girl said, handing over her autograph book. The other canaries cheeped in agreement.

Violet laughingly joked, "Do you want *my* name?"

"Oh," the flock quickly conferred. "Not really. Just write down that you work with Danny O!"

Violet forced a smile, considered for a moment telling them that Danny had dandruff and fallen arches, decided against it, and made her way through all the proffered autograph books: "I WORK WITH DANNY O. vcw"

The canaries thanked her, and then asked if she knew when Danny would be arriving.

"He should show up pretty soon, I'd say," she said, a fixed smile now firmly in place. And with that, the flock fluttered away to stand vigil in the back alley.

Violet knocked on the front door, and was admitted by one of the ushers. She looked around the gorgeous theatre and decided to talk with the tall, militaristic young attendant about just what she was seeing. In giving her a tour, he pointed out that the lobby and foyer were filled with white-and-green marble, burnished brass, leather-upholstered furniture, large plate mirrors, and enormous panel paintings by the Roman artist Tojetti. In fact, the usher noted, the late Mr. Keith had commissioned Tojetti to create several panel paintings above the huge and heavily gilded proscenium arch inside the auditorium. These were made to complement the ornate white-and-gold balconies, twelve private boxes, and walls of green and rose, which were painted to take on a faux brocaded silk effect. Violet noted that the design of Keith's New Theatre overlooked not a single, exquisite detail. From the elaborate hand-painted ceiling to "the finest toilet and retiring rooms in the country," as the usher told her they advertised, to the number of fragrant floral displays; this was truly one of the premier vaudeville houses in the country. The theatre offered "the purest artesian well water" and writing materials which were furnished at no charge to patrons—gold pens and monogrammed paper, with embossed envelopes. Everything conveyed a feeling of abundance, coupled with elegance. The usher mentioned to Violet that even the boiler room featured a thick carpet and a whitewashed coal bin. She was impressed, which, of course, had been Keith and Albee's intention. She thanked the young man for the tour, and made off on her own.

Violet looked around the vast lobby as if she were an audience member, not a performer—after all, it had only been a short time

since that was the case. She knew just what a thrilling experience it
would be for those who passed through these gorgeous halls. She then
noticed a sign which had been posted for the theatregoers:

```
Gentlemen will kindly avoid carrying
cigars or cigarettes in their mouths
while in the building, and greatly
oblige.

Gentlemen will kindly avoid the stamp-
ing of feet and pounding of canes on
the floor. All applause is best shown by
clapping of hands.

Please don't talk during acts, as it
annoys those about you, and prevents
a perfect hearing of the entertain-
ment.

The Management
```

Violet smiled, thinking of the signs posted in the backstage areas
for performers. The management certainly wanted to control both the
front *and* the back of the house!

She quickly made her way past the lobby and into the auditorium,
watching as even more uniform-clad ushers cleaned the carpets and
made sure all would be ready for the evening's performance.

Running up the steps on the left side of the stage and into backstage, she saw Danny speaking with the man who must be the manager. She dutifully signed the call sheet, glanced at the postings on the
bulletin board, then made her way to their dressing room.

Opening the door, she stopped short. A scantily clad blonde reclined suggestively on the sofa, puffing away at a cigarette in a long
ivory holder.

"Oh, I'm sorry," the girl said barely above a whisper, rising languidly and approaching the door, "I thought this was Danny O'Brien's dressing room."

"It *is*," Violet said icily.

The blonde slowly gave Violet the once-over, made a barely audible snorting sound, then took another languorous draw on the extended cigarette. She blew the smoke out in Violet's direction, her red lips remaining pursed long after the smoke had made its way to its intended target.

"Oh, well, just tell him that Thelma shimmied by—he'll know what to do," she leered. She wiggled out into the hallway, followed by the stench of strong, cheap perfume. She looked like the kind of girl who changed *smoldering* from an adjective to a verb.

Violet was indignant. Danny had mentioned a girl by the name of Thelma, with whom he had a fling a year ago. But Violet had to wonder if *this* Thelma was indeed from the past—or was she his date after tonight's show? Surely not—not with his ribs in their present condition. Only ... the problem was that she and Danny were not really anything besides professional partners. Not officially. Danny had never said he had any kind of feelings for her, nor had he said anything about a future beyond this run. He had kissed her, that is true, but perhaps he was just making time. He had shared a lot with her; probably, to Danny, they were just friends and, as she had been warned, he seemed compelled to flirt with every girl he met. She felt a black cloud forming over her. At that moment, she didn't want to do the act. Still, she was a trouper. She would definitely go on, do her lines and sing her dumb little song. But she didn't have to like it.

She heatedly slapped on her make-up, getting black lash bead smeared on her cheeks several times, and yanked on her costume. Using the same force to tug on her new silk hosiery, she immediately put a run in the right one and began another internal blue streak. Luckily, she had a spare and had just pulled it on when Danny came in. And to make matters worse, he was humming. Like a happy man.

"Hi, honey!" he said perkily. "Did you get a gander at this place? Ain't it a beaut? I think it's one of the fanciest on the tour. And you know, I think I am really doing better. I bet I'm almost back to my old timing tonight." He crossed through the small room to behind the dressing screen, and began carefully shedding his clothes. Not hearing any response after a while, Danny poked his head around the partition. "Vi, you okay?"

"Just *peachy*," she answered emphatically, crossing her arms in front of her. *Feeling better enough for a date with Thelma?* she thought.

Danny shook his head and continued dressing—and resumed that blasted hum.

Violet couldn't stand it anymore. "*Who* is Thelma?" she asked in a tone which was far shriller than she had intended.

"Thelma?" Danny thought for a moment. "Oh, there is a girl named Thelma I went out with a few times a year ago. Why?"

"Well, she just slithered by and asked for you." Violet was beginning to feel ridiculous, but couldn't help herself.

"Oh, did she?" Danny mumbled. He came around the screen, sat on the sofa, and slowly put on his hose. "She must be here in whichever tab show she's dancing with now."

This, for some reason, made Violet even angrier. She stormed out of the small room, ran down the stairs, and stood in a quiet area of the wings. She knew Danny had a past, after all, that he had dated quite a few girls, in fact. But he didn't even have the decency to be embarrassed or ashamed—*or dead*. Being angry about this situation was silly, she comprehended, but she couldn't help it. She also realized that it really wasn't Thelma who was upsetting her so. Well, she would be damned—yes, *damned*—if she would allow him to turn her into a jealous woman. It was time to start acting like a New Woman, and she had already begun by think-swearing, and that felt pretty dang, *damn*, good. After all, it was 1925, for goodness sake. What a *fool* she would have been had she told him she loved him! She was angry with herself for taking this relationship so seriously. Well, that was about to change—and how!

When he caught up with her, she turned and made a point of beaming at him, practicing her new I-really-don't-care-I'm-just-here-to-have-fun attitude. He looked at her as if she had just told him that she had walked on the moon.

Women, he thought.

They took their places and the orchestra leader signaled the downbeat: the quaint strains of "Love Me, and the World Is Mine" echoed through the packed auditorium. The two glided through the routine without a hitch, with Danny's timing much improved. But he knew he hadn't heard the last of what was on Violet's mind.

After their curtain call, Violet shot ahead of Danny and made for their dressing room. She ran a Pullman cloth under the hot tap until it was steaming. Lying down on the small couch, she put the cloth over her face to melt the wax off her eyelashes. While waiting, she overheard Danny talking to a girl down the hall. *Thelma*. She froze and strained to hear the conversation.

"Oh, come on, Danny boy," she overheard the girl say in a whining tone, "let's just go out for a little fun, grab some laughs, like the old days." And then Thelma added, "I'll kiss it and make it *all* better."

"No, thanks, not interested," was all Danny said.

"Why not, lover?" she sniveled.

"Because I *have* a girl. So leave me alone, Thelma."

Danny was angry that this girl clung to him the way she did, like they were a couple. Thelma was so *needy*. He took a deep breath and got himself together. Only then did he walk down the short hallway and into the dressing room, closing the door with purpose. He looked at Violet lying on the couch, head covered with a steaming towel. She was probably giving him the cold shoulder again. He couldn't help it: he walked over and slowly lifted the cloth. Underneath, he found a blotchy, make-up smeared, sweetly smiling Violet. He carefully set the cloth back and walked behind the screen.

WOMEN!

CHAPTER ELEVEN

THE DECISION

November 1925

T he next few stops on the route went just as planned. Erie, Cleveland, and Columbus had provided wonderful accommodations, great theatres, and marvelous audiences. Having gone to a doctor to remove the stitches in his forehead, Danny no longer had to use the surgical tape, which made the job of applying his make-up much easier. One snag that did arise was in Cleveland when, at the train station, the porters couldn't find the team's theatrical trunk. All hands were on deck to try to locate it, and Danny had the sinking feeling that perhaps it was still in Erie, at that station. The team went to the theatre where, twenty minutes before they were scheduled to go on, the trunk finally showed up. They were grateful, but, as a result, began their sketch without their normal spot-on timing. Danny, the one who was rushing, realized his error and slowed down before morphing into his third character.

At the theatre they were greeted by Sally and Thomas, and also met some new acts. They had the pleasure of working with Harry Richman, a singer/dancer with a larger-than-life personality and performance style. And it was here that they met a vocalist by the name of Leonardo Rossi, an Italian tenor who had received wide acclaim in Europe as an opera virtuoso. He had come to America and was immediately snapped up by the Keith-Albee management. They knew that women would fall for his exotically dark, European good looks (he was called "The Valentino of Opera"), and that all theatregoers would be amazed by his singing virtuosity. Indeed, he was a popular draw on the circuit, with female fans practically falling over themselves just to get his autograph. In fact, the new sensation was co-headlining the bill with Danny and Violet.

Violet's initial encounter with Signor Rossi came when she was exiting into the wings, directly after finishing their routine.

"May I, please-a to tell you, how a-perfect you are a-look tonight, *Viola*," he said in his alluring broken English. He took her hand and kissed it, palm-side up (just like Valentino), gazing upon her with his piercing ice-blue eyes. He then simply held her hand in his, smiling down upon her like a mythological seducer. She stood immovable, noticing how his thick, curly, dark hair curved around his high white collar. He wore a black tuxedo effortlessly, gracefully, as if a tuxedo was simply what a man *should* wear at all times. Violet inhaled his rich, spicy scent and felt a bit lightheaded. She kept her hand in his and, staring into his hypnotic eyes that rendered her unable to come up with something—*anything*—to say, slowly become aware that far too long a time had passed and that she was starting to look foolish. Violet finally opened her mouth to speak.

"Danny O'Brien," came a strong voice in back of her. A hand shot out in front of Violet's face, obscuring her view of the Italian, and forcing her to let go of his hand. Leonardo, looking slightly disappointed, shook Danny's hand. "We're glad to have you on the bill," Danny continued, angling in and moving Violet to the side.

"Pleased-a to make-a the bill with you," he said to Danny, then glancing back to Violet, "We will have-a talking again soon-a, *mio bella Viola*?"

"Thank you," was all Violet could say. She walked with Danny up to their dressing room, and sat at the table, dipping into the Ponds jar to remove her make-up.

"Nice guy," Danny said, looking at Violet. "And he *is* a great singer."

She nodded, not saying a word. What Danny had said about not having a jealous bone in his body must be true, Violet disappointingly realized.

Thanksgiving rolled around on Thursday, November 26, and the vaudeville world barely took notice. Shows went on as usual, and most performers were glad to be away from family during what could often become a stressful holiday. A lot of relatives didn't approve of the gypsy-like aspect of a vaudevillian's life, and the performers were loath to hear about it every time they attended a family reunion.

Violet decided that she would put together something for their fellow performers that afternoon, something which would be a special way to observe the holiday. She had arranged with a local restaurant to deliver a full Thanksgiving meal, which the establishment was more than happy to do given the fact that Violet prepaid (and included a generous tip) for a feast designed to feed forty people. This restaurant had been preparing the same meal since 1905 for the holiday:

> Oysters on the half-shell with cocktail sauce in pepper shells
> Radishes, celery, salted nuts
>
> Clear consommé with tapioca
>
> Filet of flounder with pimentos and olives;
> Dressed cucumbers
>
> Roast turkey; cranberry jelly in small molds;
> Creamed chestnuts; Glazed sweet-potatoes
>
> Cider frappé in orange-cups

Quail in bread croustades;
Dressed lettuce

Mince pie
Cheese with almonds; Wafers;
Angel parfait in glasses; Small cakes

Violet had the stagehands clear and reset the backstage area by 4:00, and set up as many tables for dining as could be found, creating one long bench covered by table cloths supplied by the restaurant. Chairs were brought in from dressing rooms and backstage lounge areas. Every performer and stagehand was invited, as were any lost souls who didn't have somewhere else to go. Violet was excited by the dozens of people who showed up, serving themselves from the huge buffet, and then taking their places around the massive table. Violet put Danny and Grace to work serving drinks—lemonade, iced tea, or coffee—which they did with the skill of professional waiters. From all around the stage could be heard the merry sounds of knives and forks being put to good use, laughter, and the familiar patter accompanying stories of the trade. Violet had never been happier, feeling that she had actually contributed something to her new family of vaudevillians. It meant a lot to the theatre folks, and almost everyone, including Leonardo, came up after the repast to thank her for creating this event. Standing in front of her, flashing a warm and inviting smile, he once again held her in his compelling gaze.

"This-a Giving-thanks-day, as you say, it—" he offered, his eyebrows knitting with concentration, then gradually giving way to the relaxed confidence of returning to one's intrinsic language. "*Era davvero delizioso. E tu sei molto bella.*"

"You are welcome?" Violet said rather loudly and slowly, as if this would aid in the translation.

With that, he smiled, reached for her hand and gently kissed it, then turned and walked away. A short while later, while packing up the excess food for some of the grateful performers, Violet noticed that Leonardo and Danny were talking in serious, whispered tones. Leonardo looked over at her and smiled, which made her blush, and she quickly turned back to the job at hand. They were probably just talking opera, she assumed, but Danny didn't look as if he was enjoying the conversation very much.

At the conclusion of the festivities, the stage was hastily cleared as the audience members, many of whom appeared to be stuffed from their own family gatherings, began to file in, eventually filling the house. Everything went well for that evening's show, except that the troupe of acrobats had to work carefully around some spilled cranberry jelly that had somehow been overlooked by the cleaning crew.

Violet lay in bed that night with a huge sense of satisfaction and gratitude that she could do something to show these wonderful folks how much they meant to her. She sighed contentedly and drifted off to a deep sleep.

Danny, on the other hand, tossed and turned all night. Murray, usually comfortably snuggled up by Danny's side, had jumped up on a chair to give the restless sleeper a wide berth. Just thinking of how Violet was looking into that Italian clown's eyes made him mad—*damned* mad. He also knew enough Italian to put together that he had told her she was beautiful. Told her—right to her face. Did she understand him? Could she be taken in by his cheesy act? Stupid tuxedo and accent. And her name is VIOLET, not *viola*. Danny had seen Leonardo flirting with the other girls, although he didn't pay them *half* the attention he did Violet. *His Vi.* To think, this—this Italian even had the nerve of asking him if he and Vi were serious or engaged. Imagine the gall! And kissing her palm, well, that was going way overboard, to the point of indecency. Did Violet feel … anything? He couldn't really tell. Danny turned over, hitting his pillow with his fist, not caring that his sudden movement sent pain rippling through his body from his still-healing ribs. He preferred that pain to what was going on in his mind. No, he thought, not by a long shot would he let anyone near her. He finally sat up, running his hands through his hair, feeling a shadow of a headache forming. He wondered just how much longer he could take it. He may just have to do something drastic.

The next few performances sailed by quickly, and soon enough O'Brien & Williams were in Detroit with several well-received shows under their belts. They found some of the audiences less than stellar, but discovered that they could hold their rhythm and make it through the routine without milking the laughs the way they had grown accustomed to doing. What didn't help (in fact, what didn't help one little bit, Violet thought) was that for the past week Danny had not been himself. He was constantly distracted; alternately demonstrative and aloof, hot and cold. To be fair, Violet reasoned, he was always professional and thoughtful, but she knew that something was going on in that thick head of his, and she was afraid that she knew what it was.

Thelma.

Violet was concerned that, even though she had heard Danny tell the chorine that it was over between them, he might be having second thoughts. Did he love this girl? Was there more to their relationship than met the eye—or than he made it sound? Maybe Danny merely felt that he owed Violet and couldn't, for the time being, openly date. But Thelma wasn't on this leg of the tour, not yet, at least. Violet didn't want him to stop dating this woman if he *loved* her, certainly not on her account. But, at the same time, she knew that she really cared for Danny and that seeing him with another woman—well, it would destroy her. She decided to wait it out, knowing that he would tip his hand sooner or later. And, opting for the former as Danny usually did, it was one evening while Violet was applying her make-up for the final show in Detroit that Danny came rushing into their dressing room.

"Hope we have a decent crowd tonight," Violet said while beading her eyelashes. She had completed the right one and was just starting the left when he dropped the bomb.

"Violet, I have an idea and I want you to hear me out," he said in a rush, pacing the small dressing room.

Before turning away from the mirror she realized what a strange sight she was, with mismatching eyes, but this was no time for vanity. She had never seen Danny this agitated. She felt unnerved, but knew that she had to remain as calm as possible—at least outwardly. "I'm listening."

"I've been thinking about this, and we should get married. To-morrow morning at the Detroit City Hall. Then we can go to Chicago and, well, things will be much smoother. We can get a nice room with a bath, and it would—"

"Okay," Violet said quietly.

"—make traveling so much, wait, wh–what did you say?"

"I said, fine. I think it's a good idea, too." Having said that, Violet, the very picture of nonchalance, returned to her make-up application. At least, that was how she appeared on the outside; on the inside, her stomach was doing a belly flop, and her right hand was shaking so badly that she had to steady it with the left just to finish applying the warm beading wax. A small smile formed on her lips. Ha!—*so there, Thelma*, she thought. We all know to whom Danny's heart belongs now.

But he still hadn't said those words; *that* phrase which seems al-most impossible to be formed by some male lips. She had to wonder: *did he*?

They arrived at the Detroit City Hall exactly at 8:00 the next morning, just as the doors were opening. Violet wore her light blue traveling en-semble, and Danny wore his white linen suit. They took along Thomas to be Danny's Best Man, and Grace to stand up for Violet. Grace shed more tears than Violet, which broke the bride's heart.

The ceremony was simple, straightforward, and quick. Danny had convinced a jeweler to open early that morning of December 12, 1925, and secured two gold bands for the service. And, in true Danny style, he fudged the waiting time on the marriage license by slipping the court reporter a Hamilton. And so, by the power vested in the clerk by the state of Michigan, county of Wayne, they were pronounced O'Brien & O'Brien (only offstage; professionally they were keeping their original billing). Danny took a deep breath and, turning to Violet, gave her a sweet, lingering kiss. She thought this was a good omen, and beamed just thinking of the life which lay ahead.

The couple stopped by Western Union to telegraph Violet's family, Danny's mother, and Uncle Patrick. The latter gave Danny pause, but it would have to be done. Now the two weren't just friends, or even agent and client; they were uncle and nephew. Danny thought that, after the initial tirade, Patrick would actually take to the idea. Even so, he was glad that he wouldn't be there when the telegram arrived.

The vaudeville troupe taking this leg of the journey scrambled on the train just as it was leaving the magnificent Michigan Central Station. Danny noted that the Italian who seemed to prompt this latest turn of events had, in fact, been booked in a different theatre. *Good,* he thought. The clown was already out of their lives. Making a stop in the men's lavatory, he looked at his tired reflection in the large mirror as he washed his hands. He paused, wet hands reaching for a towel. A tiny notion scratched at the back of his brain. He hadn't been hasty with the whole marriage thing, had he?

Violet was comfortably settled in their private drawing room, something which Danny had arranged for their nine-hour trip. She looked out the window at the buildings of concrete and steel which eventually fell away to pastureland. Murray loved the private space as he could stretch his legs during the ride instead of being relegated to his grip. He ended up in Violet's lap, purring vociferously as she scratched his chin. "If I could, I would purr right along with you," she said to the contented cat. Pure bliss.

Upon hearing the news of the impromptu wedding, shouts of congratulations could be heard from various sections of the Pullman, and each performer had to stop by to shake Danny's hand and give the bride a kiss. The couple invited Grace to join them, which she did happily. Thomas, who had checked in on Sally in her special crate in the baggage car, brought them a bottle of champagne and some glasses.

"From my bootlegger," Thomas smiled conspiratorially. Holding his handkerchief over the cork, he popped it, and a small stream of bubbles ran down the side of the iced bottled. He poured the sparkling wine into four champagne saucers, then, after handing a drink to each of the four, he raised his glass in a toast: "To the newlyweds! May your marriage outlive your act, and may your act outlive radio."

Danny and Violet hooted, toasted, and took a sip of the bubble water. The four friends talked and laughed together for a long time, celebrating life and the joy of a memorable afternoon. After some time, Violet and Grace excused themselves to freshen up. Thomas and Danny chatted about old times, but after a while Thomas looked at his friend with a serious expression. "Danny, you know I have really come to care for Vi. I wouldn't want to see her hurt. Some guys, well, they only marry their partners to keep the act together. Please say that ain't so."

"Tommy," Danny started hesitantly, shifting uncomfortably on the seat. "I, of course, want Vi to be in the act for a long time, and maybe I'm afraid she'll leave. Maybe I'm being selfish. I'll be honest; in some ways I don't know why I married her—although jealousy could be a reason, I don't know. I told myself I would never marry, but here we are ..."

The two were so deep in conversation that they didn't hear the footsteps outside the room. What Violet didn't stay to hear was the most important part of Danny's answer: "The only thing I *do* know is that before I met Vi I was ready to cash in my chips and walk away from everything. She has given me life; she makes me laugh and enjoy work again. I would do anything to keep her safe and to make her as happy as she makes me."

But in the cramped train lavatory, Violet huddled in a small chair, tears streaming down her face.

"I can't believe it," Grace said, crouching beside Violet and rubbing her back. "I *know* he loves you."

"I know he loves our *act*," Violet snapped. "O'Brien & Williams. *That* is why he married me—you heard him say it! I know he feels obligated to me, but I think that maybe he loves Thelma. You know, he has never told me that he loves *me*."

"Now you are just talking gibberish. I can tell you that Danny never loved Thelma and never will. You are the only woman who's captured his heart—I am sure of it. Men—" at this point Grace stood, went over to the counter, retrieved a handkerchief from her purse, and handed it to her friend, "well, men are pretty slow to discover what they are feeling. But I *know* he loves you."

Violet took the proffered hankie and blotted her eyes. She was quiet for a moment, her mind a kaleidoscope of all the ideas she had imagined Danny felt, as well as the cold, hard facts. Trying to decipher what was real at this moment was simply impossible, and she felt exhausted and defeated. "You are a good friend, Gracie. I only know that this will take some time."

"Talk to him, honey. You've got to clear this up before it gets any worse."

Violet half nodded, but knew that she couldn't discuss it today. She pulled herself up, washed her face, and reapplied powder. Together they walked back to the drawing room.

Thomas and Danny rose as they entered. "Well, I should let you lovebirds be alone," Thomas said as he started to leave, "besides, I have to go check on my girl."

"Thanks, Tommy, for everything," Danny said as he shook his friend's hand.

"I'd love to say hello to Sally, too, Tommy," Grace added quickly. "I'm right behind you."

Violet gave Thomas a kiss on the cheek and hugged Grace.

"*Talk*," Grace whispered in her ear before disappearing into the hall.

Violet closed the drawing-room door after them. All alone in the room, Violet looked at Danny, not being able to start the conversation she knew they would eventually have to have. Danny looked at Violet, not understanding the desolate, defeated air she now radiated. Neither could find the words. So, exhausted, they journeyed the rest of the way in the kind of silence borne not of companionability, but of possible regret.

They arrived in Chicago just as night was emerging, so Thomas and Danny quickly arranged for their theatrical trunks to be forwarded, then got Violet, Grace, Sally, Murray, their personal trunks, and themselves onto a bus to go to the biggest boarding house known to show folk far and near—The Rose and Thorne Inn. Located right next to Keith's Orpheum Theatre, it was a melting pot of every act imaginable—a place where seals and cats were as welcome as jugglers and contortionists. Established in the early 1900s, the inn grew from a large Victorian house that featured a massive kitchen, large front parlor, and more than a dozen bedrooms of varying sizes. Entertainers knew which room they wanted by color— recognizing, for instance, that the blue room was a small niche on the third floor, and the rose suite was the largest on the first. The Rose and Thorne Inn was famous for offering good food and clean rooms with a generous spirit. This loving atmosphere was a reflection of its proprietress: Mrs. Bridget Finnegan, a small, plump woman who was just about to make her entrance.

"Danny O'Brien? Have ya come to see your old friend, now?" she queried, a bit of old Ireland in her voice. Mrs. Finnegan wore a long, faded housecoat and an equally faded apron, but one that was brightened by splotches of color from joyful cooking. Her long salt-and-pepper hair was tied up in a bun that was always granting leave to some errant tendrils. Her small, heart-shaped face featured two bright green eyes, a pug nose, and chubby cheeks which always sported a red glow. She ran into Danny's open arms, rising on her tip toes to give him a quick buss on his forehead. "I've missed ya, dear boy—it has been too long a time."

"And I've missed you, Mrs. Finnegan. I have someone I want you to meet—my wife, Violet O'Brien."

"That is Violet Williams, professionally," Violet said to deaf ears as the bundle of affection that was Mrs. Finnegan flew into her arms.

"Danny's *wife*! Saints preserve us! I never thought I'd see the day! I'm so glad to have ya here with us, Violet darlin'." Mrs. Finnegan stood back and looked at Violet, smiling and nodding. "You've got the beauty of an angel about ya now."

"Thank you," Danny said modestly. "Oh—you mean *Violet*!" Danny gave Violet a smile, which was not returned. Ignoring her off-mood, he happily registered as "Mr. & Mrs. Danny O'Brien," and, sure enough, got the rose suite—with an attached bath. Danny handed over a large amount of cash to Mrs. Finnegan, who shook her head and tried to hand some of it back. "Danny, ya don't have to be doin' this, now," she said softly.

"It would make me happy if you were to keep it. And, besides, I plan to eat you out of house and home during the next week!" And, turning to Violet, he declared: "Our Mrs. Finnegan is the best chef I have ever had the pleasure of meeting. Her biscuits will make your tongue fall out of your mouth and slap your face!"

The landlady smiled and put the money in her apron pocket. "And ya have the little rascal with ya, I presume?"

"Yes," and Danny picked up the satchel that contained Murray, unzipping the top and giving the cat a chance to surface and greet his favorite landlady. Mrs. Finnegan looked at him and smiled. "I have plenty of tuna and cream for ya, young master," she said, scratching his chin. His purr was loud and rumbling, just like Danny's stomach.

"And *you* will eat in an hour, so go and clean up," she told Danny, giving his arm a pat. Then, seeing Grace, she went to the girl and threw her arms around her as well. The two disappeared into the kitchen, talking in low voices, which Danny knew meant that Grace was pouring her heart out.

The repast they shared that evening was truly remarkable: ham with pineapple chutney, roasted potatoes with butter and chives, fruit salad, maple-glazed carrots, a large salad with Roquefort dressing, the heavenly biscuits with golden Irish butter, and homemade vanilla ice cream with fresh berries and Scottish oat cookies. Violet was amazed at how much both Danny and Thomas ate, and had to admit that the food raised her spirits—albeit by a very small degree.

After thanking Mrs. Finnegan and saying a goodnight to Thomas, Grace, and other assorted guests of the inn, Violet and Danny made their way to their room on the first floor. It was, as Danny said it would be, large and airy, quite beautifully appointed in shades of antique rose and gray. The bed was a large double, and their trunks had been placed where a wardrobe would have been located, in one of the corners of the suite.

"I have just been living out of the trunk, and not really unpacking," Violet said, wondering if that was protocol.

"Yeah, that's kinda what we all do." Danny was unsure what to do next, but he decided to test the waters. He came around and gave Violet a kiss on the back of her neck. She was tempted to let him kiss her a little longer, so extraordinary did his hot breath and lips feel on her skin, but she moved away. Just then, there was a knock on the door.

It was Thomas, who wanted a word with Danny in the hallway. "Say, since you have a private tub and are on the first floor, would you let Her Majesty use it tonight? She could do with a long soak."

"I'm sure it would be no problem; let me just check with Vi," Danny said nonchalantly and closed the door. He went to Violet, who was taking off her make-up. "Honey, would it be okay for Sally to spend the night in the tub?" he asked, not paying much attention to her response.

"But, dearest," Violet said, looking him straight in the eye, "where will *you* sleep tonight?" Violet had made one steadfast decision: she would be polite with Danny, but she would not allow him to share her bed until he told her that he loved her. And he would have to solve that riddle all by himself.

"Oh," Danny looked at her with genuine surprise, "well, now that we are married, I naturally assumed—"

"Well, you assumed wrong. That tub is *your* bed. This marriage—*'It's for the act,'* remember? And not for any 'evening shows,' if you catch my meaning." She threw down the towel she was using for emphasis, breaking eye contact.

"Violet, I—" Danny said, anger slowly beginning to brew inside. But he decided now was not the time for a heated discussion. He swallowed his pride and walked back to the hallway, and to the waiting Thomas.

"Sorry, but, well, we want to be alone tonight," he said quietly, hoping that it would sound convincing.

"Of course, sure, I shouldn't have—I'm sorry to have bothered you. I can set up her tub on the back porch." Thomas said, making a quick exit.

Danny locked the door and turned around to find Violet taking the counterpane off the bed and carrying it, along with a pillow, into the bathroom. *She was serious?* he thought. When she came out, he got his pajamas and went into the room, closing the door rather forcefully behind him. He was getting one of his headaches, and had no one to blame but himself. And, of course, he had neither aspirin nor Violet's gentle hands to take away the pain. As he brushed his teeth he tried to make sense of what was happening to his world. What did she mean, *it's for the act*? He felt at odds with her; not knowing why she was so moody, not understanding her one bit. He had imagined that tonight—well, tonight would have culminated differently. He brushed his teeth so hard he practically scrubbed off the enamel.

After finally spitting out the paste he got into the tub, his legs dangling awkwardly off the side.

It was going to be a long night.

The next morning Danny woke early, emerging slowly from his porcelain bed, unkinking his body and rubbing his aching muscles. He walked into the bedroom to find Violet asleep with Murray curled up in her arms. The cat opened his eyes and blinked at Danny.

"Traitor," he snapped aloud at Murray, who simply put down his head with a grunt of satisfaction and dozed off again.

Getting dressed, Danny vowed to make things right with Violet. No matter the cause of her change of heart, he would win her over—of that he was certain. He went into the kitchen and asked Mrs. Finnegan if he could get together a breakfast tray for his bride. She readily agreed, taking charge and putting thick slices of buttered soda bread, homemade blackberry jam, sections of oranges, and coffee on a tray.

"How does the dear girl take her coffee?" she asked.

"I'm not sure. Probably black. But I'll need a saucer of cream for Murray."

"And a kipper," the sweet lady added. She put the cream in a little jug, making it easier to carry. After putting the finishing touches on the heavy tray she handed it to Danny, who spirited it to their room.

When he walked in, Violet was just waking up.

"Here you go, honey," he said, setting the full tray on the bed and offering her a bright smile.

"Oh, thank you," she yawned. "And thanks for remembering the cream for my coffee."

"Of course," he said, being glad he had the Traitor after all. He placed the plate containing the kipper on the floor, and gave Murray a conciliatory ear scratch.

After breakfast Violet took a long bath and dressed, getting ready for the matinee. She turned the bathroom over to Danny when she was finished, allowing him to bathe and dress as well. She sat on the bed, playing with Murray, who had decided that the tassel on her belt was there for sport. He batted it and attempted to grab the leather, finally rolling on his back in surrender.

"You give up too easily," she said, laughing.

"Sorry—what?" Danny said, coming out of the bathroom with shaving soap lathered on his face, his damp hair rumpled, and wearing just a T-shirt and trousers.

Violet, still laughing, pointed to Murray, who was lying on his back, legs sticking up in the air. Danny chuckled at the silly cat, and went back into the bathroom, with Violet following on his heels. She wanted to see him again, catching too brief a glimpse before. She knew he was handsome, but somehow seeing him in this very personal, un-affected light, he was impossible to ignore. She felt her resolution slip ever so slightly—or perhaps she felt it fall right on the bathroom floor.

He looked at her in the mirror and raised his eyebrows, as if to ask if she needed anything.

"I just want to watch you shave," she said, sitting on the counter.

He looked at her again for a time, then smiled and shook his head, getting back to the task at hand. "Is this some fetish I should know about?"

"I don't know yet," Violet grinned, wiggling her eyebrows.

This was more like his Vi. Where had she been? He quickly fin-ished shaving, then wiped the remaining soap off his face. She watched him pick up a clear deco bottle filled with amber liquid and, uncapping the top, put some of the cologne on his hands, and slapping it on his face and neck. The scent hit her—that wonderful deep wood fragrance with leather and vanilla notes. This was Danny, and she longed to be close to him. Extending her arm, she gently ran her finger along the scar on his forehead. She would always love that scar, for what it said about his protective character, and his refusal to be intimidated. He was so brave. Her finger continued down his face, across his jaw, and to his lips.

Danny took both of her hands in his, not wanting to just be taken up in her mood. He looked deep into her clear, brown eyes with a gaze of sincerity which grabbed at her heart. "Vi, honey, we need to talk. I am—"

He was interrupted by loud knocking. He begrudgingly let go of her hands.

At the door was one of the Orpheum's stagehands who reported that he couldn't locate Danny and Violet's theatrical trunk; Danny, muttering under his breath, said that he would leave immediately. He walked into the bathroom, pulling on his shirt as he went.

"We will continue this later, okay?" he asked.

"Okay," she said, softly.

He kissed her on the forehead, and, with a nod and a "Be good, old man" to Murray, grabbed his coat, and was gone. Violet felt hopeful that, just maybe, they could work through this. No, she thought, they *would* work through this.

She finished dressing and grabbed a sweater to wear over her dress. On her way out, she stopped in the kitchen to thank Mrs. Finnegan for the breakfast and return the tray and dishes. She and the kind landlady had a nice chat over coffee and freshly baked sugar cookies.

"Do you enjoy running this inn?" Violet asked while breaking off a small piece of cookie sitting on her plate.

"Oh, yes I do, honey. Gives me a chance to be around some of the most interesting people in the world, and to be able to take care of 'em is a real treat."

Grace drifted into the kitchen, looking as if she didn't want to intrude.

"Come over and sit by me," Violet said, moving over one seat. "How is your room?"

"Just lovely. I enjoy looking out the window at the theatre—you can see the marquee clearly." She took a proffered cup of coffee and looked at Violet. "Tell me now, seriously, how is Danny?"

"Yes, what happened to him?" Mrs. Finnegan asked with great concern. "The poor boy's wearin' a terrible scar."

Around bites of the tender sugar treats, Violet told an expurgated version which didn't mention any specific names at all. She tried to ease Grace's guilty conscience while telling a story interesting enough to satisfy the twinkle in the bright-green eyes of Mrs. Finnegan. Grace knew what she was doing, took her hand, and squeezed a thank you.

"The main challenge now is just to go about our sketch in a completely normal way," Violet mumbled in the language of cookie. "We have been compensating so long, I've almost forgotten just how it is supposed to go!"

"Mrs. Finnegan," Grace enthused, "you have got to see Danny and Violet's sketch. It is really good. Why, you won't recognize Danny at all!"

"'Twould be a shame," Mrs. Finnegan said defensively. "Danny reminds me of me late Walter, and I love him singin'."

The girls were quiet for a moment. Then Violet ventured a conciliatory thought: "You know, Danny plays a very convincing Valentino type!"

The idea of that didn't just make Mrs. Finnegan laugh: She turned beet red. Her whole body shook. She squealed. It was a wonderful moment.

Violet and Grace insisted upon washing their cups and straightening the kitchen. Grace asked about Mrs. Finnegan's husband.

"He passed away ten years ago, honey," she said with a faraway look in her eyes. "I miss him every day."

"I'm so sorry," Violet said, taking her hand. "You must have loved him an awful lot."

"Yes, like you and Danny," the wise woman said, telling the young newlywed what she wanted to hear.

The girls got up to leave, Grace going back to her room to dress, and Violet heading out for the theatre. Grace pulled Violet aside.

"You know what I meant by asking how Danny was doing, it wasn't just about his physical condition," she whispered. "Did you talk things out? Is everything resolved?"

"Not exactly, but we will get everything settled right after the show. Don't worry, honey, things will be boffo!"

Violet hugged Grace, then set off for the theatre.

Violet confidently walked through the stage-door entrance. She saw the now-familiar group of canaries awaiting the star, and decided to slip past them.

"Violet! Violet!" she heard a couple of them chirrup. "Hello! Can we have your autograph?"

"*My* autograph?" She smiled, and soon was signing her own name, feeling like she had met yet another rite of passage. Besides the typical flock, a young boy emerged, lingering a bit longer to have her sign his book.

"You—you are the most beautiful woman I have ever seen in my entire life," said the timid boy, whose life must have encompassed all of thirteen years.

"What is your name?" she asked.

"Herman," he said in a whisper, finally being bold enough to look her in the eye. Violet took his book and signed the page, "To my friend Herman. Love, Violet." She then kissed it, leaving a perfect lip print.

"Oh, thank you! Thank you! I'll treasure this forever!" And with that proclamation, he flew off.

She chuckled and made her way into the theatre. Luckily, the trunk had been located and was in its proper position in the wings.

"Hey, did you see this?" one of her fellow performers asked as he approached her with a copy of the *New Yorker* magazine in his hands. "*Look!*"

She took the proffered magazine and saw a cartoon of a frustrated young fellow looking at a girl who was filing her nails while sitting on a couch. The caption read: "Lady, do you *eat?*"

"Oh, my gosh," Violet gasped, putting her hand over her mouth. "Th–that's *us!*" She got so excited she took the magazine and started running off, then ran back to the smiling actor.

"May I have this?" she asked as an apology.

"Of course, Vi!" he said, laughing.

"Thanks!" she smiled, and then was off again. Violet ran to the backstage area, peeking into the auditorium and saw Danny talking with the theatre's manager, Douglass Harlan. He was a small, nervous-looking man who seemed to take on a surly and impatient air with Danny. This conversation didn't look easy and she knew that Danny could probably use a smile. Running into their dressing room, she got to work. She cut the cartoon out of the magazine and taped it to the mirror, smack in the center. Then Violet cut out the logo for the magazine and taped that above the cartoon. She took her lipstick and drew a big red heart around the two items, then the words: *We have arrived!*

Violet had heard that certain lines in the routine were being quoted by the public and other performers. It seems as though that one line—which had almost been an afterthought during the writing phase—took off the most. It got the loudest laugh of the sketch, and had become slang, used by college boys if a girl turned them down for a date. She thought how funny it was to be a part of changing the national lexicon. But this … this was really something special.

She stood back, admiring the scene which would surely catch Danny's eye and make him beam with pride. She decided to go looking for him and would drag him into their dressing room, if need be. She was walking just in front of the oleo curtain when she detected an odd, hot smell, then heard a buzzing sound followed by a loud *pop*! She froze, looking up. One of the arc lights positioned right above her short circuited, causing sparks to fly, quickly igniting a heavily oil-painted drop. A stagehand swiftly tried to douse the fire with the Kilfyre canister, which was a mainstay in every theatre, but the fire flared, quickly following a downward path. Immediately Violet's sleeve ignited, drawing a blazing knife quickly through the thin layers of material. She reacted slowly, seeing the flames uncomprehendingly. By the time she did realize what was happening, she was already feeling the fire scorch her skin. Douglass Harlan, who immediately flew to the stage, tried to lower the asbestos fire curtain to throw around her, but it snagged. Danny, who was right on Harlan's heels, took off his coat and wrapped it around Violet, finally smothering out the fire. Violet fell to the floor, gasping for air. Harlan immediately yelled for the house doctor, only to have someone shout back that he wasn't in the theatre. All the while, several other stagehands and actors worked to put out the fire on the oleo, which they did posthaste. The smoke was so thick, however, that everyone was instructed to evacuate the building. Danny picked up the coughing Violet and took her out, carrying her to their nearby inn. As he began running into their room, he yelled to Mrs. Finnegan to call a doctor. She took one look at Violet, crossed herself, then ran to the telephone.

Laying Violet on the bed, he saw the black sleeve of her sweater and smelled the singed flesh. He felt sick to his stomach. The doctor arrived, took one look at Violet, and recommended a specialist in burn treatment. Then he was gone. Violet was white with pain, gasping as tears coursed down her cheeks. Within twenty minutes a second doctor arrived with a nurse in tow, and immediately ordered Danny out of the room. But he couldn't leave, staying right where he was and watching them slowly remove the burned clothing—some of which had melted onto her skin—revealing a red-and-black blistered wound that reached from her shoulder to midway down her right forearm. The pain from this procedure caused Violet to lose consciousness. The doctor looked at the arm and shook his head, conferring briefly with his nurse, then began to mix a watery solution. Putting towels carefully under the arm, he slowly drizzled the mixture onto her skin, irrigating and sterilizing the wound. After making sure every part of the burned area had been doused with the liquid, they left her side to let it dry. The doctor approached a terrified Danny.

"You are her husband?" he inquired.

"Yes, yes I am," Danny said seriously. "Will she be alright? Should she go to a hospital?"

"Well, my boy, I would prefer that she stay where it is quiet. As for the injury, there is a new procedure, only a few years old. It originated in France, and involves paraffin wax. The skin must dry as much as possible, and then a thin coating of wax is applied to the infected area. Because air doesn't get to the burn, it is less painful for the patient than the old methods we used and, ostensibly, the wax keeps out infection. I would like to give that a try, if you consent. The burned area is large; the problem is that I don't have an atomizer to spray the wax on, but I could use a brush. This treatment has worked for my patients many times."

"Whatever would work best and get her out of pain the most quickly. And, I want the best care possible for her, regardless of the cost."

"Very well, we can proceed," the doctor said and, noticing that Violet was beginning to moan, took the nurse aside and spoke to her under his breath. She nodded and retrieved a vial and a syringe from his black bag. She gave the patient a shot, and mentioned something to the doctor.

"My nurse can go and fetch the things we will need. Is there a burner on the premises?"

Danny quickly made his way into the kitchen and asked a concerned Mrs. Finnegan if there was a burner: an item strictly forbidden in any boarding house's bedroom. "Luckily, me boarders don't listen to me. I think Mr. Southwick has one in room three."

"Bless you, thank you," Danny said as he ran upstairs to the room. In no time, he had a burner for the doctor to use.

"Anything else?" he asked, breathless from his run up the stairs.

"No, we have a bathroom right here, which is a good thing."

"What about Vi? Is she in any pain right now?" he asked, looking at the small figure in the bed.

"We gave her a shot of morphine. That will help, but it won't take away all the pain. And you, my boy, will need to get yourself together."

Danny nodded, running his hands through his hair and taking a deep breath. He stood aside as the nurse rushed past him into the room. Going to Violet's side, he took her left hand in his, whispering, "It's okay, honey, we'll get through this together." Her eyes fluttered open briefly, then closed.

The procedure was excruciating. They used a brush to apply the wax, which covered the affected skin, extending an inch onto the unburned area. Violet moaned and gasped a few times, squeezing Danny's hand so hard that he was sure she would break a bone. But he held firm, speaking softly to her the entire time. After a while she seemed to fall into a deep sleep, utterly exhausted by the pain. When they were done, the doctor again pulled Danny aside.

"We'll remove the wax, re-sterilize the wound, and then reapply it once a day. She should be fine unless an infection develops, but chances are that won't happen."

Danny nodded. He walked the doctor to the door; the nurse would spend the rest of the day and night caring for Violet.

Thomas and Grace stopped by, wanting to know how Violet was doing and if there was anything that she, or Danny, needed. Danny thanked them, but said there was nothing else to be done at the moment. The two left and reported to the concerned group of entertainers and theatre workers who had amassed in the parlor. They all sat in complete silence, worried about a member of their family.

Time went by very slowly, with Danny sitting up by the bed all night long. At one point he could hear her moan, and was afraid that perhaps she was in pain. The nurse assured him that sounds like these were normal, and that he, too, should try to get some sleep.

Danny chose, instead, to pray.

CHAPTER TWELVE

THE GIFT

December 1925

The dull color of a new day seeped through the curtains and onto the floor in front of Danny's feet. He looked up, realizing he had dozed off. Rubbing the sleep from his eyes, he peered at the bed and saw Murray curled up by Violet's left arm, just looking back at him. *He knew*, Danny thought. Somehow, he just knew.

Danny looked around the dark room. The nurse, apparently, had to step out. He stood slowly and walked to the bathroom, trying to be as quiet as possible so as not to awaken the sleeping patient. After using the facility, he returned to find the nurse bending over Violet, closely monitoring her heartbeat. When she saw Danny, she nodded.

"Mrs. O'Brien seems to be comfortable, and everything looks good this morning," she said.

Danny breathed for what felt like the first time in a dozen or more hours. "Oh, thank God," he said.

"Danny?" came a weak voice from the bed.

He walked over to Violet and, moving Murray's paw, took her hand. "I'm here, honey, what do you need? Are you comfortable? Are you hungry?"

Violet gave Danny a weak smile. "I'm okay, although my arm throbs, and I'm terribly thirsty."

Danny looked at the nurse, who immediately went to the black bag and removed a vial and syringe. She injected Violet, who soon began to get a glazed look in her eyes.

"May I give her some water?" he asked the nurse.

"Yes, but just a little." She handed a glass to Danny, who carefully lifted Violet's head and put the glass to her lips. She took a few sips, and then Danny laid her back onto the pillow.

"Just sleep, dear heart," Danny said, rubbing and kissing her hand.

Mrs. Finnegan came into the room with fresh towels, and stopped to pat Danny on the shoulder for moral support.

The doctor came in shortly thereafter, and, using a type of twee-zer, removed the wax coating in one piece. He and the nurse again made up the Dakin's solution. The doctor explained to Danny that this old-fashioned sterilizing compound, comprised of a highly di-luted combination of sodium hypochlorite and boric acid, had to be made up on the spot, as it was unstable and lost its effectiveness after standing for more than six hours. Danny watched as they melted the wax, then poured it into an atomizer. They sprayed this onto the burn, which was much less painful for Violet. Even so, she was obviously in a great deal of discomfort.

"Let's try to get some beef broth down her today," the doctor told Danny and Mrs. Finnegan. "Something nourishing." Mrs. Finnegan went into her kitchen straightway and heated up a can of Campbell's Ox-Tail soup. Back in their room in a flash, she handed the steam-ing mug to Danny, who spoon-fed Violet, coaxing her the entire time. She ate as much as she could, but found the whole process exhausting. Soon she was again fast asleep.

Danny was ordered by the nurse to have a decent meal, so he joined the others for dinner that evening. No one commented on his disheveled appearance, or the fact that he barely had two mouthfuls of food. The assembled troupe determined to entertain him by telling stories of encouragement, or of humorous situations from the road. Mrs. Finnegan made him his favorite egg custard for dessert, which he found easy to eat. Danny recognized these precious gifts he was being presented and, as soon as was polite, he rose, thanked everyone for their support, and then left to rejoin his little family.

This group which kept a vigil in the parlor, featuring an ever-changing assemblage of faces, became a mainstay throughout this time. They would see Danny only briefly as he left for or returned from the nearby Catholic church, where he would go to light a candle and pray. They would eat with him, seeing him push food around his plate wearing a heartbreaking expression of concern, then quickly return to his room. They would talk among themselves in guilty whispers: there, but for the grace of God, they could be.

The following morning found Danny much stronger. He bathed and shaved, changing his clothing and making himself more presentable. Unbeknown to him, the nurse noticed some red streaks coming out from the bottom of the wax, and noted that Violet was running a fever. An infection had begun to develop. After breaking this news to Danny, the nurse immediately called the doctor, who came straightway and removed the wax. He found edema, more redness, and pus. Immediately they mixed up the Dakin's solution and bathed the arm.

"Now, we must leave the wax off until the infection is gone," the doctor told Danny, who was extremely concerned.

"But she'll be okay, right?" he said, looking at Violet on the bed.

"The burn covers such a large area; an infection like this is not a good sign. But, well, we will be positive, my boy."

Danny walked the doctor out of the room.

"Oh, by the way, Mr. O'Brien, I've been meaning to tell you that I saw your show last week. You know what you should do? Have the doctor character come in with a big cigar. We are always joking about the fact that we all smoke big cigars, and yet we're constantly telling our patients to cut down on smoking!" The doctor laughed boisterously.

Danny just stared at the man. "Thank you for coming over, doctor."

"Of course, see you tomorrow," he said, walking by the parlor and noticing the cold stares coming from the individuals seated there. He cleared his throat and stepped out onto the street.

Danny felt his hands turn into fists. He was ready to knock something—or someone—down and out. Didn't that quack know that vaudeville routines aren't real life? The only thing that was real was the girl in that bed, fighting for survival.

"Imagine such a thing," Mrs. Finnegan said, speaking for those who had overheard the comment. "You're a fine man not to have hauled off and punched him, Danny. Just the gall—"

"It's okay, Mrs. Finnegan," Danny said as he drew the little woman to him, giving her a big hug. She dried her tears with a dish towel and kissed his cheek before hurrying back to her kitchen. Danny gave a nod of acknowledgment to the group in the parlor, all of whom seemed to relax a bit, and then made his way back to the room.

Danny immediately prepared a cold-water compress. He sat by the side of the bed, laying the cloth across Violet's unsettlingly warm forehead. She was mumbling and shaking, twisting her head back and forth.

"It will be okay, dear heart. Don't worry about a thing." He softly sang "Too-Ra-Loo-Ra-Loo-Ral," holding her hand in his. Soon she quieted down and began sleeping peacefully.

Murray lifted his head and meowed, causing Danny to smile. "You have been so good, old man, and you deserve something special." After cooling off the warmed cloth and placing it once again on her forehead, Danny went downstairs and asked Mrs. Finnegan for some scraps for the loyal feline. When he re-entered the bedroom he saw the nurse—was she a different nurse? She didn't look familiar. How long had she been here?—making up the Dakin's solution to bathe the arm.

In no time the gentle landlady brought up a platter of seafood and chicken, and a small bowl of cream. Murray abandoned his position long enough to partake of the repast, then, after a good stretch and post-meal groom, reclaimed his post. Both he and Violet slept soundly through the night.

⊷⇌　⇌⊶

Danny, however, didn't sleep, not really. The few times he would begin to nod off, he experienced horrific nightmares: he saw Violet on fire, but he was prevented from getting to her by some unseen, unknown force. After enough of these ghastly visions he decided to stay awake.

He was constantly re-cooling the cloth on her forehead, and wiping down her left arm. He lost track of the number of prayers he offered up, and how many times he told her something which he needed to believe: that everything would be alright. The following day brought no relief from the worry, as the infection was still extant. The nurse was sure that the constant irrigation of the wound would eventually kill the infection, and kept a regular schedule of mixing the potion and pouring it carefully over her arm.

The doctor stopped by. Time passed. The doctor left. Mrs. Finnegan insisted that Danny eat something—anything, as he was looking pale and gaunt. He went downstairs to eat, only to return as soon as he could. He talked to Murray, who stayed glued to Violet's side. The nurse irrigated the wound. And more time passed.

He had to get some fresh air. Fearing a headache, he took off to walk the night-blanketed streets. He pulled his coat up close around his neck and strode as fast as he could, head down. Passing a store which had bundles of newspapers outside, he saw the headline: "ORPHEUM BACKDROP UP IN FLAMES!" He picked up the paper.

The Fire Spread with Deadly Rapidity on the Oilcloth

ONE GIRL SEVERELY BURNED, FIGHTING INFECTION

Theatre Manager Worked to Put Out Flames Before Entire Theatre Went Up

A curtain in the Orpheum Theatre went up in flames Thursday
mid-morning when an arc-light
short-circuited, setting an oiled
backdrop on fire. The flames
set the sleeve of one vaudeville
performer, Mrs. Daniel (Violet)
O'Brien, on fire, causing second-
and third-degree burns on her
arm. As of this morning, Mrs.
O'Brien was battling infection.

Several theatre employees,
including the theatre manager,
Mr. Douglass Harlan, worked
quickly to put out the flames.

Mrs. O'Brien, who goes by the
stage name of Violet Williams, is
new to vaudeville, having joined
her husband on the circuit only
a couple of months ago. Her
husband, Daniel O'Brien, is best
known to vaudeville audiences...

He dropped the paper and walked. Tears stung his eyes, blurring
his vision. He couldn't get away from this—this turmoil. Moving as
fast as he could along the dark streets, he thought about Violet until his
throbbing head felt like it would split open. He could think of nothing
else. What if she were to—? People *did* die from infection. He would
lose the only one who truly meant anything to him. As he walked,
music kept going through his head, which didn't help the ache at all.
Finally, he recognized it: the ironic "Ah! Fuyez, douce image," from
Manon. So, now he knew how that guy felt. His Vi—his Manon—his
obsession. Thinking back to the last time he played the piece, a few
short months ago, he didn't believe that such a feeling was even real;

he felt that he was immune and would never experience it. He stopped dead in his tracks. He *was* feeling it. Love. The reality of caring about someone so much that it hurt, that taking on her pain and experiencing it for her would somehow be more tolerable, that life without her would be worthless. That was it. He loved Violet completely and utterly. He could deny that fact no longer.

Danny turned around and made his way slowly back to the boarding house. He paced around the empty parlor, then saw Thomas and Grace walking in from outside. He looked at them, the tears gathering in his eyes. They ran to his side, guiding him to the sofa and sitting down on either side.

"She didn't—" Grace began, looking horrified.

"No, no. It's just, I don't know what to do—what if I *did* lose her?" he asked pitifully.

"We have an excellent doctor here," Thomas said consolingly, "he'll take good care of her."

"If it hadn't been for me, she wouldn't have been in show business in the first place," Danny said, raking his fingers through his hair.

"But she obviously wanted to do it," Grace countered. "This was just an accident."

Danny got up and moved toward the window. "I know I'm not a good husband."

"Why would you say—?" Thomas began, but looked at Grace. She didn't make any move to contradict him.

"I–I married her because I was jealous," he confessed, tears now streaking down his cheeks. "That is the truth, *jealous.* I haven't told her that I love her, although I do, more than my own life. But I have this fear that somehow I could end up like my father. He beat my mother and said that is just what marriage—what love—is."

Grace walked over to him and took his hands. "No, no, no. You need to work this out with Violet. That is what I told her on the train—"

"What? Why would you have said we needed to work things out on the train?" Danny questioned.

"Because she—*we*—overheard you tell Tommy that you didn't know why you married her. That it was just for the act."

Thomas sat up straight. "No, Gracie, you're wrong. Danny said, to be precise, that he didn't know what love was, and that he might have made a mistake in actually getting married. But he made it clear that he wanted to take care of Vi for the rest of her life. You've seen him fussing over her now, after the accident, the love he has for her is evident in everything he does."

"I agree," Grace began. "Danny, you are *nothing* like your father. You are compassionate, and strong, and respectful. I know what a man is like who would do such a thing, who would beat a woman. But you aren't like that. That was *their* life—it's not *yours*. And it is not what marriage has to be. She loves you, and I know you love her. That's all that matters."

At these simple words, Danny wept.

Finally, after the third day, the infection was gone. Danny thought he would fairly burst with relief and happiness. Their room was filled with violets, a gesture that made Violet feel better, just knowing that Danny was feeling up to his old tricks. He also tried to keep her spirits up and left unusual things on the bedside table for her to find. One afternoon she awoke to find an open can of sweetened condensed milk and a spoon.

Danny knew he had to send a couple of telegrams, and dreaded the task. First, to Patrick, to explain what happened, although chances are he had already heard about it. But he needed to hear it from Danny directly. Then, he had to get the news to Violet's family. He didn't know what to say, as he felt so responsible. He begged their forgiveness, told them that he loved their daughter, and promised to take better care of their precious girl.

He got back home and saw the sight he was yearning to see: Violet, with the roses back in her cheeks, contentedly sitting up in bed and languidly perusing a magazine. He spoke with the nurse and requested some time alone with his wife. She didn't have to be asked twice. Murray, however, made no move to get up, looking at Danny as if to say, "Whatever you have to say, I'm on her side."

Sitting on the bed and taking Violet's left hand in his, he spoke softly: "Vi, sweetheart, I need to tell you something I think you know, but which I haven't actually said out loud." He paused, feeling oddly nervous. Clearing his throat, he looked up, into her eyes, into the captivating brown of them, into the deep love he found in them. "The act we created for the stage … I could throw away tomorrow. It means nothing without you—life, well, *nothing* means *anything* without you. I love you. I adore you. I cherish you."

"You fool, I've been waiting an awful long time to hear that," she said, her eyes now glistening with tears.

They kissed over Murray, who purred his approval.

It didn't take long for the story to get around about the accident. Folks who had met Violet just in passing or had seen their act sent get-well notes. Some of the managers of the Keith-Albee theatres sent flowers. The largest bouquet was sent by Douglass Harlan, who checked in on her several times, showing that he had a kind nature to rival his dour one. Those performers with whom she had shared a bill—or that memorable Thanksgiving dinner—expressed their wishes for her speedy recovery in notes or wires. Violet got a beautiful bouquet of pink roses from Grace, and a handsome bunch of fall-colored flowers from Thomas and Sally.

Edward F. Albee himself came to check on his theatre—and his new vaudeville star. Whereas lawsuits brought against theatres by performers were few and far between, the men in the Keith-Albee home office knew they could be held liable. Albee first spoke with Danny, getting the particulars and an update on Violet's condition. He casually mentioned that all medical bills, naturally, would be picked up by his office. Albee's visit with Violet was short, but he could see why Danny was so enchanted with the dark-haired beauty. She joked about the accident, which Albee thought was highly refreshing, and then assured *him* that she would be working again in no time. Even the most seasoned of his vaudeville stars wouldn't have handled this situation with such aplomb and bravery. After telling Danny that he was quite taken with Mrs. O'Brien, he left. The Orpheum was closed for a full week while the drops were fixed and the house allowed to air, and no one even mentioned the gigs lost.

Patrick came to Chicago to see Violet and report directly to her worried family. When her uncle made his appearance, Violet was sitting up in a chair looking just perfect—even with one arm propped up on a pillow and covered in paraffin. She told him not to worry, and to let her parents know that she was just fine. It was only a little burn, she contended, not something for them to be concerned about. Danny was not unhappy that she downplayed the severity of her condition. Patrick asked him if he was interested in picking up some time, maybe singing a little, as they didn't know how long Violet would be laid up.

"I've saved my money for a rainy day, and I'd say it has been pretty stormy lately," Danny said with a smile. "I've got a job right now, and that's taking care of my wife."

"That's right, you two are married," Patrick said, as though to remind himself of the fact. "Well, congratulations, Daniel." He formally held out his hand.

"Oh, come here, Uncle Pat," and with that, Danny threw his arms around the stunned man. Patrick stayed stiff as a board, and Danny soon retreated, laughing. He realized that, for the first time in what seemed like months, he felt free.

Patrick enjoyed his short stay, during which he had taken a special shine to Mrs. Finnegan's delectable cooking. The little landlady didn't know what to make of the grim, thin man at first, but soon learned that a platter of scrambled eggs and crisp bacon with a side of her fluffy biscuits slathered with butter and fresh blackberry jam made him seem almost human. She stood by his side, watching him eat the breakfast of two men, relishing every bite. Her smile was that of a maternal figure feeling a little better for her charge's immoderation. Patrick left with a good report to share with family and a few new recipes for Mavis to try.

Christmas was evident in the colorful decorations around town, but the O'Briens hadn't given it much thought. Danny had arranged for some special gifts, which he hid in a drawer in his trunk. But when it came to his attention that it was already Christmas Eve, Danny resolved to do everything in his power to create a merry setting. Deciding to make this a surprise for Violet, he walked her over to the festively decorated front parlor of the inn, seating her with her back to the entrance. This gave Violet a chance to chat with the residents who had been so supportive of Danny and her throughout this ordeal. Grace made a pot of tea and they all had a wonderful chat, Violet looking almost the picture of health.

Danny, meanwhile, smuggled a small, spindly tree into their apartment and called in Mrs. Finnegan for decorating ideas. She offered to remove several ornaments from the front parlor tree's overladen boughs, but Danny wouldn't hear of it: he would come up with a theme and decorate the tree with "found items." His one concession was some Cheer-I-Lights (spending $2.35 for the long string), and they began the decorating process by winding these around the tree. The pine-cone-shaped, small lamps were colorful and added a beautiful glow to the corner of the room. The two conspirators then dashed around, trying to find anything that would emulate a Christmas ornament. Mrs. Finnegan held up some knives, forks, and spoons, which Danny said he could wire onto the tree. To this, he added some small scalloped Jell-O molds, five old wooden pestles, a wire whisk, and a few tins of sardines (which would double as Murray's Christmas gifts). He also couldn't resist making a few paper-clip chains to hang throughout the tree, which were sure to make Violet smile. He borrowed a skein of bright red yarn and wound it artfully around the tree, creating the illusion of red spider webs here and there. But something was needed for the very top, and, by this point, Danny had run out of ideas. Mrs. Finnegan took off for her workshop/kitchen and returned a short time later with a small, colorful, metal tea caddy which, when turned upside down, perfectly fit over the thin top. The tree had a stand of crossed wood that was nailed to the bottom of the slim trunk, and they both agreed that this needed to be covered with something. *A shawl*, Mrs. Finnegan thought, and was back in no time with a beautiful red creation which she wound around the bottom. Danny retrieved the small gifts from his trunk and tucked them into the shawl's folds. When they decided that they had conceived of every possible decoration, Danny went to the parlor and invited Violet back to the suite. Upon seeing the results, she clapped her hands together and declared it the most beautiful tree she could ever imagine. Danny announced the theme of the Christmas tree: "There *Was* Room at the Inn."

Underneath the tree was a small robin's egg–blue box, tied with a white ribbon, and adorned with the inscription "TIFFANY & CO." Violet could hardly wait to open it, so Danny naturally obliged. What lay inside took her breath away. It was an ornate deco sterling silver bracelet, engraved on the inside with the words, "Love Me, and the World Is Mine."

"This," Danny said, taking the bracelet and placing it upon her right wrist, "is for your beautiful arm." He kissed her, and she melted into him, the discomfort for that day all but forgotten.

"And we couldn't forget *you*, Mrs. Finnegan," Danny said as he handed her a box wrapped in silver paper and tied with red-and-green ribbons. Inside lay a beautiful cut-crystal relish tray.

"Oh, now, you shouldn't have," said the little woman, rubbing her roughened hands over the sparkling surface. She held it to her ample bosom, and then, after heartfelt thanks, made her way out of the room.

Violet had received a large package, postmarked Portland, Oregon, which she opened and therein found some of her favorite chocolates, a new bathrobe, and letters from her sisters, mother, and father. There was even a package for Danny: a beautiful box of monogrammed stationery. Danny was touched by this thoughtful gesture. He looked around and noticed that, squeezed into the corner by the tree, something was hidden under a sheet.

"What is that?" he asked innocently.

"Well, perhaps after *Herr* Doctor could change the bandage, he could find out!" she said, offering her arm to the task. After the paraffin treatment was completed, and bandages were utilized to protect the sensitive skin, Danny took over Violet's care. Her favorite moments of the day now came when Danny fell into one of the comic characters he donned to distract her from the uncomfortable job.

"Ja. Unt now, Fräulein?"

"Ja, doctor," she replied with a giggle.

After the bandages were duly changed, with Danny's running Dutch comic monologue, he asked if he could find out what was under that sheet. Came the nod from Violet, so he raised the covering to reveal a new Victrola Granada, one of the first Orthophonic Victrola models introduced late that year. It was a flat-top console machine.

"Oh, Vi, it's beautiful! Thank you so very much. But how did you arrange this?"

"Well, I had some help from Thomas," Violet confessed. "He knows this sort of machine so well. He even arranged to have a few of your favorite recordings!"

Sure enough, Danny found a stack of records featuring some wonderfully familiar titles. They spent the next hour listening to Puccini, Verdi, and some popular favorites, including "Love Me, and the World Is Mine."

"You have outdone yourself, Vi. I can't thank you enough for making this day so special," Danny said, kissing her hand. "How would you feel about attending midnight Mass with me? It's such a beautiful December evening, and I bet you would love some fresh air."

She nodded enthusiastically.

Danny gently helped her slip into her warm coat, getting her gloves and hat as well. After dressing for the cold weather himself, they went out, arm in arm, and strolled down the street, falling in step with the ever-present crowd of Chicagoans. Violet took a deep breath and loved how the night smelled of fresh pine. Long, green garlands stretched and arched across the streets, and tall candy canes were propped up in front of shops' doorways. Electric lights were plentiful, and could be seen shining and winking in windows, both professional and homey. A few fat snowflakes silently drifted down from the dark sky, and were soon joined by more gliding puffs of white. It was a beautiful, magical place.

They made their way to the ethereally lit and decorated church, once inside saying many prayers of thanks for Violet's healing. Danny knew the spot well, having spent hours there praying for a miracle. He felt that God had given him much more than he had requested.

Upon their return to the boarding house, they found Thomas and Grace waiting for them in the warm parlor.

"Come in, you two," Grace requested. "We have some hot toddies and gifts!"

"Perfect," Danny said, carefully divesting Violet of her coat. "Vi, dear, you go in and sit and I will be right with you."

As soon as Violet had taken a chair, Thomas handed her a small plain box, which was followed by Grace handing her a larger, elaborately wrapped one. "Oh, no, but we don't have anything for you two!" she said with a furrow in her brow.

"Not so fast," Danny said, coming around the corner with two gifts for their two good friends.

"Well, there you have it," Violet laughed. "My husband is very good at sneaking out and getting wonderful gifts!"

Thomas opened his and found a beautiful new pipe. "Oh, say, I like that. Thanks, Danny O, and Vi."

Grace was next up, and was overjoyed to find a beautiful crystal perfume bottle. "Oh, how exquisite! I love it, thank you so much."

"Oh, you're more than welcome," Violet joked. "I planned it for months. And you, my dearest, are marvelous," she said to Danny, who bent down to give her a kiss.

"Now open our gifts," Thomas and Grace said in unison.

"But mine first," Thomas said, smiling.

Violet opened the box Thomas had given her and found a small slip of paper inside.

"March 16, 1926," Violet read out loud. "Thank you, I think! What could this mean?"

"Open mine next," Grace said, wearing a bigger smile than Violet had seen her don in ages.

After making quick time of stripping the box of paper and ribbon, she opened it to find a bride-and-groom wedding-cake topper.

"This is lovely, thank you, although a little too late for us," Violet said, studying the delicate porcelain figures.

Violet heard Grace hiccup. She looked up and found Thomas and Grace sitting hand in hand, and beaming.

A week later, on New Year's Eve, Danny made a special trip to the Orpheum to confer with the manager. He had offered to personally oversee the installation of a proper fire curtain so that the safeguard would be working and in place. It took him the better part of a day, and when he finally made it back to the boarding house it was late in the evening. Reaching the door to their room, he heard a commotion emanating from inside. Walking in, he found Sally cavorting in the tub, playfully splashing a very grumpy Murray. Violet welcomed Danny with a broad smile.

"What's this?" Danny asked, perplexed. "Why is Sally in my bed?"

"Oh, I was thinking that we can arrange another place for you to sleep tonight," Violet whispered, a blush creeping up her cheeks.

"Really?" Danny choked out the word.

"You dope. I love you, too. And I think it's about time, don't you?" Violet put one arm around Danny's neck and kissed him passionately.

"Sorry, old man," Danny said to a damp Murray, who was grooming on the bathroom rug. "Looks like you will be keeping Sally company for a while."

He quickly closed the door.

CHAPTER THIRTEEN

THE PALACE

February 1926

Violet sat quietly at the office desk, its surface and shape so familiar to her. Her left hand self-consciously traveled to her right arm, feeling the large scar on her shoulder which still felt tender; perhaps it would always be as tender as the memory of that accident. Her hand moved down the mottled skin until it rested on the silver bracelet. She smiled.

She was onstage at the Palace Theatre at Forty-Seventh and Broadway in New York: the pinnacle for vaudevillians, the flagship of the Keith-Albee organization, the most desired booking in the country. Acts had to be perfect, and other players were quick to try and take your place. But now was her time—hers and Danny's. This was it. After weeks of recovery, she had wanted nothing more than to rejoin the circuit and, with a couple of weeks of intensive practice, they were both back to their exquisite timing. She knew that tonight they could pull off a show-stopping performance and give each audience member what they wanted: to have excitement hit them in their solar plexus.

Designed by Milwaukee architects Kirchoff & Rose, the 1,740-seat Palace Theatre opened on March 24, 1913, with headliner Ed Wynn. It was not an instant success and was negatively received, due in no small part to its outrageous $2 top. It took the prestige of two major legitimate theatre actresses, Ethel Barrymore and the Divine Sarah Bernhardt, to turn it into the foremost vaudeville theatre in the world. Other performers who graced the stage included Will Rogers, The Marx Brothers, Fanny Brice, Al Jolson, Lillian Russell, and Blossom Seeley. Movie actors also appeared, in one guise or another, and included Rudolph Valentino, Harry Langdon, Francis X. Bushman, and Marie Dressler.

In the stillness of the darkened stage Violet closed her eyes and took a deep breath. The rancid scent of greasepaint was one she had missed, she thought incredulously. She could hear the faint rustle of the audience: the movement of programs, the occasional cough, the hushed whispers between friends. These sounds she had all but forgotten, but now took the time to savor. In fact, that feeling of nervousness she felt coursing through her body was something she had missed— that sense of being so completely alive that every nerve in the body was shouting for attention. That was the rush a performer craved, and she was proud to be a part of that vibrant alliance.

From across the stage she saw Danny, waiting in the wings, in his Delivery Boy costume. She gave him a wink and he winked back. Feeling utter joy, Danny thought back to a time when playing this theatre meant little to him. Only months ago he felt as if he could hang it all up. But tonight reminded him of why he loved this life: the pride he felt in his profession, the confidence he had that the audience would be thoroughly entertained by his efforts, the sense of home he always felt when embraced by a theatre's ambience. And that beautiful girl across the stage—the one he had never met until seven short months ago—she had become his entire world. Life no longer made sense without her.

Violet heard their theme music start up, and, slowly, the curtain ascended. The audience began applauding as usual, but this time they didn't stop. In fact, they kept applauding, adding whistles and cheers in good measure. She couldn't understand what was going on—this was not the way their act began. While this expression of appreciation washed over them, Danny sauntered onstage, the embodiment of the experienced vaudevillian, and took her hand, walking her front and center. He knew what the audience was saying; what they wanted. He stepped back, leaving Violet alone, and joined in the ovation.

Then Edward F. Albee entered from the wings and presented her with a bouquet of violets. Putting his arm gently around her shoulder, he silenced and then addressed the crowd: "We are so pleased to have our newest star, Violet Williams, with us tonight. This courageous woman has come back from a horrific injury, only to work once again alongside her husband, Danny O'Brien. Let us tonight welcome her back into our fold and celebrate her vivacity. She has the heart and soul of a true vaudevillian." Then he, too, stepped back, adding his personal applause to the now-deafening ovation.

Violet reached for Danny. As the sound washed over her, she acknowledged the audience and thanked them for the support they had so generously given. She and Danny stepped back, allowing the curtain to be closed in order that they might start their routine.

For just a moment she stood there, holding Danny's hand, not wanting to let go—now or ever. She looked into his warm, inviting eyes and saw herself as she wanted to be: inspired, magical, strong, and loved.

Danny looked into the depths of Violet's eyes and saw his future with more worth than he could ever have conceived: his longing sated; his heart overflowing. Life now had reason.

Two old souls had indeed found each other, and continued their eternal flirtation.

The End

ABOUT THE AUTHOR

DEBRA L. DAVIS (née LaCoe) was born and raised in San Diego County, California. A communications/sociology major at the University of California at San Diego (La Jolla), she was elected to the National Dean's List and was a member of Phi Beta Kappa. At that time, she and fellow student Lon Davis began collaborating on books covering the silent film industry. As freelance editors, Debra and Lon have edited literally hundreds of academic books on the performing arts, history, and literature. Her eclectic tastes include a love of tennis, zombie films/television, and German Lieder music. *Flirtation Act: The Story of a Boy, a Girl, and Vaudeville* is Debra's first novel.